Fragma

Mojca Kumerdej

FRAGMA

Translated from the Slovene by Rawley Grau

DALKEY ARCHIVE PRESS

McLean, IL / Dublin

Originally published in Slovenian by Študentska založba as *Fragma* in 2003.

Copyright © by Mojca Kumerdej, 2003.

Translation copyright © by Rawley Grau, 2019.

Introduction copyright © by Blanka Bošnjak, 2019.

Introduction translation copyright © by Nada Grošelj, 2019.

First Dalkey Archive edition, 2019.

Names: Kumerdej, Mojca, author.

Title: Fragma / Mojca Kumerdej ; translated from the Slovene by Rawley Grau.

Description: First Dalkey Archive edition. | McLean Il : Dalkey Archive Press, 2019.

Identifiers: LCCN 2019030344 | ISBN 9781628973198 (pbk. : alk. paper)

Classification: LCC PG1919.21.U46 F7313 2019 | DDC 891.8/436--dc23

LC record available at https://lccn.loc.gov/2019030344

Published in cooperation with the Slovene Writers' Association—Litterae Slovenicae Series. This work has been published with the support of the Trubar Foundation, located at the Slovene Writers' Association, Ljubljana, Slovenia. This translation has been financially supported by the Slovenian Book Agency.

Printed on permanent/durable acid-free paper.

McLean, IL / Dublin

www.dalkeyarchive.com

Contents

Introduction

Subversion, Topicality, and Critical Consciousness in the Writings of Mojca Kumerdej

Blanka Bošnjak

By Way of Introduction

HIGHLY ARTICULATE, PASSIONATELY involved, and sweepingly erudite – such is the approach of Mojca Kumerdej to crafting her writings, which focus on longer and shorter prose. She is successful in a number of other fields as well: the performance *Projektator*,[1] for example, where she collaborated as dramaturge and as one of the authors of the text, received, at Borštnikovo srečanje, the central Slovenian theatre festival, the 2016 Borštnik Prize for Best Dramaturgy. Her rich and heterogeneous oeuvre testifies to her meticulous research prior to writing, especially on historical or scientific themes. The most precious aspect of her work, however, is her authentic and original poetics appealing to a more demanding readership, as the following analytical interpretation of her seminal literary work shall attempt to show.

The Subversion of the Subject in *Baptism over Mount Triglav*

Mojca Kumerdej's début, *Krst nad Triglavom* (Baptism over

---

1 The performance was directed by Dragan Živadinov. The text was co-authored by Dragan Živadinov, Lotos Vincenc Šparovec, and Mojca Kumerdej.

Mount Triglav, 2001), a short novel of elusive genre, took shape primarily as an intertextual reference to France Prešeren's long poem of national significance, *Krst pri Savici* (*Baptism on the Savica*, 1836). This subversive text metafictionally undermines faith in grand and great narratives, particularly through the ironic distance of the authorial narrator. Ironic, allegorical and imbued with pronounced philosophical elements, the text is crucially marked by all-pervasive doubt about the existence of a single reality. After the long disappearance of the protagonist Janko Pretnar (which is never explained but attributed to an encounter with extraterrestrials) and his subsequent return to everyday life by Lake Bohinj, his discourse assumes a verse form: the hendecasyllable. The verse form expresses visions transcending our civilisation, as well as deep insights into existential issues. This trait, the main departure from the subject's formerly tractable personality, may well be related to a contact with the unconscious, which is (in Lacanian terms) suggested by the changed structure of the protagonist's discourse. Lacan does designate the enunciating subject, 'but does not signify him. This is obvious from the fact that there may be no signifier of the enunciating subject in the statement – not to mention that there are signifiers that differ from *I*, and not only those that are inadequately called cases of the first person singular, even if we add that it can be lodged in the plural invocation or even in the Self [*Soi*] of auto-suggestion', and '[t]his cut in the signifying chain alone verifies the structure of the subject as discontinuity in the real' (Lacan 2006: 677–678).

Because of his hermetic discourse and obstinate adherence to his visions and principles, the protagonist is subjected to repression by various characters. These represent important social entities but are morally dubious, especially because of religious fanaticism, homophobia, sexism, and aggression: priest Vinko Ogrizek acts in the name of religion, police inspector and criminalist Ernest Gorjanc in the name of the police, and Dr Marjan Kukec in the name of psychiatry. The wave of institutional violence is raised by Janko's wife, Malči, whose domineering behaviour is intolerably degrading for her husband. With Janko's unexplained disappearance and his sudden return, with changed perceptions, the individual's intimate sphere opens to the public against the backdrop of the village community, which mangles the 'truth' of the individual's destiny in its own way. The opposite pole in this subversive text is realised in such subjects as the 'aethereally fragile' Lili, a doctor of psychiatry who regards alternative theories of extraterrestrial civilisations with favour, the inspector's assistant Mirko, or Daft Franček, the village idiot, who likewise believes in the existence of other civilisations.

The text was published ten years after Slovenia's declaration of independence, which suggests a deliberate choice on the author's part. It may be perceived in her juxtaposition of two watershed national discourses, both set in the context of political actions which were of crucial importance to the Slovenians. The first discourse refers to the victory of Christianity over pagan beliefs (or belief in Slavic mythological creatures) through the matricial text *Krst pri Savici*, which thematises this seminal historical epoch in both private (the love of Bogomila and Črtomir) and public spheres (by Christianisation, including the acceptance of Christianity by both protagonists, which separates them in this world and postpones the happiness of their union beyond the grave). The second discourse is linked to the acquisition of an independent state, which had perhaps failed to meet its citizens' expectations by its tenth anniversary. Or as phrased in rhymes by Janko, the protagonist, in the intertextual context of the subversion of the subject:

There hatches, independent, as is proper,
a hen – the symbol of Slovene expanses,
and starts to peck at democratic fodder,
but hens are not at home in legal science:
Slovenia's towns are overrun by tyrants –
whose blood runs thick with toxins and with madness
(Kumerdej 2001: 65).

In addition to other possibilities, the text invites interpretation along the lines of conspiracy theories: this is what Lili, open to new ideas, mulls over in the end. An example is the notion that the Ten Commandments given to Moses and the ancient

Jewish Arc of the Covenant were computer software, which may have strayed into Jewish hands by accident (ibid.: 101).

There may be a further association with Dragan Živadinov's performance *Krst pod Triglavom*, staged by Gledališče sester Scipion Nasice (GSSN) and other groups of Neue Slowenische Kunst (Irwin, Laibach) on February 6, 1986. This performance left a deep mark on the Slovenian theatre and resonated abroad as well. On its 25th anniversary, Živadinov emphasised that it had struggled to achieve abstraction, that is, to separate theatre from *mimesis* in the manner of Marcel Duchamp (Krečič 2011). Philosophically, this is closely linked to the subversion of the protagonist or subject in Mojca Kumerdej's work, but in her version the baptism takes place *over* Mount Triglav, implying that the encounter with extra-terrestrials is a baptism *above*. The text is thus highly topical at various levels: politics, transformation of important historical truths, convergence of public and private, and the subject's desire to flee from profanity to a quest for transcendence.[2]

The Topical and Apocalyptic Qualities of the Novel *Kronosova žetev*[3]

The very title of Kumerdej's (long) second novel, *Kronosova žetev* (2016; *The Harvest of Chronos*, 2017), is significant: two concepts – the name of Chronos, the Greek god of time, and the notion of harvest from the Biblical passage 'The Harvest of the Earth' in the Book of Revelation (Apocalypse) – are singled out and joined in a tightly knit phrase. This establishes semantic links between different ideational discourses: Greek mythology and Christianity. The author's stance shifts to a critical contemplation of the political apparatus of religion, which destroys innocent victims in the name of ideology. This multi-layered historical

---

2 In the text analysed, this happens through 'close encounters of the third kind', which may replace belief in God with belief in other civilisations. This change washes away the subject's guilty feelings, liberating him (Kumerdej 2001: 81).

3 The novel *Kronosova žetev* was hailed in 2017 with a nomination for the Kresnik Prize (for the best novel of the previous year) and with the Critical Sieve Award (presented by the Slovenian Literary Critics' Association for the best book of the previous year) as well as the Prešeren Foundation Prize.

novel with a characteristic polyphony of narrators treats and philosophically accentuates the events in Inner Austrian lands, the heart of the Slovenian ethnic territory, at the close of the 16th century, when the struggle for supremacy between Protestant *Landstände* and the Catholic Habsburg monarchy peaked. The work rests on exceptionally thorough studies, starting from a bulk of extraliterary archive sources (including a report by Bishop Thomas Chrön), which is masterfully leavened with literary quality and fiction. With a particular feeling for detail, the author depicts the invasive Catholic policy against Lutherans, adding metafictional time leaps into the future in order to show the pattern of the past repeating itself: the future trickles through the past in seemingly simultaneous action. The novel links the past and present in various segments, mainly in a well-nigh apocalyptic portrayal of the consequences brought on by the emphatic ties between ideology, politics, and economy in the past and present.

The time of the tempestuous and groundbreaking 16th century, when medieval monolithic seclusion is invaded by free will and the accompanying polyphony, is portrayed with a critical distance. With its carefully orchestrated polyphony of perspectives, discussions, insights, opinions and actions of its numerous characters, the novel is a subtle criticism of our time as well. There is an emphasis on the different views on existential questions, religion, and power which are held by the most prominent characters: Prince-Bishop Wolfgang as a representative of the clergy, Count Friedrich, and Nikolai the scrivener. In contrast to the upper class representatives, the voices of the populace are not differentiated, with the occasional exception of an individual shepherd or a clever girl. The author introduces an innovation, *the collective subject of the populace*, presenting the pogroms, book-burning, witch-burning, etc., as happening in its name and thus obscuring the responsibility of the initiators. On the other hand, the book presents the colourful Renaissance spiritual and historical climate with its revival of classical antiquity, scientific discoveries and new geographical spaces, lively philosophical and theological discussions, and introduction of such mythological creatures as the Jewish golems. These may even assume the form of a threatening female figure, especially in the context of the so-called familiarisation of the world and carnival culture in a Bakhtinian sense.

Through the processes of critical irony, a pungent, revealing humour, and elements of alienation, the faith of Catholics is shown to weaken the higher they climb on the social ladder. Such is the emphatically negative and bizarre character of Prince-Bishop Wolfgang, who admits at the end that 'my entire life, my mouth was full of God' because of his vocation, but he had only believed in God when he was young, and later less and less (Kumerdej 2017: 359). With his devilish lack of feeling, promiscuity, and delight in cruelty, killing, paedophilia, etc., which seem more appropriate for the Antichrist in the Christian imaginary than for a Church dignitary, his character is evil incarnate. As he puts it in his deathbed monologue: 'After all, no matter what I did I was never punished, and meanwhile I watched innocent people suffering and nobody heard them – neither God nor any other divinity, and not people either. God is not someone I'd like to meet' (ibid.: 359).

The critical gaze of ironic perspective likewise falls on patriarchal lines of force, which dominated during the successful Counter-Reformation in the Slovenian lands, for example, through the character of Agnes Hypatia, Count Friedrich's daughter. She suddenly dies in the flower of her youth, which the narrator's comment blames on her mother's too-liberal upbringing: she had allowed her daughter to engage not only in what befits a woman's role inside the family, but also in excessive reflection, book-reading, men's studies, and all this must have overburdened her female brain (ibid.: 85). The novel repeatedly stresses the historically suppressed but important role of certain women in the past, mostly the victims of witch trials in the context of patriarchal discourse. From a critical distance but with sympathy for the victims, there are depictions of countless pogroms, witch trials, murders, sexism, racism, homophobia, etc., in apocalyptic dimensions. They turn out to be orchestrated from the background of the power centres – by the guided interests of religious ideology allied with the political and economic supremacy of the ruling structures. How topical!

The Snarl of Madness and Pain in Mojca Kumerdej's Short Fiction

The author's very first collection of short fiction, *Fragma* (2003), revealed the full intensity of her writing and her ability to express several levels: private and intimate relationships as well as social criticism, unmasking the subjects' weaknesses, intrigues, obsessions, selfishness, aggression. All this is depicted with intelligence and a sardonic humour, but also with a feeling for the pain of the subjects, be they people or animals. In this collection, individual violence may take the form of destructive possessiveness in partnerships and friendships, which degenerates into parasitic appropriation, in the narratives 'Pod gladino' (Beneath the Surface),[4] 'Maščevalec' (The Avenger), 'Angel varuh' (Guardian Angel), and 'Mernik sreče' (Yardstick of Happiness). Another line of individual violence emerges in sadistic and masochistic relations within partnerships – in the stories 'Ponovitev' (Repetition), 'V roju kresnic' (A Swarm of Fireflies), and 'Nekakšen sindrom' (A Kind of Syndrome) – or in the unwholesome relation of mutual addiction in the tale 'Roka' (Her Hand). It is precisely 'Roka' that provides a broad range of violent acts perpetrated against oneself and others (the psychological or physical violence of mother against daughter, emotional neglect, paedophilia, alcoholism, drug abuse, bulimia, suicide). Finally, the short narrative 'Moj najdražji' (My Dearest) seems at first glance to depict an individual's violence against a girl because of the male protagonist's obsession with a new BMW, but the whole narrative actually implies a criticism of collective violence in the contemporary neoliberal system (Bošnjak 2015: 80). This converges with Foucault's concept of the 'constitutive subject', which belongs to late capitalism but nevertheless underpins the society of control and punishment (Foucault 2008: 118).

Kumerdej's second short fiction collection, *Temna snov* (*Dark*

---

4 The story *Pod gladino* from this collection received the Crystal Vilenica Award at the International Literary Festival Vilenica in 2006.

Matter, 2011),[5] continues to break down a variety of stereotypes and taboos: the unconditionally loving mother, good and non-violent children, family happiness, the wholesomeness of institutions (ecclesiastical, medical, educational, social). A case in point is the story 'Včasih Mihael molči' (Sometimes Mihael is Silent),[6] a highly sensitive, multi-layered rendering of a paedophiliac and incestuous relationship between father and underage daughter, with all psychological consequences (especially for the daughter).

In addition, the collection tackles various human ideals, from eternal life or youth in 'Jetrnik' (Hepatica) to the power of wealth in 'Siromaki' (The Poor) and the power of science in 'Kača'. New levels of relationship are established: coexistence between man and robot in 'Božič s Hirošijem' (Christmas with Hiroshi), or between man and animal – or, more particularly, a cat – in 'Vsiljivec' (Intruder).[7] One dystopian story, 'Program nacionalne obnove' (The Programme of National Reformation), depicts the intrusion of ideology into the private human sphere, which leads to collective violence. Individual violence (including death and various forms of abuse) features relatively frequently in this collection, in the stories 'Vanda', 'Čas potem' (Aftermath), 'Na terasi Marija' (On the Terrace, Marija), 'Včasih Mihael molči', and 'Zdaj spita' (Now the Two Are Asleep).

The stories of both collections are set in the present time, usually in an urban environment. Throughout Kumerdej's short fiction, misunderstandings between protagonists cause frustrations, and with these the accumulated hate, self-love and sadistic or masochistic character traits of both men and women may escalate into extreme psychological and physical violence. In

---

5 The collection, translated by Ana Ristović, was published in 2015 by Geopoetika, a Serbian publishing house. In 2016 it won the Kočić's Pen Award (bestowed for important achievements in contemporary literature).

6 The story has a child focaliser, a little girl observing the events and commenting on them from her own perspective. A child focaliser, this time a boy, likewise appears in Kumerdej's story 'Bela brada' (White Beard).

7 This story is included in a selection of short fiction written by Slovenian women writers, *Kliči me po imenu: izbor iz krajše proze slovenskih avtoric* (Call Me by My Name: A Selection of Short Prose by Slovenian Women Writers). The book was edited and furnished with an accompanying study by Silvija Borovnik (2013: 350–354).

Fromm's terms, we can detect symptoms of the so-called "malign aggression", which stems from the agents' unsatisfied existential needs and is a predominantly human trait (Fromm 1980: 13–31).

By Way of Conclusion: An Attempt at Outlining the Author's Poetics of 'Truth'

According to Foucault, the question of truth is linked mainly to political economy and stems from the scientific discourse by which truth is produced. Truth is subject to both economic and political evaluation, which means truth for the purposes of economic production and political power. Moreover, it is an object of social confrontations in the form of ideological struggles, as well as an object of consumption, circulating though educational and informational channels; last but not least, it is produced and mediated under the control of large political and economic systems (Foucault 2008: 118–119). This synopsis is perhaps the best general characterisation of Mojca Kumerdej's poetics, especially with regard to the simultaneous intertwining of past and present in both novels discussed above. The intimist paradigm prevalent in her short fiction, on the other hand, additionally underlines a re-valued view of social and gender stereotypes, which displays an open eco-feminist-oriented (Zimmerman 1994: 233–235) criticism of various forms of structures prevailing in society, from ideological to patriarchal and political ones.

Translated by Nada Grošelj

Works Cited

Blanka Bošnjak, 2015: *Med sodobnostjo in tradicijo* (*Between Contemporaneity and Tradition*). Maribor: Pivec.

Michel Foucault, 2001: *Arheologija vednosti* (*L'archéologie du savoir*). Slovenian translation. Ljubljana: SH.

——, 2008: *Vednost – oblast – subjekt* (*Knowledge – Power – Subject*). Slovenian translation. Ljubljana: Krtina.

Erich Fromm, 1980: *Anatomija ljudske destruktivnosti. Druga knjiga* (*Anatomie der menschlichen Destruktivität:* vol. 2). Croatian translation. Zagreb: Naprijed.

Jela Krečič, 2011: 'Ob 25. obletnici Krsta pod Triglavom' (On the 25th Anniversary of *Baptism under Mount Triglav*). http://www.delo.si/kultura/ob-25-obletnici-krsta-pod-triglavom.html.

Mojca Kumerdej, 2001: *Krst nad Triglavom* (*Baptism over Mount Triglav*). Ljubljana: Študentska založba.

——, 2003: *Fragma*. Ljubljana: Študentska založba.

——, 2011: *Temna snov* (*Dark Matter*). Ljubljana: Študentska založba.

——, 2012: 'Bela brada' (White Beard). In: *Dan zmage* (*Victory Day*). Ljubljana: Študentska založba, 37–53.

——, 2013: 'Vsiljivec' (Intruder). In: Silvija Borovnik [ed., accompanying study]: *Kliči me po imenu: izbor iz krajše proze slovenskih avtoric* (*Call Me by My Name: A Selection of Short Prose by Slovenian Women Writers*). Ljubljana: Študentska založba, 350–354.

——, 2015: 'Pauli.' In: *Moč lažnega* (*The Power of Deception*). Ljubljana: Beletrina, 77–98.

——, 2017: *The Harvest of Chronos*. Translated by Rawley Grau. London: Istros Books.

———, 2017: 'Poteza z amarantno figuro' (A Move with an Amaranth Figure). In: Gabriela Babnik [ed.]: *Opazovani: kratke zgodbe* (*The Watched: Short Stories*). Ljubljana: Društvo slovenskih pisateljev & UMco, 35–54.

Jacques Lacan, 2006: *Écrits: The First Complete Edition in English*. Translated by Bruce Fink in collaboration with Héloïse Fink and Russell Grigg. New York, London: W. W. Norton. https://archive.org/details/pdfy-I3ZjI2B47rFvMjBd.

Michael E. Zimmerman, 1994: *Contesting Earth's Future: Radical Ecology and Postmodernity*. Los Angeles, London: University of California Press, Berkeley.

Fragma

Beneath the Surface

"So you're really not going swimming with me?" he asked as he walked across the pebbles into the cold water of the lake.

"You know I'm not. You know how I hate swimming," I replied, just as I do every time he asks. It's like he's forgotten, or maybe he does this because he doesn't want to remember.

You will never learn the real reason. I'll never tell you. It's our third summer now, just the two of us, our very own summer with no one to bother us, and for this a sacrifice was required. On that early afternoon in July, it wasn't only that I saw it all happen, but that I did nothing, and by doing nothing, did everything. It was probably fate—that I left the beach and went into the house because I'd been nauseous since the morning and felt like I was going to vomit. Maybe I was reading, or maybe not; I probably wasn't doing anything except walking around the house and going out on the terrace a few times. I saw you playing on the beach, you and the kid with her long, curly blond hair. I can't say I had never thought about the thing that happened later that afternoon or that I hadn't desired it. I had never been particularly fond of children, had never even thought about them, in fact, and the only reason it seemed like we might have one was because that's what usually happens when two people love each other. I doubt I would have given the matter any serious thought if I hadn't noticed that calculating woman hanging around you, buttering you up, the way she would deliberately adjust a strand of hair whenever she was talking to you, and the corners of her mouth would tremble before she uttered a word, the way she'd

3

bite her lower lip and then—nonchalantly it seemed, but in fact despicably and deviously—lick it with her tongue, and the way your eyes became moist and frozen when she did this.

That's when I knew I had to do something. Not least because she was more attractive than me and had the ability to produce a kind of warm magnetic field around herself, which I simply do not know how to do. So that's how it happened. The first time you placed your hand on my belly, I knew I had you, and I decided then and there that I would have you forever, entirely and completely, with nothing in between, no troublesome elements that might threaten our love.

But when the kid was born, you changed; you looked at me differently, not like you used to. Like I wasn't your lover anymore, but the mother of your child. The mother of the kid, who soon turned into a little girl, and then more and more, I noticed, into a little woman. Every day when you came home from work, the first thing you'd do was give her a big hug, play with her honey-blond hair, and kiss her on both cheeks, and only then was it my turn. And how the kid cried those first few months—I can't describe how much she cried. Even then I was thinking that something had to be done. She woke me up every night with those ear-splitting squeals, and I'd climb out of bed and try to quiet her down—but you almost never got up, because you needed to be well rested for work the next morning, and presumably I didn't, since I was staying home with her. To look after her. To look after your child, your dearest darling, as you so often called her and never noticed how much that hurt me. She knew very well that she came first, that you loved her more than you loved me. More than once I saw that self-satisfied smile in her big bright eyes when you hugged her, with me on the sidelines waiting my turn, waiting for the two of you to grow tired of each other. The kid could be nasty, really nasty sometimes, and conceited. She'd make things up that were total lies, like saying that she hadn't been given the food she wanted that day, or the food that I'd promised her the day before, or that I had slapped her a few times in the department store when she wouldn't obey me, when she bolted from my hands just to get attention, and then the store's employees had to search for her over the PA system, and the salesgirls, and me with them, rummaged and poked through the clothes racks until finally she was found in the athletic department. She was laughing in my face, as if to say, look how many people have been searching for me, everyone was trying to find me, including you, who don't have anyone in the world who loves you best. And it was then, right when they brought her to me, that I didn't really slap her, I just grabbed her a little hard and gave her a tap on the head, but she started screaming as if I'd hurt her. But she wasn't hurt; it was me who was in pain, because, like so often before, she had disgraced me: all eyes were looking at me, asking, How could I have raised her so badly? What sort of mother was I? and so on—that's what I saw in their eyes. And then later, at home, you were furious, not at her but at me, because I had let her out of my sight, because I had allowed her, your child, to bolt away from the safety of her mother's arms.

She did this I don't know how many times, just so she could be the center of attention. When friends came to visit, she would sit in the armchair, cross her legs, and like a little woman ask our guests the sort of questions you don't expect to hear from a child, some of them even about sex. Oh, they adored her—she's a real femme fatale, they said; she'll keep men on a tight leash; you can already see how bright she is, and to top it all off, she's going to be a real beauty too. Smart and beautiful, our guests would say, as they glanced in your direction. Her father's daughter—I'm sure that's what they were thinking—thank god she doesn't take after her mother so much. She has his blue-green eyes, thick lips, and that disarming smile which will get her everything she wants, as well as his extraordinary communication skills . . . Many of them must have wondered what you saw in me. Sure, now we had a child, but what had you seen in me then, when in all probability you must have fallen in love with me? People always make a sort of calculation, and fall in love with those whose beauty is similar to their own; they're always making assessments: who is too far out of their league and who is beneath them. And when people looked at us, they probably noticed, and thought to themselves, that you deserved a woman who was prettier than me. But no one in the world could ever love you as fiercely as I do; no one could ever have done the thing that I did, when at that critical, fateful moment I did nothing.

With the kid's arrival, everything changed. There were no more Sundays like we used to have, lying in bed until noon, with a big wooden tray on the floor loaded with fruit, whole-grain bread, cheese, and cardamom coffee. No, instead, just when we were starting to wake up and you had wrapped your arms around me, usually the door would open and she'd come bounding into our room in her nightdress, jump on the bed and give you a big hug. And everything was over for that Sunday, for the entire week. More and more, our time became her time; she set the rhythm for our mornings and our nights. You always objected whenever I suggested locking the door—you never know when she's going to get the urge to leave her room and come crawling into ours, I said. But it's not right, it's not humane, you would tell me; she's just a child, she needs us . . . Yes, of course, I said, but not anytime she feels like it—what about us? But she's our daughter, you said and would always give me a dirty look, as if reproaching me for not loving your child enough. Whenever I'd wake up in the morning and feel you next to me and start to touch you, I would always be looking at the door in dread, straining my ears, hoping not to hear those tiny footsteps heading towards our bedroom, fearing the turn of the door handle.

She always managed to steal the show. Even on my birthday. I would prepare everything very carefully, do myself up nicely, and it would all be perfect, and then, when the guests arrived, some of them with their children—because that's what happens when your birthday is in the summer and everyone's delighted by an outdoor grill, so the kids can run around the yard safely without any fear—the kid again became the focus of attention and interest. People would give me their presents and a moment later forget why they were there in the first place. Twice I told you that I wanted to celebrate my birthday differently, not in the afternoon outside in the yard with all those children, but in the evening, just the two of us, alone, and we'd give the kid to our parents to look after. Both times you were against it; you said my birthday was a family occasion and that our parents would be offended if we didn't invite them. I gave in, but only because I would do anything for you, because I love you so much, like I have never loved anyone before, and, indeed, like I myself have never been loved. But you don't know what that's like, loving somebody more than he loves you, knowing that his hands and arms are able to embrace somebody else even more tightly, while you are ready to give him everything you have, to find something, to do anything, so you can give him even what you don't have yourself. And that is exactly what I did for you, and for once in my life I reclaimed the thing that meant the most to me and that for five years had been dwindling in front of my eyes.

The kid was four and a half that summer. It was a very hot summer, the kind we used to relish, like those summers before she was born which we spent on the Adriatic, just the two of us. But with her arrival, we started taking "family vacations" with our friends and their children. The couple we spent July with three years ago also had a child—though she had not been a child for a long time. The girl was fifteen, tall and slender, even a bit taller than me, and with the kind of perfect skin few teenagers have. You don't think I noticed the puma-like way she stretched out her young, long, and not yet fully developed body, how she'd purr and pout her lips whenever you asked her something, how she'd chat with you, seemingly with no particular interest but actually head over heels in love? What in the world could they be talking about? I wondered as I watched you from a distance. I couldn't hear what you were saying; I only saw your body language, which was clear and unambiguous: you liked each other a lot. I'm sure you would never have attempted anything—she was only fifteen, after all, the daughter of our friends, and just ten years older than your own daughter. But the more I watched that creature, that emerging woman—who a few years later, maybe three, and in a different setting I have no doubt you would make a pass at, and not stop at silly conversations (and I ask you, what can you even talk about with a teenage girl, unless the conversation is just an excuse to be with her, in such a way and to the precise degree that the rules of decency allow?)—the more I could see the kid in her.

It must have been fate—the fact that at noon on that July day I stood up, left the beach, and went into the house above the shore. I don't remember exactly what I did next, probably nothing special except go out to the terrace a few times and watch as you chatted with that fifteen-year-old and played with the kid. The next time I looked, you and your sea princess were sculpting castles out of sand. The two of you were alone; our friends had left the beach for the shade, and the girl had followed them.

The last time I looked out the window, I saw your tanned body lying beneath the umbrella. The kid was playing on the sand next to you. The inflated plastic dolphin, which you had left on the sand by the edge of the sea, started shifting as the tide came in. She noticed it. When the sea was lapping at the dolphin and the first bigger wave began to carry it away, she ran after it. I went out onto the terrace and at that moment wished for exactly what was starting to happen. You were still asleep. She was scampering after the dolphin and trying to grab it, but it was too slippery and kept drifting away from her. I knew I only needed to call out, one big powerful yell, and you'd wake up, leap after her, grab her, and pull her out of the sea foam, which was lathering her body in salty bubbles. That was the moment I saw a chance for everything to be the way it used to be. You and me, just the two of us, with no one in between setting the rhythm of our hours, days, and nights, our future years. Everything around me seemed to have stopped, sounds faded to nothing and the light was a blinding white. With half-closed eyes I watched the scene below and seemed to feel nothing. No pain, no fear of any sort; I was watching only what I was thinking moment by moment. At one point the kid was clinging to the dolphin's handle-like fins, but then a big wave, at full force, ripped the inflated animal out of her hands and she helplessly let go. I saw her tiny arms trying to wrap themselves around it and then how she was being pulled under . . . I didn't watch any more. I turned and went into the house, poured myself a glass of cognac, and collapsed on the bed. I shut my eyes and the world went dark, in front of me and behind me. I fell into a sleepless sleep. And when some time later I felt a hand and looked into the watery eyes of the wife of the couple we were on vacation with, I knew what had happened. The story was over. Your little girl!—she put her arms around me and held me tight—Your little girl is dead!—the woman burst into tears. I stood up, woozy from the cognac, and probably from the strange sleep too, and saw you sitting in an armchair in the living room with a sand-white blanket around you, hugging the little inflated dolphin. Our friend was sitting on the sofa next to you, and next to him was his fifteen-year-old daughter, who had just seen death for the first time in her life. There were a few others in the house too, and then the police and the coroner arrived. It was the girl who had found her. She had come back to the beach after lunch and seen her body floating on the surface face down. You had jumped into the water like a man gone mad and tried to revive your sea princess, but by then she had gone to other seas, oceans, rivers, and lakes. Yes, even though we buried her body in the ground, I feel like she has somehow spilled into the waters of the earth. There are times when I even seem to remember that, just as she was trying with her last strength to hold on to the dolphin, our eyes met and she saw that I was watching the whole thing and was doing nothing to help her. That I was simply letting her die.

It's not that I didn't feel terrible after she died—after all, she was my daughter too. But during those few long months, it was you I felt the worst for, you who blamed yourself for her death because, as can happen, you fell asleep on the beach for half an hour at the wrong time. And you also felt guilty towards me, the mother of the child you couldn't keep from dying. But I was full of love for you, so very full of love and understanding. I tried to assure you, to console you. I told you it was an accident, that you weren't to blame, that it had simply happened. I think that her death sealed your total commitment to me, even if I know that what you feel for me is not so much love but guilt.

Once, for just a moment, it seemed as if you doubted me. You asked me, You loved her too, didn't you? Of course, I said; she was our child. I remember the look in your eyes, as if you weren't happy with my answer and wanted to hear something more.

And I put my arms around you, pressed myself very tightly against you, and slowly, tenderly, began making love to you. It was a Sunday morning and there was nothing to interrupt us. After the kid died, you changed. You became softer and more vulnerable, and you stopped flirting with other women and girls. Whenever you mention to me, warily, that you would like to have another, second child, I sadly look away and say, You know I can't; it's much too painful. You caress me and, with a kiss, let me know that you understand. But you don't understand. You will never know the truth—that I hate swimming because I'm afraid that as soon as I dive into the water I will feel her soft, honey-blond hair on my skin, that her tiny arms will cling to me and pull me with all their might beneath the surface.

Sometimes I dream that the sea is carrying her away on a blue dolphin and I start to run after her, and at other times, that she and the dolphin grab me and pull me to the bottom of the sea. And I always wake up from these dreams with a horrific pain that holds me in a paralyzing cramp, barely breathing, my heart pounding—and not just one, but next to the sound of my own heart, I hear the slightly faster beating of another, smaller heart. I never wake you. I wait for it to pass, and then I go into the bathroom and take a shower. Afterwards, I return to bed, lie down next to you and passionately, very passionately, with boundless love, kiss you and press myself right up against you.

The Avenger

AFTER A FEW months with no improvement in your condition, I'd had enough. I couldn't look at you anymore. You were like a crumbling medieval fresco, faded and totally lifeless. You even seemed to have aged. And this was you, who in your best moments were unstoppable and in your passions often nothing short of ravenous. When I first met you, I thought you must be living the typical duality of the femme fatale, who, even as men dream about her, lies at home in bed alone and lonely. But that's not how it was with you. Whenever you mentioned the name of a man, I always listened to how you said it—did you simply toss it out, more or less casually, or was there a curious emphasis in your voice?—and I would try to deduce whether you were already somehow involved with him, or only hoped to be, and probably would be too. You collected men and boys—sometimes, my dear, boys much too young for you, younger even than me!—it all depended on your mood and the given circumstances. This really drove me crazy sometimes, but it was what made you who you are: different from every other woman I know. Because despite your throng of guys, you did not actually belong to anyone. And in fact, the way you lived never seriously bothered me. In any case, we were only friends. Friends first and foremost. Very good, very close friends. I liked you a lot more than I really should have. I had a girlfriend, after all. And yes, I genuinely loved my girlfriend. But you I loved in a very special way. What I felt for you was much more than just love.

And then like a bolt from the blue he showed up. I had been feeling for a while that something was going on with you (well, there was always *something* going on with you) and I knew that sooner or later you would tell me: whenever you were happy or unhappy, it was hard for you to keep it to yourself. That muggy afternoon in early July we were sitting on the patio of some silly Latino bar sipping cheap Cuba libre counterfeits. They were making you more animated: you were talking a lot, taunting the waiter, teasing and flattering me, and then suddenly you mentioned him.

"Who?" I asked, startled out of my lascivious rhythm.

"He told me he was coming for a visit."

And then nothing could stop you: when and where you first saw him (it was some cultural workers' protest march, I gathered), how you found him so extremely interesting—a little tipsy, you went on and on—and not just interesting but, and here's the main thing, you wanted him, you wanted him so much, like you hadn't wanted anyone in a very long time. I bit my lip and was seriously angry. What about that freezing night when we were wandering around town—we'd only known each other a few months—and you pushed me against a wall and started kissing me? I'm not saying I didn't like it; on the contrary, afterwards I couldn't sleep for days, and not just because I wanted to see what it would be like with a different woman but mainly because I wanted to do it with you. Even then I suspected that when the urge struck, you moved fast and with no reservations. I could sense that you liked me, just as I liked you too, but I was in a relationship, and you had a few yourself (although I wasn't entirely sure about this at the time), so I turned you down that night. It wasn't because you were older, and not just a few years but an entire decade older—no, it was because you did this with such nonchalance, such lightness, as if you were ordering dinner in a restaurant.

I adored you—I adored how you talked, how you moved your lips, how you paused between phrases to take a breath and joined them into very particular meanings. At times you seemed soft and feminine, but at other times you were like a well-trained

East German swimmer, with a stiff gait and much less charming
gestures. At times your insults were very blunt, and you could
even be a bit rude to me, but at other times you would tenderly
stroke my hair and kiss me on the cheek, and on the mouth too.
And then, sometimes, something would again be aroused within
you and you kissed me like you meant it. Almost always I wanted
to respond the same way, but I stopped myself. I knew we would
be closest to each other only if we stayed friends first and foremost, and nothing but friends, without sleeping together, but
that was something you never fully understood. All your life
you'd been getting these concepts confused. If you felt a strong
attraction to somebody and were getting close to him, it seemed
natural that you should sleep with him too. It's simply communication, you laughed, it's always about language, sometimes the
messages are in words, at other times, touches and kisses. When
you talked like this, I could never decide if you were being vulgar
or not, but you always pulled it off with such naïve purity that
in fact I saw nothing obscene in your behavior. And besides, I
enjoyed your stories immensely, even if sometimes, when we
were together with other men, what I wanted to do most was
grab you by the hair and drag you from the table. A few times I
even leaned over and hissed in your ear that you really didn't have
to be flirting right and left. But I'm not, you defended yourself,
at least not intentionally, or so you tried to convince me. At such
moments I just wanted to smack you, and then smack all those
idiots who swooned as you ground them into a little packet, all
the while preserving the impression of innocent enthusiasm.
You'll see, I thought; one day you too will get caught, and it will
teach you a lesson, if only because you will feel what the others
feel when you crush them with a smile as they're falling apart,
and then later, when they are home—unless, of course, you've
taken them home with you—they struggle to reassemble themselves piece by piece.

And then it actually happened. Never before had you talked
with such fervor about anyone. You described him so precisely
that when I finally met him, I was shocked. Sure, the guy wasn't
really all that good-looking; yes, he was tall and I won't say he

wasn't smart—after all, he'd climbed his way into that stupid job at the European Commission and was rather crassly hawking his latest book, which wasn't even his but just a collection of essays he'd compiled on cultural politics. From the first moment you mentioned him he got on my nerves. That conceited Euro careerist! Right away I suspected that the guy had no balls. Just another bureaucratic sellout, who had swallowed shit for years to work his way up to that imbecilic job and bought third-rate secondhand sports cars, which he pompously drove from conference to conference around Europe. In other words, a dutiful, wonkish poser!

"So if I understand you correctly, my dear, you're in love with a Eurocrat."

"He's not just a Eurocrat—he has a doctorate!"

"Like I said: a dutiful, wonkish poser," I repeated, and you were offended and pretended to strangle me.

But what I didn't understand was why him. Why was he the one who opened up an abyss in you that could not be closed, who awakened in you such powerful desire that it pressed me to the wall that summer afternoon, as you sang praises to his looks, his intelligence, and his sense of humor? Especially, my dear, because as I later discovered, he had no sense of humor whatsoever. And your praises were merely the result of your hormonal algorithms, which, apart from you being in love, had nothing to do with the truth.

The powerful desire he had triggered in you bathed you in such radiance that you were more attractive than ever. I was desperately curious to know what it was about this idiot that had catapulted you through the stratosphere, to somewhere none of us who knew you had access. Sometimes we would get together just to discuss your flights of euphoria, and we would try to remember when we had last seen a movie where someone was so head-over-heels in love, and how it was even possible that a woman normally so smart could fall so unreservedly in love, with no safety mechanisms. "With all my heart," one of our friends remarked, "I hope it ends well. Or doesn't end at all, because when it does, she'll come crashing to the ground and it will be really terrible. She'll get sick, with lots of aches and pains, imaginary cancers, swollen glands, an ashen, expressionless face, wordless, with a wounded, dead look in her eyes."

"I'll kill him if he's just toying with her," I said at the time. And that same friend replied: "Well, I hope you keep your word." We laughed; what else could we do? It was summer; the evening was warm, and it seemed, probably because of your boundless infatuation, that nothing was out of bounds and everything was possible. Absolutely everything.

And then the guy really did come for a visit. But no one got to see what he looked like. Because the evening he was supposed to arrive, probably in some flashy convertible, you shut off your phone and hid him from the rest of us like a cat hiding her kittens. A few days later (at last!) my cell phone rang.

"Are you on magic mushrooms?" I interjected and held the phone away from my ear as you squealed euphorically that you'd never had so much fun with anybody—and similar nonsense. If the guy had been anywhere near me at that moment, I'd have punched him in the mouth for sure. Just like that, no fuss. I could sense that it wouldn't end well. You didn't even know him. You just decided to direct some romantic telenovela in your head and picked him as your leading man. It could have been anyone at all, but at the moment you met him and later started exchanging emails with him, you were simply ready for love. Fine, maybe you were inspired by his contrived writing style, although he wrote to you much less often than you wrote to him. But it could easily have been somebody else, from some other country, who looked nothing like him; no need for him to be a few years older than you or have such a silly job. Yes, ultimately, it could even have been me. That is, of course, if you didn't live the way you do. If I wasn't in a serious relationship. If . . .

In that early period you exuded enough energy to raise the dead. On evenings when the rest of us would wrap ourselves in cardigans and pullovers, you would be waving your bare arms as you sang his praises and transmitting bodily heat.

"My dear, I think you must be entering that change of life," I taunted you.

"Absolutely!" you replied. "My life is entering a completely new phase."

From time to time you would confide to me some detail about your relationship, which I found most interesting. But at the same time, I was becoming more and more furious with him. And I was furious with you too—for hiding him from all of us and especially for hiding from me. If I had met him then, at the very beginning, I could have spared you a lot of pain. I would undoubtedly have seen him for what he is and discerned his character—lackluster and cowardly, and at the same time full of himself. Not only was he not in love with you; he didn't even like you, and I was more and more convinced that he was with you only to get revenge, because he envied your passion and capacity for pleasure. In you he was taking revenge on all the women who, in his dewy youth, when he hadn't yet mastered the art of seduction, had in some way destroyed him or remained out of reach.

In less than a month it was clear that he was a total selfish prick. "Well, has your Eurocrat been writing to you at all?" I would goad you. "Sure," you said at first. Then a little while later: "Not so often." And the one day you mumbled out: "Pretty seldom, actually—or rather, no, not really," and your face was no longer aglow. You added that in any case you intended to visit him. "Well, I hope you'll have a good time," I said as you left on the train for Brussels, but what I really hoped was that you would come back disappointed, get over him as soon as possible, forget about him, and be like you used to be. That time when you were away visiting him I had trouble sleeping—I'd get anxious in the evening and couldn't help sending you at least one text message. Only with great effort did I keep myself from calling you at six in the morning, and at eight o'clock, I told myself: enough already, time to get out of bed. Then I would text you some nice thought, saying I wished you a nice day, to which I couldn't resist adding some cynical barb at his expense.

After your return, your delight subsided a little and evened out. I was surprised at this and wondered if your biochemical infatuation was turning into partnership love. But it soon became clear that I had been right all along.

"So how's it going with your bureaucrat? Heard from him recently?" I teased you. You were sending each other text messages every day, you told me at first, then that he was taking longer and longer to respond, and after a few weeks you were flinching whenever I asked you that. You said I was doing it on purpose and knew very well that the question tormented you. Once when I was looking at some photos I had taken over the summer and compared them with the ones from the fall, after you came back from your visit, I noticed that your eyes, and your whole appearance too, were losing their fire. Your voice was becoming softer and your words sparser. Your sense of humor dried up, you stopped taunting me with your witty remarks, and I could see how badly you were hurting. I don't know how such an intelligent woman doesn't see—I said, trying to wake you up—I don't know how you can't see that you mean nothing to him, that for him you are nothing more than one of his chess pieces. I don't know—I said in amazement—how an Amazon like you could be so besotted with some slutty Eurocreep. "But I'm in love with him," you replied in a voice that was increasingly a monotone. More and more seldom were you willing to get together with your friends, more and more seldom were you texting me, and you stopped answering my emails altogether. It was so unbearably painful to see you in such pain. What a prick, I kept repeating to myself, and I imagined how one day I'd meet him, stuff him in a grinder, make mincemeat of him, and toss it to the filthy birds in the nearest park, so they could feast on his disintegrated body—the same body you said you so passionately adored.

But there was something about him you didn't want to talk about, something you couldn't mention to anyone, you once told me in a whisper. "So what is it?" I asked. But you got very quiet and said only that you were certain you had touched him deeply.

"That pragmatist is much too calculating to let anything touch him," I tried to convince you, "unless he got something out of it. You never saw his game. You walked right into it, wholly and completely, and he was like a puppet-master. Who knows where this preacher is spreading his EU gospel now?

Maybe in Hungary or the Czech Republic he's persuading candidate members to join, and all the while, with no emotion—since he's incapable of it (you really didn't notice?)—he's mercilessly banging them."

My coarse commentary no longer angered you; you just kept repeating softly that you didn't know how it would end (something that had never begun!), that you couldn't take it anymore, and that you would probably go mad from such immense desire, if you didn't die first, that your heart would break . . .

"Your heart break?" The pathetic cliché disappointed me; never would I have expected that from you. "You don't have heart disease; you're just in love—and with a total jerk! You deserve something infinitely better; he's not worthy of you," I persisted, but you said nothing and only went on staring into space, and it hurt me to see you slowly but surely imploding like this.

That's when I made my decision and once more told myself what I had said before in jest (but half in earnest too): I'm gonna kill the bastard! Not physically, no; his death will be educational. I'll ruin him so badly and completely that, for a while at least, his career as a bureaucrat will be going nowhere.

That summer afternoon on the patio of that cheesy pseudo-Latino bar, you mentioned in passing that you thought that he wasn't only into women but men too. Later, however, it apparently proved otherwise: he was only into women and, especially, into you. I knew you were never wrong about these things and that if you later forgot your initial deduction, it was only because the serotonin in your brain was distorting your perception and you were adjusting reality to match your desires. My decision—to rescue and avenge you in the most effective way possible—calmed my nerves. Of course I didn't mention it to anyone. A few days later I had worked out a detailed plan. It was absolutely foul, but just. And then—I'll admit it—with a pleasure such as few things had ever given me, I set about executing it. First, I bought all his books and articles over the internet and quickly skimmed them. There wasn't a lot, far from it, particularly since they were all compilations of the same material. Next came communication. I discovered his email address, which isn't very hard with EU officials, and got in touch. In my email, I introduced myself as a journalist (not far from the truth) who was writing something about European cultural policy and said I'd like to do an interview with him (of course I didn't mention you). I flattered him with superlatives about his articles, tossed in a few thoughts about his Euro-gospel, and let him know that I wasn't someone who could be easily converted by half-baked platitudes. I threw down the gauntlet and attached a picture of myself, one of the ones where I thought I looked really hot. The idiot naturally took the bait and wrote back right away that he found my comments extremely interesting and would be happy to talk to me. Clearly, he was caught like a fat fly on the lid of a jam jar, and all I had to do was twist the lid back on the jar and the insect would be smothered in sugary sweetness.

"Do you want to do it over the internet?" he asked in his email, and I enthusiastically replied that in two weeks I'd be traveling to the Rotterdam Film Festival and could stop by his office on the way there. "That sounds really great," he replied. The carp was caught securely on the hook and all I had to do was pull him off and roast him on the spit.

Two days before my departure I went to the stylist, got a trim, and had him dye my hair Scandinavian blond. On the way home I picked up *Death in Venice* at the video store and then, frame by frame, studied a few of Tadzio's preadolescent poses, practicing them in front of the mirror. I went through the trendier part of my wardrobe and picked out a few things by Gap. So get ready—I whetted my thoughts as I tried on the clothes— because I'm gonna crush you like the Taliban, I'm gonna bring you down like the Twin Towers, I threatened him mentally, and sincerely enjoyed myself.

As I was leaving, of course I didn't tell you that I was planning to meet with him, or even that I had been in touch with him and that his emails to me were far more frequent than the ones he was sending you, and that often his reply to my messages arrived the very same day, sometimes in just a few hours. Oh, how I was looking forward to that meeting! I'm going to destroy you,

I'm going to fry you, like no one has ever done to you before, I thought as I plotted my lethal schemes. Such thoughts and my plan made me diabolically attractive. I really liked myself like this, and in a gas station bathroom I put a little gel in my hair, so I looked like an Arian lover at some chic spa resort. "You'll be sorry you were ever born," I perfected the words in English and then typed him a text to say I was having problems with my car, which meant that right now, somewhere in the middle of Germany, in the cold rain, I was all alone, abandoned by the world, waiting on the side of the road for a kind soul to help me. And that there was no way I could make it to his office by one o'clock, as we had agreed, but with a little luck, if I didn't have to spend the night in a roadside motel waiting for my car to be fixed, I would get there before evening. A minute after I sent the text, I got a response full of good cheer and sympathy: he said he hoped everything would be OK with the car, that it was cloudy in Brussels too but not raining, and that he'd like to invite me to dinner at an excellent Italian place near his office. An Italian restaurant? Really? I considered the prospect with disdain as I cut into the chicken and stabbed the salad at the gas station's self-service buffet. Obviously. What else should I have expected from one of those politically correct types from a grim and frustrated Western European country who finds his notion of freedom in the Mediterranean lands, where it doesn't rain every single day, where the sun is hot and so are the women, while pleasure is tediously reduced to traditional rule-breaking. But even more than the Mediterranean, those bleeding-heart Euro-leftists prefer to enthuse over some trendy Cuba, where, while screwing the natives, they cleanse their conscience by spending money earned in globalist offices to correct the wrongs of the exotic communist exclave (the wrongs of both communism and globalist capital-ism) and improve the standard of living for the Cuban people, all under the illusion that the hot chicks and Castro-machos are fucking them out of sheer pleasure! Well, fine, if he insists, but then he'd better pay for my pasta, but it won't happen until at least seven.

I arrived at his office building strategically late, at seven thirty.

As soon as he saw me, his blue, angled eyes grew wide and his pupils glistened. You were right, my dear, at least until your brain started rotting like a bad mushroom: what he liked more than you, far more than any of you, was us. And me. He especially liked me. When we did the customary handshake in front of the building, I made a point of giving his hand a firmer squeeze. And for a few moments I could read in his eyes what this might mean, even as I pretended that I didn't have a clue about anything and it had happened spontaneously. I could see that he was trying to be witty and amuse me however he could. At the restaurant, he naturally asked me about my car. I made up a story about hearing a clunking noise in the engine, so I pulled over right away and, for nearly half an hour, waited by the side the of road for some cold Protestant heart to be moved by my plight—all in vain of course—but finally a bearded Hungarian stopped, and although I could barely understand his bad German, he took a tool and some cables out of the trunk of his car, lifted the hood and fiddled with the engine, and then, when he closed the hood, turned to me and poked his thumb optimistically in the air a few times, from which I understood that there was nothing to worry about and I could continue on my way. I concluded my fabrication with an ominous-sounding bronchial cough.

"You haven't caught a cold, have you?" he asked. I told him I really hoped not, but that I had first tried to deal with the engine myself in the pouring rain, and then, soaking wet, waited at least twenty minutes for that Hungarian to appear, and that I didn't change my clothes until after he had fixed it.

As we were finishing our meal, I looked around the room with a slight frown and said I doubted we'd be able to do the interview here because it was so noisy and that I needed to be in Rotterdam first thing in the morning. Clearly, there was only one solution.

The two-room apartment was just as you had described it to me. Huge, with only a little furniture, the orangish yellow walls in the living room painted with deliberate carelessness to create a kind of Flemish baroque patina, or something like that. The guy walked over to a cabinet, opened it, and started offering me expensive brandies, whiskeys, and all sorts of wines from his Euro-missionary travels.

"Why, you've got the entire EU in your liquor cabinet, candidate members included," I observed, and then went to the little bar and started poking through the bottles. I knew what I was looking for and found it. A Slovenian teran wine from the Karst and a gentian brandy from the Soča Valley were hidden far behind the French, Spanish, and Portuguese wines, and even behind a Moldovan cognac. Clearly, that bastard had never even touched them, nor had he offered them to me.

"Hmm . . . What exquisite taste!" I noted with the air of a connoisseur. "Oh, look, something from my country," I said, as I rotated the bottle of teran in my hand. "A gift?"

He didn't remember who gave it to him, he said, denying your existence. But if I liked, we could open it. The prick has no balls, I thought as I remembered with what passion you had bought that wine and that brandy, both of superior quality and by no means cheap.

We took our glasses and the booze and went to the other room, which was both his office and bedroom. An antique desk and chair stood in front of a big window; he then dragged a cushioned armchair closer to the desk, and I casually fell into it.

"This really is excellent," he said knowledgeably, cautiously sipping the wine (earlier, over pasta, we had drained a bottle of Spanish red), while I tried to discern if he had devoted even a moment's thought to the person who had given him the wine. There was no indication of it; he had obviously forgotten. My scrutiny, however, he understood differently. I knew what he was thinking: was I not perhaps looking at him so intently because there was something else I wanted to convey? Dear friend, who if not you taught me the arcane art of interpreting gay codes? It was you who taught me to pay close attention to the details of body language, and as you know, I am an excellent pupil.

Sprawled out in the armchair, I switched on the cassette recorder and turned into a journalist.

I knew he was nervous and excited—and wanted me. During the interview I kept track of the amount of alcohol consumed, while my strategy was first to flatter him a little, then blast him with a comment and follow-up question. I was the embodiment of the driven young man. He was twenty years older and no doubt saw something in me that he had never had, in particular, the freedom he had never been able to seize for himself, had never had the guts to claim, and which he had also seen in you. But you, as a woman, were someone he had been taking out his revenge on, while I, on the contrary, was someone he desired. Desired a lot.

As we were talking, I made a little grimace, which I then dramaturgically developed.

"Aren't you feeling well?" he asked.

"Oh, I've got a headache coming on. Maybe I did catch a small cold."

He pouted his lips a little to express sympathy. When I was later quizzing him about some comparative statistics between the EU member states and non-members, he turned on his laptop, which had been my intention all along. I had quite correctly reasoned that it would be password-protected.

When the cassette reached the end, I started to unwrap a new one, without, however, putting down my wine glass, so I spilled wine on myself. Intentionally, of course.

"Oh, fuck!" I cried, and apologized: I hoped he didn't mind if I took off my shirt to wash out the stain. Of course, he replied, already opening his wardrobe and looking for something of his I could wear. As I removed my shirt, I positioned myself next to a floor lamp, specifically so its light would fall on my body, and contorted myself like St. Sebastian pierced by arrows. As he raced off to the bathroom with my stained shirt and I waited for him to give me a fresh one, I placed my hand on my waist, turned towards the window, and stood like Tadzio on the Lido's sandy beach in the last scene from *Death in Venice*. In the reflection (by now it was dark outside) I saw how closely, how attentively, he was watching me. I turned at once to face him and he quickly looked away. Something wrong, sweetie? Getting some ideas in that head of yours? I could see that everything was going like clockwork. I put on his shirt, more or less, not really buttoning

it up, and said it felt a little hot in here, then did the rest of the
interview half naked. His responses were increasingly less for-
mulaic, less precise; he was correcting himself more and more,
checking things on the computer, and more than once his eyes
wandered to my chest, which I could tell he wanted to lick like a
schoolboy with an ice cream cone. I pretended not to notice, that
I was merely an ambitious young journalist, so dedicated I had
no interest in anything unrelated to my work. When we finished
the interview, I grimaced again, more expressively this time, then
took my head in both hands and ran my fingers through my hair.

"I think I might have a fever," I said, and felt his gaze following my every motion, how it was riveted to my armpits. I held
the pose for some twenty seconds, so it wouldn't seem too contrived, and fell back in the armchair like jelly. Slightly narrowing
my eyes, I gave him a piercing look, presumably showing a headache, and again he was left to wonder if I was staring at him like
that because my head was splitting or was I trying to send him a
different message? Since he was in fact very shy (which I realized
when we first began our communications), I knew he wouldn't
be bold enough to make the first move. With my eyes apparently
closed—although actually squinting at the big bed across the
room—I thought of you, of the two of you rolling around on
that bed a few months earlier and everything you did with him.
What I most wanted to do right then was stand up, jump on the
bed, and piss all over it. But I had an even more perfidious strategy, and now, with the interview over, I asked him politely, with
the beseeching eyes of an injured German shepherd, if I might
lie down for a few minutes, since I was feeling dizzy, and if he
wouldn't mind turning off the ceiling lamp, which was hurting
my eyes, and switching on the floor lamp by the bed. "No problem," he said, as he hurried to tidy up the bed linen. My dear, his
level of hygiene was definitely below European standards! You
really had to be in love to lie down in that mess, or did you perhaps insist that he first change the sheets? Knowing you, probably not; you were in too much a hurry . . . I ran my eyes across
the little shelf next to the bed: there was a big box of condoms
(does he buy them in bulk?) and next to it a big jar of lubricant.

I carefully arranged the duvet around me, in just such a way that he got a good look at my casually exposed torso, and then, as I lay there, I started massaging my head. He obligingly brought me a glass of water with an aspirin dissolved in it.

"Oh no, anything but aspirin!" I cried. "I have a very sensitive stomach." After this lie, I moaned that I needed something stronger, something for the flu or a stomach virus, which I thought might be the source of my troubles, at which point I ran my hand down my body and started rubbing my abdomen, sliding my little finger a few times to just above my zipper and loosening my belt. He stood by the bed and was visibly perspiring. As he apparently had no intention of ever moving from that spot, I asked if maybe he too had caught something.

"No, no, I'm fine," he said. "I'm quite all right." And then—at last!—he asked if he could do anything to help. That was exactly what I wanted to hear.

"I'd be really grateful if you could go to the pharmacy and get me something for the flu and this stomach virus, something that won't damage the stomach tissue."

"Absolutely. I'd be glad to."

"I hope I'm not asking too much," I added, "and that the all-night pharmacy isn't too far away."

"Not at all. I'll be back in less than forty-five minutes," he replied, and as if in pain, I stammered out how deeply I appreciated his kindness.

He threw on his coat and ran out of the apartment like my personal caregiver. When I heard him go down in the elevator, I went over to the window so I could see what direction he went. So forty-five minutes, I said to myself, half an hour to be on the safe side. Then I sat down at his computer and went to work. I couldn't care less about the articles he had written, but I pounced on his email. You weren't the only one, dear friend; there were a few other lambs like you roasting on his spit, from both inside and outside the EU. There were no emails from you in his inbox; he must have deleted them, just as he had deleted you. Now there was a certain Chiara, an Ingrid, and a Katalin, along with a few other pigeons. And not all female, either.

And so I embarked on the chief part of my plan. I wrote you a letter in his name. I had the text already prepared; you had shown me a fair number of the fictions you'd received from him, so I was familiar with his style. The letter was polite and, in a way, even contrite. The main message was that he was in love with an Italian woman he had met last spring, and when they saw each other again in the early fall, they fell in love; they had decided to live together because in mid-July they were expecting a baby. He couldn't bring himself to tell you about it earlier because he didn't want to upset you, but now he had to because you kept on sending him text messages and emails and the relationship between you didn't make sense anymore. Although he liked you, he was never truly in love with you and it would be best to cut off all contact and let it end. I sent the email and, of course, deleted it. I knew you would be crushed by this letter, but I had to be cruel; I put a woman in the scenario because if I had mentioned a man, your affection for gays might even make you sympathize with him and you'd probably try to stay in touch.

With my mission accomplished in under half an hour, I next sat on the bed and rummaged through his drawers a little. I found a few silly sex toys—the guy really had no imagination!—and then looked through some of his business cards and noted the names and addresses.

He came back with an entire small pharmacy and at once started preparing herbal teas and medicinal beverages. I was lying on the bed sprawled out like a poisoned fox, then drank every remedy he offered, wincing only at the possibility that the cunning bastard might have slipped me a roofie. Then he suggested I spend the night. In your dreams, prick, I thought.

"Thanks for the offer, but I have to be on the road first thing in the morning. I do have another favor to ask, though"—I spun my lie slowly, with calculated pauses between the words—"I'd be very grateful if you wouldn't mind giving me a head massage."

"Just tell me how," he said eagerly, and I turned onto my stomach and instructed him to rub my temples and the back of my neck. To tell you the truth, he wasn't so bad at it. But when I felt his fingers getting more and more expressive, and mainly they were expressing the desire to please me, I stopped him and said I felt better now, that the medicines were kicking in and that the massage especially had worked miracles.

I stood up and was about to take off the shirt he had lent me, when he said I may as well keep it since it looked so good on me. Then he gave me a plastic bag with the shirt I had spilled the teran on, which he had washed out manually while I was in bed. As I put my coat on, he watched me with slightly parted lips. I knew he wanted to say something but didn't have the courage. When I was about to leave, I offered him my hand, gave him a diplomatic hug and, with my lips by his ear, whispered: "You're a wonderful man." He gave a little start and pulled me into his arms. I'm not exactly sure what happened next. As we were embracing, body to body, I felt his rigid dick against my pelvis. I don't know, it wasn't part of the plan, but when I felt the pulse of his body against my lower abdomen, I thought of you, of everything you had done with him, how you had touched him, the way you had taken him in your hand, and probably in your mouth too. And at that moment, as I really did start to feel hot, without looking at him, my eyes closed, I kissed him and shoved my tongue deep into his mouth. It was a passionate kiss—at least it looked that way—and long. I felt the beating of his heart and the hot sweat on his hands as he stroked my neck. He tenderly caressed my head, the back of my neck, and then my back, but when his hand slid down to my butt, I gently pushed it away.

"No, please, I need to get back to the hotel. I'm leaving early tomorrow and I still don't feel very well," I hastily explained, hoping to forestall any attempt to get me to change my mind.

"How about I give you a full-body massage?" he offered.

"Another time. There will definitely be other times," I replied warmly; then I kissed him again, now on the forehead, and left.

When I got in my car, I hunted around the glove compartment for some menthol candies and stuffed them in my mouth. I didn't know why, but in a way I had really enjoyed that kiss. Not because I was attracted to the guy—never in my life had I even imagined French-kissing a man—but something about my tongue being intertwined with his deeply excited me. And my

dick had gotten hard—right when I was thinking about what
you had done with him, and feeling what you had touched, what
you had so desperately desired, what had made you so happy
and later, when you no longer had it, had sent you into such
utter despair . . . It was your desire I had felt against my body.

Back in my hotel room I turned on the television, opened
the minibar, and had myself a party. Which ended in the wee
hours with me bending over the toilet bowl, having chased the
recently imbibed medications with the minibar's entire selection
of Belgian beer and tiny bottles of liquor. In fact, I had such pain
in my stomach, I was vomiting mercilessly for nearly an hour.

But when things calmed down and I was lying there in bed, I
was content. I knew that my project could not have gone better.
And I felt a deep peace. Or at least it seemed that way.

The next morning I didn't wake up until I got a call from
hotel reception in which a dry female voice said I had to leave
the room by noon. In other words, in fifteen minutes. I had
a murderous headache—for real this time. I dug through my
toiletry bag, found three aspirins, and dissolved them in water.
But even after drinking this, there was still a strange menthol
taste in my mouth.

On the way to Rotterdam I was bombarded by his text messages and when the phone rang it was usually his name on the
screen. Naturally, I didn't answer his calls; I only sent him a short
text message to say that my health was stable, thanks to him of
course, and then shut off the phone.

At home I found a thick folder of emails from him waiting
on my computer and a few days later I wrote back: I too was
really delighted that we had met, I thought about him a lot, and
other such nonsense. He only became mushier. I, meanwhile,
always made him wait, sending one email for every five of his,
and only with much delay, sometimes a few days but more often
a few weeks. So now do you see what it's like when someone toys
around with you, when someone abuses your emotions? Are you
feeling the same pain that she felt? That's what I was thinking
as I read his troubadour poetry; then I would compose some

schmaltz of my own and send it off to him.

You were even gloomier when I got back and wouldn't say why. But only a few weeks later your mood began to change. You were returning to your old self, slowly becoming the person I had known. Never again did I ask you about him, but I did publish that interview in a magazine you don't read. If by some chance you do see it, I'll say that the editor assigned it to me and I didn't mention it because I didn't want to upset you. As for him, not even I know for sure what's going on. I still get messages from him, invitations and offers to visit, and every now and then I like to torture him, put him on the rack as it were. Whenever some higher-up gives me a hard time or I'm agonizing over an article, or when I'm fighting with my parents or my girlfriend's in a mood, or my car breaks down, or I'm simply having a bad day—I sit down at the computer and write him some sugary letter about how he's such a great guy and I'd love to see him too only right now I can't because I'm too busy or I'm sick or someone in my family is sick or if nothing else I'll use the dog as my excuse. Basically, I lie to him, and I like it that he believes me and pines for me. I do exactly what he did to you. And whenever I send him an email from my computer at home, I go to bed satisfied, pick up the phone, call you, and we chat a while as I lie there. You are again full of witty remarks and quick responses; your voice is vibrant again. You taunt me and joke with me, but we also talk about very serious matters. You ask about this and that, comment on some article I've written, and every so often, in passing as it were, you tell me you love me. When you say this I know you are sincere, that you really mean it. I say I feel the same, that I'm glad I know you. And when we say good night and I hang up, I add something out loud that I never tell you: I don't just love you, I love you very much, so much more than love . . . My dearest friend . . . My dearest woman!

Guardian Angel

I AM SURE you have never noticed me. And have no idea I exist. Because you despise men with puny bodies, as you once exclaimed in a burst of noisy laughter at the next table over, which is when I first noticed you. Your appearance is cheap and vulgar. With tacky makeup and messy red hair, which you adjust with your arms raised so high and wide that your half-shaven armpits are exposed and the sickly-sweet odor of your sweat permeates the entire area around you.

When you left the table that afternoon and went, key in hand, to the elevator, I followed you, unnoticed, and waited to see where it stopped. Seventh floor. I worked your name out from the mailbox. It was clear to me at once that you live alone. The male voice on your answering machine is, perhaps, a sign that you are not quite sure that the world you live in is safe.

The desk in my office faces the entrance to your apartment building. At eight in the morning, when I sit down at my computer, you are still fast asleep. With no sense of decency or time, no sense of responsibility to life, to the start of the day, which for you begins whenever you wake up and feel like getting out of bed. When sometime before noon you step out of the elevator, you move slowly, nonchalantly. You're in no hurry. That's because you live alone. Out of selfishness—so you don't have to accommodate anyone, don't have to coordinate your time and obligations with anyone. For you, hours are the same as minutes, and minutes the same as days. It makes no difference to you if you return to the apartment at six in the evening or midnight. I myself frequently go back to the office at night because my work demands it. I always recognize the sound of your red car, the way you slam the door—brusquely, with no sensitivity. And even if I didn't know your license plate by heart, I'm sure I'd be able to pick your car out from all the other Opels: it's the one with the ashy blotches of stale, cemented dust and the filthy windows.

Because of your disorderly work week—if you feel like it, you can work at home, not in an office like others do, like most people do, like I do—I have to be careful. You are negligent and forget things, and when you step out of the elevator you often have to go back to the apartment, so I always wait thirty minutes until I'm sure you won't be returning for at least a few hours. You probably don't know there's a drying room on the top floor of your building, and from there a person can slip out onto the roof. And then it's just a matter of agility—the kind we puny men have—to climb down from the roof onto your balcony. I don't understand your naïveté, how you can be so careless as to leave the balcony door open.

Your blithe disregard is profoundly offensive to the people around you. Once when I was standing behind you at the checkout in a store, I glanced into your open shoulder bag; it was crammed with all sorts of useless things. As you searched for your wallet, and the debit card inside it, you loaded the counter with crumpled scraps of paper, pens, a small toiletry bag, and then, for everyone to see—your tampons! You act like the world is your oyster and nothing can ever happen to you.

The first time I stepped into your apartment, I was shocked. I knew you were sloppy, but I was horrified to see your dirty underwear strewn across the living room sofa, the towels and dresses hanging off the chairs, the dishes in the sink with bits of food stuck to them, the table covered in books and piles of paper, and the bedroom, with your enormous unmade bed and the windowsill above it lined with condoms. You never notice when I make some alteration in your apartment—when I move a plant, for instance, or open the curtains, or mix up your papers. Once I even washed a dish for you, and the next day, when you stepped out of the elevator breezily twirling your car keys, you didn't seem the least bit upset, let alone alarmed. Sometimes I

go through your drawers, the months-overdue bills and remind-
ers, the illegible Post-It notes stuck to the table by the phone—
that's how I learn in advance when you probably won't be home.
Sometimes I read your email. The way you talk to men is direct
and dirty. You disgust me; everything about you makes me want
to vomit. Your face shines from the powder you use to cover
your dried-out skin after nights of not sleeping. And probably
from alcohol too: seven times I found empty wine bottles in
the trash can in your kitchen. And two unwashed wineglasses
on the counter. Once even three, two of which had no trace of
lipstick on them.

A few days ago I came in through the balcony door right
when you were doing the thing you normally do—irresponsi-
bly and unemotionally—with one of your men. I crept up to
the open bedroom door and glanced at the bed. Neither of you
heard me. How could you? You were going at it like street dogs.
When I steal into your apartment at night (which is less often,
of course, than during the day), I always wear my track suit and
sneakers. Because I take care of my health. I know that without
a healthy body there's no healthy mind. No soul. And you are
completely soulless. You are nothing but an impudent mass of
flesh, inside of which organs are pulsating, beneath the skin of
which infected blood is circulating, urine and lymphatic fluids
gurgling, excrement making its way towards the rectum . . .

How is it possible that men don't notice the vileness veiled
by your skin? How do they put up with the words you throw
around, with no responsibility at all, when you're sitting in the
bar beneath your building? Or when they're getting out of your
car, or you're getting out of theirs? It's vulgar the way you speak
to them. And when you leave the apartment with one of them,
it's shameless how your arm weaves around his butt and how,
when you're saying goodbye, you shove your right leg deep
between his thighs. I watch their faces, I read it in their eyes: you
are a spreading carcinoma. And when one of these men walks
away with barely a glance at you, it really makes my day. I want
him to wound you. To make you hurt. To make you hurt bad.

Lately you've been metastasizing into my home. Into my

dreams. You're affecting my sleep. Four days ago, when I was sleeping with my wife, you slinked into my field of vision just before I climaxed. I shut my eyes and you were everywhere. When I opened them again, I saw your smeary brick-red lipstick on my wife's face, and my stomach started twitching; with my hand over my mouth I ran to the bathroom, bent over the commode, and threw up. I ate too much at supper, I told my wife, who is not at all like you. She is pure, with no slimy thoughts that wrap themselves glutinously around the head and body of a man, without him even knowing it, and then with sharp-pointed tentacles pierce deep inside him.

Whenever I see you in front of your building, my vision sharpens and I can peer into your viscera. All my life I've been fascinated by the way an organism looks on the inside. Like leather gloves when you turn them inside out. Like the gloves I always put on before I enter your apartment. Before I examine the place where you feel safest. One day I will do to you what I do at home. What I have been doing for years. In the basement. Something nobody knows about. When I go running in my track suit, I set traps in the park and collect the animals' little cadavers, which I secretly bring home and stick in the basement freezer. And when I'm at home alone, I reach down to the bottom of the freezer and take out a little wren, a frog, or a squirrel, and dissect the animal with a scalpel on the metal table. Slowly and very carefully, I open its body, place the little organs on the table, and meticulously examine them, weigh them, measure them, study them.

One night when you are lying alone in that enormous, unmade, messy, semen-soaked bed of yours, I will step into your apartment through the open balcony door, go through the kitchen, and enter the bedroom. You will look at me and won't have the faintest idea that you've ever met me. That I even exist. But I have been by your side the whole time. Right next to you. Much closer than you can imagine, closer than you could ever fear. I am your dark angel, in whose wings you have glutinously, slimily entangled yourself and who, for now, watches over you, so that nothing happens to you. An invisible angel, who, unobserved, touches your body with his sharp scalpel and waits for the right moment to open it and turn you inside out. I don't know yet what I will do with that which remains unseen by others, but I notice every time you appear in a tight dress the color of raw, flayed meat. Most likely, I will leave you like that on the bed, turned inside out, but first I will clean your organs, wash them, and spread you out piece by piece. For once in your life, things will be in their proper place, pristine. You will lie there on the bed, unable to say anything ever again. You will disappear from the world, and soon from my dreams too, and from my most intimate moments. No one will ever find out it was me. Who would imagine that such a puny man could have any connection to you? After all, we don't know each other. At least you don't know me. But there is still time before that happens. I am a patient man. I'm in no hurry. And as I wait, I feel immense satisfaction. Because I know something that you don't know: I know that you are constantly and completely under my surveillance. Every step you take. Your comings and goings. Your every routine, every bad habit, even the tiniest things that go unnoticed by others.

On days when I can't get you out of my head, not for a single moment, I go down to the basement. I lock the door and put on a clean white lab coat. I wash my hands, open the freezer, and reach towards the bottom. I pull out a pigeon, a blackbird, a mouse, or a sparrow. I stick the little corpse in the microwave and wait for it to thaw a bit. Then I put on my surgical gloves, pick up the scalpel, make an incision—and think of you.

Love Is Energy

DESPITE HIS NAME, Felix was not a happy man. Every day at the end of his shift in the factory's boiler division, he raced like a scared rat through streets where the plaster was flaking off the buildings like dry skin, then slipped into the one-room basement apartment he had been given by the factory for a small monthly rent, after fourteen years of assembling heating equipment. He and his now departed mother had moved there from their privately rented apartment to escape his father, who two years after Felix's mother's death was himself finished off by alcohol. There, alone in the basement, Felix would whimper and moan, and not infrequently ask himself the ever-popular questions about human fate, loneliness, and the meaning of life.

It wasn't that he was a loner by nature or didn't want company. On the contrary, he gazed with envy at his neighbor, a warehouse worker from the same factory, whose apartment, in its dynamics and colorful goings-on, resembled nothing less than a railway yard. He watched through his grated window in the late afternoon as the women's thin pumps—black and red, sometimes even a pair of green ones turned up in the mix, and the white ones with the slender high heels (oh, those he liked best!)—scurried past his basement apartment, entered the building, climbed to the second floor, and a few hours later scampered off in the direction they had come from. Other than one or two, when he happened to be carrying a black plastic bag out to the dumpster, he had never seen their owners, so with every pair of shoes he would harness his rich imagination, attach it to the

35

women's feet, and conjure up various bodies, personalities, and faces, most often resembling the women he saw on his way to work. But how does he manage it, that debauched neighbor of his? How does he have sex with so many women? One of them, it's true, wasn't much to look at, but this was hardly the point. He wasn't choosy; he'd be content with the worst of his neighbor's visitors, because in fact there was no worst—they were all good, too good, it seemed, for him, Felix Gril, a man of small physique, with modest muscle mass, thin bones, brown-bean eyes, and a nondescript complexion that more than anything else resembled the pale beige walls of the factory corridor. He thought and thought but just didn't know how to approach them. Fervidly, he examined the women and girls he passed and tried to come up with some secret method for making them see that he too existed in this world. But Felix might as well have been made of spiderweb, not soul, blood, and flesh like other men, who clearly possessed something else, some ingredient that he sadly lacked. He would watch the women at work and try in his own inimitable, timid way to win their favor. He was always ready to leap to their aid, whether by covering for them on their cigarette breaks or filling in when they called in sick under dubious pretenses, because of some female trouble or a problem with the kids. As he diligently did his work, he would look up from time to time to see if any of his female colleagues were expressing some intention. As soon as the large mannish woman and petite pimply-faced girl pulled their rumpled cigarettes and lighters from the pockets of their blue smocks, he would send them a protective glance and calmly pick up the pace of his hands, doing the work of three for as long as their break lasted, whether five minutes or twenty. The women did not view such attention as an expression of love; they didn't think about it at all, and shamelessly, blithely, instinctively took advantage of the man, this thirty-seven-year-old "boy"—a frequent designation for the unmarried male, regardless of his age.

And just as with his nimble hands he helped the women assemble the boilers, so too at home, lonely and desperately desiring female company, he had no choice but to help himself with those same hands. Despite his uninteresting fate—or maybe, indeed, because of it—the boy was blessed with a most vivacious nature, to put it politely. His body may have been small and frail, but for all his slight appearance, energy was coursing inside him as in the factory's voracious generator. He had only one option left to him, one sordid, lonely option: Felix did a lot of masturbating.

His narrow wooden bed hovered above piles of colorful stained and gummed-up magazines. There weren't many words in them, but plenty of full-color photos. More than a few times he had wanted to scoop them all up, stuff them in black plastic bags, and distribute the bags at night to different dumpsters in the area. But you never know; somebody could see you, and then, after you've dumped the things and left, run over and go through them to see what was hiding in the bags that couldn't be disposed of during the day. They would find lots of things in Felix's bags. The worst times were rainy, moonless nights, when he couldn't sleep and felt the gnawing of some inner anxiety, that fragile condition of the soul which in its extreme stages, in keeping with local custom, most of his coworkers alleviated with alcohol. Felix, however, never touched a drop. He had learned this lesson at home, on those evenings when his mother would point her finger at his father and uncle, press him to her breast, and implore him, "Don't you ever become like those drunken pigs!" as the tears ran down her fleshy cheeks. He had never even tasted alcohol, no matter how much his coworkers made fun of him at holiday parties and factory anniversaries. But the big stack of magazines beneath his bed was driving him to despair. Countless times he swore to himself never to buy another one. For several days he would avoid the red newsstand that lay in wait for him between the factory and home and deliberately took a different, if much longer, route. But when he began to feel that the temptation had been vanquished, that nothing in this world could ever again lead him astray, he returned to the old, shorter, but more dangerous streets. With his hands in the front pockets of his shabby brown polyester jacket and with his brownish gray beret on his head, he would hurry along and in a half-whisper repeat to himself that this time would be different. No, he wouldn't stop, he'd just walk right past it, straight home. Because it was the right thing to do, and what he had been doing was unforgivable and very, very wrong. So when, from a distance, he saw the newsstand waiting for him, he took a deep breath and walked right past it without changing his stride. But the end of the story was always the same. Just when he thought it was over, some mysterious force would make him turn around on the sidewalk, drag him back to the half-open window, electrify his right hand, pull it out of the front pocket of his jacket, guide it past his hip, and shove it into the back pocket of his faded gray wool pants, from which he pulled out some crumpled banknotes, grabbed the magazine, and ran home. It'll just be today, he told himself. I'll quickly, very quickly, skim through it and throw it away. But it was never that simple. A quick look at such magazines just wasn't possible. Some photos he had to return to again and again. Five times, twenty-five times, six hundred and twenty-five times, and on and on.

Without success he battled with his conscience, which told him clearly and distinctly that he was just your typical male pig. Yes, exactly the kind of man his mother had hated and who had caused her so many tears. And ultimately, it wasn't just the magazines; there were actual living women too—Felix's coworkers, the random women and acquaintances he encountered every day on his way to and from the factory, and the women he saw on television: news announcers, variety show hosts, reporters. These women—such was his personal philosophy—you couldn't just scoop up, cram into black plastic bags, and dump into different trash cans in the area.

All these secrets, worries, fears, and guilty feelings, like timid mistresses, remained silently concealed in the always well-tidied corners of Felix's one-room dwelling. Life was hard going, but somehow it went. Right up until one winter evening when, as usual after the afternoon shift, he returned to the apartment feeling tired. As he warmed up a pot of two-day-old goulash on the stove, he warmed up his frozen hands on the radiator. They were his weak point. They were very sensitive hands, with tender fair skin that turned red in the cold, even inside his wool gloves. He was often washing them—before eating, after eating, before work, after work, after shaking hands, in the morning, in the evening, and countless times between; indeed, whenever it was necessary. What particularly troubled him was the unpleasant sweating. Whenever he became self-conscious, which was not seldom, he felt a heat mixed with cold spreading from his palms, which would leave a sticky bodily fluid on the tender surface of his skin.

That cold winter evening he cut off two slices of brown bread, turned on the TV, and sank into his gray-brown armchair with a bowl of the hot goulash. As he dunked the toasted heel of the bread into the thick, greasy liquid, he would now and then hop up, run over to the TV, bowl in hand, and change the channel. There was nothing on but boring programs, weird movies, stupid commercials, crazy music—and then suddenly he couldn't move. On Channel 1 of the national television station, a woman with fiery red hair and a generous figure, in a group of portly and scrawny men, a scientist in her mature years, Dr. Evica Tomič, according to the name at the bottom of the screen, was taking part in a panel. It was obvious that this energy expert knew her field backwards and forwards. With her knowledge and even more with her inner certainty she was—it seemed to him—crushing every possible objection and comment, no matter how germane, from her male colleagues.

Felix could feel the melodious current of her charged voice as it traveled along the red-hot neural fibers of his body. By the end of the broadcast, he was actually trembling with excitement. "Such a mind in such a wonderful body!" he said out loud, and kept repeating this as he got ready for bed. He was so astonished by the televised discussion that he even forgot to wash his hands. And instead of pulling out one of the magazines from under his bed, which is what he usually did before going to sleep, he covered himself up nice and warm and gazed at the water stains on the ceiling. He didn't, couldn't, fall asleep. The moment he shut his eyes he saw Dr. Evica Tomič hovering before him, and when he opened them, the damp spots above him began to join curvaceously into her bosom, which as it rose and fell was saving the nation from the energy crisis. His hand slipped down over his skinny stomach and he began to release his thoughts about her. Quite a few times that night. And then the next night and the next . . .

He was no longer thinking about his female coworkers. The lower part of his body found strength again and again only in the thought of Evica Tomič. It was as if this thought had cocooned itself in Felix's bowels. Even at work, more and more his attention would often slither away from the boilers to the lavatories and wait there hissing at him until he followed humbly after it and thought the matter through to its conclusion. This habit became increasingly suspicious and troubling to the people around him. His coworkers could see that something was terribly wrong with Felix. He was visibly deteriorating. On the morning shift especially, he would arrive at work with a pale, rumpled face and circles beneath his eyes like burnt chocolate cookies. The unlucky fellow blamed his condition on kidney and bladder problems, but his coworkers weren't buying it. Whispers started going around that, as happens with some people, he had lost a difficult battle with alcohol, which he had been concealing hypocritically from everyone. And that hypocrisy made them like Felix even less. Such a tight-lipped fellow, you never know what's going on with him.

His body, so frail to begin with, started wasting away. His skin took on the patina of the factory walls and his lackluster eyes were like hot colorless gelatin. Only his hands grew stronger. They became sinewy. But his muscles could not endure his body's relentless demands and after a few weeks simply withered.

"It's clearly a case of overload," they determined at the health clinic. "A kind of occupational hazard," the doctors concluded. Then they wrapped his arms in bandages, supported them with braces, and advised Felix to rest for three or four days, avoid stress, and just unwind nicely at home.

"Unwind?" he thought in despair. "Oh, unwind!" he said again at home a few hours later, and that same evening he was taken to the emergency room with his head between his knees because, they said, he had slipped two discs in his neck. They kept him in the hospital for almost a week. The doctors, reasonably enough, suspected muscular dystrophy. Or some sort of muscular cramp that twists the entire body. But it was nothing as bad as that. He recovered fairly quickly, only he now was even more taciturn.

When he came home from the hospital, he collapsed on his bed and, assuming the position of an unwanted fetus, broke into loud sobbing. There was no will left in him. No drive or inspiration. Everything hurt. And he was bitterly ashamed of himself. From the nightstand he grabbed a photo of Dr. Tomič that he had cut out of the newspaper, and started crying even harder. "You are one sick bastard!" her eyes condemned him. What pained him the most was knowing that, while she was doing her best to save the country every last kilowatt, he was wasting all his energy on the basest of activities. He swore to himself, swore on his mother's grave, that he would stop this once and for all. But nothing helped. Feelings of guilt and shame were crushing his body and tearing at his soul. He felt desperately lonely, useless, and dirty.

Never until now had he thought seriously about ridding himself completely of his worthless life. "Nobody will even notice," he realized. He knew he couldn't do it with rope—he was no good at knots and, anyway, basements have low ceilings. There was no gas; the factory's apartment building had all-electric appliances and hot-water heating. Then he remembered how his mother always said: "In seven years, if not sooner, these will all come in handy." And he thought of the boxes and bottles of pills he had carefully stored away. There was a lot left over from his mother's illness. The drugs had been terrible, just like her illness. "If I have no other choice, I'll do it her way," he decided. He was already looking through the drawer and collecting the little bottles and boxes with the poisonous capsules when the ceiling lamp started flickering. The bulb's going out, he thought, and even before he finished his thought, the light flashed one last time and met its sad end. He got up, went to the kitchen cabinet, took out a new light bulb, placed a wooden kitchen chair beneath the lamp and stood on it. First he unscrewed the simple white shade and then the old extinguished bulb, with the broken filament bouncing and jingling inside as he turned it. Strange, he thought; he had replaced it not long ago. Had they sold him a bad bulb at the store or were the new ones, the kind they were making now, not very good? With his thoughts still absorbed in suicide and medical poisons, it never occurred to him to switch off the fuse, an oversight that almost cost him dearly. To be more specific, the thing he had intended to do himself, the new and entirely ordinary light bulb nearly did for him. While he was screwing it in, he received such a jolt that it knocked him clear off the chair. Onto his head. He must have been unconscious for a few seconds, since after being shrouded in primal darkness, the first thing he saw when he opened his eyes was the pale yellow ceiling, which dazzled him and seemed to be rocking above the brown and white kitchen linoleum. He tried to get up but couldn't move. The electricity he had intended for the new light bulb he could now feel flowing in his muscles, circulating through his entire body like water in a radiator. Whether it was from the fall or from the electric shock, something had startled from sleep a brilliant idea in his brain, so that the unfortunate soul cried out: "Holy Mother of God! Energy!"

In one very special respect, you see, Felix was a gifted man. He had a kind of natural intelligence. With only seven years of education, he had had no choice but to dedicate his life to assembling boilers. But even if he wasn't particularly good at reading and writing, he had no trouble at all repairing a neighbor's washing machine or putting together a moped, and he could find his way around a television set too. He understood very well that something doesn't come from nothing and doesn't vanish into nothing either. Many times he had felt how everything was connected: rain falls on the earth and evaporates back into the air; a person harvests wheat, makes it into bread, eats it and grows strong, and gives it back to nature . . . With renewed strength Felix picked himself up, propelled himself over to the desk, and slammed shut the drawer with the deadly pills. Then, his face brimming with joy, he cried, "Of course! Everything is circulation, everything is energy! In light bulbs, boilers, TV sets, and in me too! Yes, there is tremendous energy inside of me!"

Stashed beneath his bed were not only his magazines but also an old wooden crate, where he kept wires, screws, and tools, all neatly arranged and stored in cardboard boxes and cookie tins. He crouched beside this crate and with unusual mental focus dumped the machine parts and electrical elements out on the floor and started picking through them. Then he quickly stood up, put on his jacket and beret, grabbed his wallet and ran out of the building as fast as he could, hoping that the nearest store with electrical equipment wouldn't close in his face. He bought a few electric cables, some copper wire and a couple of circuit breakers. That night, before going to bed, he poked through his wardrobe and pulled out an old, red, moth-eaten, one-piece ski suit, which his mother had bought for him twenty-five years ago for a school skiing trip. He tried it on and, as he suspected, his body had not developed all that much since then or changed in any other way. The sleeves were a little short, and the pants legs could have been an inch or so longer, but this was no obstacle for what he was planning.

The next day, his heart in his throat, he went up to the foreman and in the most humble tones asked if it would be possible for him to have, from one of the discontinued or maybe flawed product lines, a transformer, a storage battery, and an oscillator. The foreman, who was surprised, not only because this was the first time the man was asking him for anything, it was the first time he had even addressed him, asked what he was planning to do with them.

Felix turned red as a beet. He needed them, he said. He needed them urgently.

"Sure, OK, but why?" the boss asked, now curious.

"I just need them," Felix said meekly and, embarrassed, looked at the floor. He was on the verge of tears.

"Well, if you need them," began the foreman, who was inclined to give in to the request of a worker who had been having health problems supposedly caused by an occupational hazard connected to his work at the factory, "then we can make some arrangement. But how's your health?" He thought he might as well use the opportunity to chat with the man. "No more problems?"

"Better . . . yes . . . getting better," Felix said shyly.

"Well, so long as it's getting better," said the foreman, who had never believed the gossip about him being an alcoholic, and to encourage him gave him a pat on the shoulder. Felix Gril was one of the few workers who had never taken a sick day; the foreman barely even knew that the man worked in his division, since he had never caused him any problems. Until recently, that is, but things happen to even the most decent people.

Over the next few days, Felix's thoughts were immersed in electrical and machine parts. In very exciting situations, it was normal for him to talk out loud to himself, but now his enormous excitement made him so chatty there might have been five people in the room: "I just can't, I can't stop doing it . . . That's no excuse . . . Now I just need that little knife . . . And a screw . . . I'll insert it here . . . What a creep, what a creep . . . What a sicko . . . OK, let's tighten this up . . ."

To the inside of the tight-fitting ski suit he had sewn a thermal grid in copper wire, corresponding to the circulation of the blood. At the nodes of the grid he inserted tiny thermocouples, which were serially connected by the wire grid into a kind of thermoelectric battery. At the top of the suit's hood and at the crotch, the grid converged into two well-insulated cables, which he connected to the other components in a carefully worked-out sequence. Thus, energy traveled from Felix's body through the two cables—one with an excess of electrons, the other with a deficit—into the storage battery, from there to the oscillator, or frequency modulator, which converted the direct current into alternating current, and from the oscillator to the transformer, which regulated the voltage. From the transformer it passed through a distributor to the electrical outlets in the apartment. Before each provision of energy, he applied an electro-conductive aftershave gel to the points on his body that touched the copper thermocouples sewn on the fabric. Then he climbed into his energy suit, down which ran a long zipper that, in the area below the abdomen, gently protected the sensitive power source—always standing at the ready, willing to gear up the body so it could discharge energy into the web of wires in the suit.

It may have looked primitive, but his invention was truly epoch-making. Felix could power everything—from the washing machine and the stove to the coffee grinder—with nothing but his own energy. The unhappy man had found a way to accept himself. Whenever he got the urge (and he got it throughout the day), he put on the ski suit, connected the cables of his power device, and the thoughts his body dictated to him were converted into practical, usable energy. He developed the conviction, the feeling, that he wasn't just wasting his time or his life. He didn't breathe a word to anyone about what he was doing or, of course, about his invention. Nor did he have any such intention (and anyway, who would he tell?). The whole thing would have remained hidden from the world, were it not for the accounting department at the state energy monopoly, which found it strange that over the past few months their meter readers, detecting no change on Felix Gril's meter, had been marking "0" in their ledgers. One of them had even rung his doorbell once, after the women in accounting instructed him to inquire if perhaps Mr. Gril had himself been fiddling with the meter. Felix opened the door an inch or so. Behind the door chain, his face turned a burning red and he was sweating from fear.

"I can hear the TV and I see you have the lights on—" That was all the meter reader had managed to say before Felix, without a word, quietly shut the door in his face.

It was all very strange, the women in accounting concluded when they heard the man's story. And it just wasn't right that some people weren't paying for the electricity they consumed. So they contacted the head of regular maintenance, the head of consumer services, and the measurements officer and, without hiding their suspicions, told them about the case of Felix Gril. These quick-witted experts realized at once that there could only be two explanations: either the meter was broken or (more likely) the fellow was simply cheating. "We'll send an inspection team to his door," the experts decided. "Nobody's going to scam us!"

A few days later, in the late morning, the doorbell rang at the apartment of Felix Gril.

"Who is it?" He looked through the peephole in the door and quickly understood that the three men, two in blue coveralls and the third in a suit, meant nothing good.

"We're from the electric company," the man in the suit said. "There seems to be something not right with your meter."

"What do you mean 'not right'?" Felix asked in a trembling voice from behind the closed door. "I don't think so. Nothing seems to be wrong."

"Oh, but something is. There is definitely a problem somewhere. Would you mind opening the door?"

For a minute or so it was quiet inside. The only sound the men heard was heavy breathing, as if the fellow had asthma, or a bad conscience!

"I'm very sick," Felix yelped. "I can't open the door."

"Mr. Gril," said the team leader, the man in the suit, as he tried the door handle, "we just have a couple of questions for you, and then we'll leave."

"What sort of questions?" Felix asked anxiously, although he had realized right away what they would ask about.

"Open the door," the leader said, "and we'll tell you."

Meanwhile one of the technicians, immersed in the electric box, was checking the mechanism on Felix's meter with a screwdriver.

But he was very ill, he was on sick leave from work, he kept insisting from inside the door.

They didn't give a damn about that, the man in the suit said—he was done with playing dumb and had had it with the whole business—and added that he'd check to see if Mr. Gril was really on sick leave, and, if necessary, he'd be back with the police.

The police! Felix thought with a shudder. He had never had any dealings with the police. But he hadn't done anything so bad. He hadn't stolen anything from anyone. On the contrary, all the energy he was using he had produced himself. Surely that couldn't be a crime. Or could it? But what if they found out about the magazines, and what had happened with his arms?

What if his energy had escaped his apparatus and gone into the wiring, and then somewhere, probably at the police station, been converted back into thoughts? Then they must know the kind of thoughts he had been having about Dr. Tomič and what he did when he thought about her. And besides, it wasn't true about him being on sick leave; he had said that just to get rid of them. And if they did check with the factory, they would be told that he wasn't sick anymore, that he was fine now and they were expecting him for the afternoon shift. And when the police heard that, he would surely be sent to prison.

He carefully unlocked the door—first the main lock, then the door chain—and opened it.

"You don't look like you're seriously ill, Mr. Gril," the official in the suit said as he pushed the door away with his right hand and strode into the apartment, followed by the two technicians. "If I'm not mistaken, I smell something cooking. So the stove must be working. But you really should turn off some lights; it's awfully bright in this basement apartment. You don't seem to be trying to save energy. Is that because you don't pay for it? So, Gril"—the suit placed himself right in front of Felix's nose—"while you've got your stew bubbling cheerfully on the stove over there, the meter in the box outside seems to be frozen. Can you explain this magic to me?"

Unhappy Felix said nothing. He was gripping the plastic table in the kitchen and looked like he was about to collapse.

"Come on, boys. Take a look around the apartment," the suit said. "As for you, Gril, it's clear you intend to say nothing. I hear you work in the division for non-ferrous metallurgy. Is that right?"

"Yes," Felix said timidly, and at once thought they must have talked to the police before coming here. How else could they have learned this about him? It wasn't written on his forehead where he worked.

"So it follows that you're not exactly ignorant when it comes to energy?" The suit had decided to take a shot in the dark even if, to judge by the fellow's appearance and behavior, he seemed a bit dense.

Felix denied everything. He knew nothing about electricity or meters; the only thing he knew was how to assemble a good, reliable boiler.

"Mr. Lovrič!" a cry came from the bathroom.

"What is it, boys?" the suit asked expectantly. "Find something?" And he headed to the bathroom.

"We almost tripped over this heap of black cables. There's a storage battery here, and a transformer—"

"Fucking hell!" the team leader swore. "There's an entire power station in here!" he exclaimed, delighted by the discovery. "Only what the hell is he doing with it? Gril!" Lovrič yelled through the open bathroom door as he turned the transformer around in his hands. "Do you have a permit for all this stuff?"

"What kind of permit?" Felix asked in a faltering voice.

"What do you mean what kind? The official kind!"

"Who from? The police?" Felix burbled.

"Don't you realize you could blow up the entire building?"

"Not the way it's set up; that's not possible," Felix replied.

"So how's it set up? What the hell is it for anyway? You got a small hydroelectric plant in the bathtub or something? I'll give you two seconds to show us how it works."

"I don't want to!" Felix replied, shyly but firmly.

"You don't want to? Well maybe what you want is for me to call the police."

"No, I don't want that."

"So there's not too much to think about, is there? Come on, Gril! What is this hocus-pocus stuff?"

"I'm not going to show you," said the inventor obstinately.

"Fine," Lovrič replied, out for revenge. "If you don't want to show us, you'll show somebody else. Now get dressed. You're going with us. Help the boys carry that apparatus out to the car, and no dawdling, or you'll be dealing with the police." (Lovrič had noticed the word's effect on Felix.) "And don't think you'll get off easy. Now every crackpot's gonna want a power station in his bachelor apartment. And with no permit!" he added with emphasis, although he himself had no idea what permit this would be or even who would issue it. Just as he didn't know where he was supposed to take all this stuff, or even take Gril. As Felix was getting dressed, Lovrič telephoned the electric company, determined to speak to the director himself.

"Mr. Rakun has left for the day," his secretary said, adding that the director was attending a symposium at the Energy Institute, but if the matter was urgent, the deputy director was standing right here.

"What's the problem, Lovrič?" The voice at the other end of the line belonged to the number-two person at the state energy monopoly, a man whose greatest desire and firmest intention was to use all possible means to become the number-one person in the shortest possible time.

"What device? Some machine, you say? Something mysterious? You don't know how it works? . . . And the guy hasn't paid for his electricity in months?" The deputy thought for a moment and saw his golden opportunity. "Call me back in five minutes."

Rigler went to his office, locked the door, picked up a pencil, and as he was thinking drew electrical symbols on his gray laminate desk. He had exactly five minutes to link his career to the dismissal of his superior. He was in the middle of doodling a serial circuit when the telephone rang again. He grabbed the receiver as if it were a revolver and right away an idea came to him.

"Lovrič," he said in a voice in which an attentive listener (which Lovrič was not) might have detected some malevolent plan, "I just spoke with the director on his cell. He said you should immediately bring the man and his apparatus to the National Energy Institute. There's a symposium there, 'The Energy-Based Development of Society,' which has been going on for three days. Ask to see Dr. Telban—he's the director of the institute—and tell him that our director, Dr. Rakun, told you to deliver this apparatus to him. He'll be most grateful," he added, barely able to keep from laughing. "As I understand it, this case involves science, so it's no concern of ours, since all we really do is send out bills and collect payments." He shut his eyes tight, hoping against hope that Lovrič would take the bait. And he did; he even thanked Rigler, who, smiling to himself, said modestly that there was no need since he was merely doing what he had been told to do. The deputy director slammed the phone down triumphantly, barked to the secretary in the shrill voice of a famished hyena that he would be out for the rest of the day, then drove as fast as he could to the institute to watch the festivities. Now in its third day, the symposium was unwinding like the bowels of a sick elephant, and Dr. Viktor Telban, the institute's director, had a foamy look, like a wounded animal. The event was taking place during the winter school break, which Dr. Telban had planned to spend with his family on a skiing trip in the French Alps. But everything had gone wrong, and he could only send his wife (with whom he had been having marital troubles these past few months) and the kids to the suite he had reserved. The receptionist now quietly approached and whispered cautiously in his ear that some people were waiting for him outside and it seemed extremely urgent. With his slender yet clearly stubborn frame, he pivoted at full speed towards the slightly open door of the large lecture hall, through which somebody was trying to tell him something in winks and grimaces. He departed the lecture hall posthaste with the firm intention of dispensing with these people quickly and brusquely, no matter who they were. In the corridor he was ambushed by two mechanics (or so they seemed) and a bureaucrat from the electric company (Lovrič), who at once started saying something about mysterious cables, an electric ski suit, and old batteries. The director was sure the man had reached the threshold of his psycho-physical capacities and was probably hallucinating. This conviction was only further confirmed when he saw a mortally terrified and exhausted man, who was leaning for support on one of the mechanics.

"We're going to need a couple of strong men to carry the transformer in from the van, and also the cables," said Lovrič deferentially.

"Just who the hell are you?" Dr. Telban asked, seriously angry, his hands on his hips, with the haughty disdain of the first-class scientist who was also an able manager. "How dare you come here and bother me in the middle of a national scientific symposium?"

"I'm here on the orders of the director of Electro-Commerce, Dr. Rakun, who said I should delivery this to your institute,"

Lovrič said, indicating both the apparatus, which had been set down in a corner, and Felix Gril next to it.

"That idiot Rakun? He told you to bring this here? What is that thing, a time machine? A machine for producing permanent revolution? Do you think this is a mental hospital? And who made that old spy your director in the first place?"

"We don't know, sir," Lovrič replied meekly. Although in certain parts of life, he was himself a man of authority, which he was constantly demonstrating through his behavior, his choice of words, and the tone in which he said them, in other contexts he was profoundly respectful of people with power.

"It's a sort of machine for producing electricity," Lovrič continued, more apologizing than explaining. "I mean, this man here, well, this device powers everything in his apartment . . . it's a scientific invention, I guess." He was beginning to wonder if he had done the right thing by consulting the deputy director of the company. How could he have so completely forgotten the rumors about the conflicts between the director and the deputy director or the enmity between Edvard Rakun of Electro-Commerce and the institute's Viktor Telban?

Dr. Telban's lungs were wheezing in fury with every breath. It was hard enough for him to even look at that communist cur Rakun, who he knew had been an informant for the secret police even in their student days. He never understood how Rakun had managed to complete his doctorate. And he could not forget that, in the iron years of the nineteen-sixties, it was Rakun who had been given a grant to study in America, and not himself, whose father had taken up arms and died during World War II on the side of those who were fighting against communist rule, among other things. He, Viktor Telban, a doctor of science esteemed by his international peers, had achieved everything through his own merits. Everything he had was entirely the result of the sweat of his intellectual brow and scientific research. He too had eventually studied abroad, which he was able to do only through immense sacrifice and talent. Not unlike Deputy Director Rigler, Viktor Telban too, after his initial rage, now saw a chance to get revenge on Rakun.

"So you say it was your director who sent you here?" Telban said sweetly. "Well, that's all right, then." He stroked his meticulously trimmed gray beard. "If it's what your director wants, then please follow me." And he was more and more certain that this was possibly a unique opportunity to thoroughly humiliate Rakun in front of state officials and the scientific public and pay him back for all the unsettled scores the two men were still arguing over even in the media.

"Yes, yes, go in, right in here," Telban was bleating like a deer. "Everything you've got, just bring it in and hook it up. For all I care, you can plug it into your director's goddamn ass!"

After the lunch break, Dr. Viktor Telban addressed the audience: "Before we begin our afternoon session, we have something to liven up our symposium a little. Our colleague, Dr. Edvard Rakun, the director of Electro-Commerce, has prepared a very special surprise for us. He wishes to present us scientists with a device which, as far as I've been able to understand"—here he lifted his eyebrows in mocking wonder—"is a machine for producing energy, a sort of perpetuum mobile."

Dr. Rakun, unpleasantly surprised, began turning his head back and forth, trying to lay eyes on the scoundrel who, besides this white-robed academic filth, had set this land mine for him. Everything became clear when he spotted Rigler in one of the back rows, hiding like a mouse amid a group of foreign attendees. As soon as his boss caught his eye, the deputy looked away. You son of a bitch, I'll make you pay dearly for this, Rakun vowed.

Meanwhile, Dr. Telban, the official host of the symposium, had Felix brought into the hall and politely asked him in front of everybody to explain and demonstrate the system he had invented. The audience was sure this must be one of those theatrical gestures, so popular in recent years, when symposium organizers invite an artist to demonstrate some eccentric connection between art and science. Their expectation was only confirmed when Felix appeared holding a bright red one-piece ski suit in his arms. Some people in the audience (the ones who had already read their papers) found this most entertaining, but a handful of others, who were still waiting to read, were upset.

The worst thing that can happen to a scientist at a symposium is for the attention of the audience to wane. Then the person at the podium can get the impression that their scientific paper, which they had perhaps been preparing for months and was the product of long years of research, was being heard only by the walls and the projection screen.

Felix, standing in front of roughly a hundred people, was experiencing the most difficult moments of his life. Powerless and in utter despair, he abandoned himself to fate, convinced that these were his final moments before being locked away in a mental hospital, or prison, for the rest of his life. But then suddenly, among the whispers and chuckles in the auditorium, he seemed to hear somewhere a familiar, charming, and much-desired voice. In horror, he scanned the faces of the crowd. There, in the middle of the second row, in a white ribbed wool sweater, sat Dr. Evica Tomič. He wanted to cry. She was far more beautiful than she was on TV or in newspaper photographs—large-bodied, of even ampler proportions than his mother and much taller too, with thick, copper-red hair as if she was carrying on her head millions of curled wires that burned bright at the slightest movement. Her hands were strong and meaty, the kind that at a glance promised protection and total care. Did she have children? He had read in a newspaper that she wasn't married. Her hips were like the biggest generator they had at the factory. And as for the upper part of her body, oh, that surpassed everything he had ever been compelled to look at by the magazines beneath his bed. But now, sadly, none of it mattered anymore. His life was over. Completely over. No more joy, not until after he died, and even then he had a hundred years of purgatory waiting for him before he could see his mother again—if God allowed it, since it was possible he'd be booted straight into hell for all eternity.

Even at the most difficult times of his life he could not have imagined a worse humiliation. How cruelly the world is contrived. It had all started because of her, and now his worthless and, as he learned today, even criminal life would end in front of her eyes. He would be fired from his job. In his haste, he had even forgotten to inform the foreman—the very person who had given him the battery, oscillator, and transformer—that he would not be coming to work this afternoon since he was being detained. As his mother had always said, sooner or later the truth will out. And so it will come out in the clear light of day just what a jerk he is. A filthy, depraved louse, who performs the vilest, most perverted acts, things far worse than drinking sprees or his neighbor's debauchery. But it is what it is. It's too late to change anything. If the mental hospital doesn't lock him up, the police will. Because he didn't have a permit! So if he must humiliate himself, then let his punishment be to humiliate himself completely.

"Well now, Mr. . . . Just who you are, anyway?" Dr. Telban addressed him in a tone of contempt.

"Gril. Felix Gril," the poor man whispered back.

"Well now, Mr. Felix Gril,"—the director of the institute was finishing his introduction—"Dr. Rakun has had you brought here because, I'm told, you have invented a system that represents a direct development of the work of the scientists Nikola Tesla and Josef Stefan, while relying on the most recent discoveries of modern physics. From this day forward, if I understand correctly, consumers of electricity—which, my esteemed audience, also includes us—will no longer have to pay such high and, especially, incomprehensible energy bills. As I understand, with this device of his this gentleman will show us scientists"—saying this, he glanced at Felix with a wry smile, which prompted a self-satisfied smirk from the audience members with doctorates and prestigious titles—"how, to put it simply, we can conserve the greatest amount of energy while spending the least amount of money."

"What the hell! I don't even know that person!" Rakun was on his feet. "But I damn well know who's setting me up!"

Everyone in the auditorium started talking at once. Now virtually nobody had any real idea what this whole thing was about.

"I hope nothing explodes!" a frightened male voice said from somewhere.

When Dr. Telban heard that, his head gave a twitch; only now did he seriously understand that the entire experiment could have dire consequences for him too. He gestured Lovrič over, and in a tone of certainty, which, however, did not entirely conceal his fear, asked him if he knew for a fact that this machine was safe. Lovrič, too, for the first time considered the possibility that this very day, in a single second, the nation could lose the cream of its scientific crop.

"I think it is," Lovrič replied.

"You *think* it is? But does that mean you don't know?" the director yelped, and felt the ulcer on his duodenum opening.

In fact, he didn't really know, Lovrič said, which is another reason he had brought the man to the institute—on Dr. Rakun's orders, naturally. They—the scientists—were supposed to figure out what this device was all about. The stove had been working and the lights were on, Lovrič said, but he didn't know how the machine worked; they had just unplugged the cables and put them in the van.

"Lovrič, you are a total idiot! Only now you tell me this! They are going to lock you up, and me too, if we even survive this circus!"

Felix, meanwhile, had been arranging the different parts of the apparatus in front of the podium and the white screen. After connecting the wires, he removed his brown pants, beige pullover, and underwear, and then, sweating profusely as the audience grew more restless, got into the electrical one-piece. But when he slipped his hand through the zipper and grabbed his penis, the women in the audience (of whom there were only a few) cried out in shock and embarrassment, while the men commented on the display with interjections like "What the hell!" "Will you look at that nut!" "Psycho!" "Sicko!" and "Get that exhibitionist out of here!" Felix could already see the insane asylum, the police, handcuffs, how he'd be led away and sent to the psych ward. He looked at Dr. Evica Tomič one last time, pulled out his rigid member, fixed his eyes on hers, and, to the furor and laughter of the audience, skillfully demonstrated.

The director of the institute, Dr. Viktor Telban, stood in the background as if frozen; Lovrič, too, had the feeling that he had sprouted roots down to the basement and would never again move from that spot; Dr. Rakun, the director of Electro-Commerce, was holding his head in his hands and wheezing like a wounded boar. After a minute and a half—which passed like a single second to the more benevolent spectators, who were bursting with laughter, while to others, and especially to the three men just mentioned, it was like being caught in a time loop and experiencing in succession all the geological ages of Planet Earth—an ear-splitting cry rang out in the auditorium. The audience was stunned: the hundred-watt light bulb attached to the system was glowing white. Felix stood there with his penis now limp and slimy, his eyes still fixed on Dr. Evica Tomič, his face grimacing (from humiliation? from pleasure?) and wet with tears.

The auditorium resounded with whoops of enthusiasm. A few of the younger attendees, mostly research assistants with MBAs, pushed their way up to the inventor. Stepping over the cables, they heaped praises, stammered, passed different parts of the apparatus from hand to hand, exchanged observations, and offered him whatever business deals were spawning lustfully in their young managerial brains eager for fame and profit. Felix stood in the midst of them bewildered, his zipper open, his face and penis both tearful.

But right then, two mammoth engineers elbowed an opening through the thronging crowd, and down this corridor, gliding in perfect safety, came Dr. Tomič. She raised Felix's head with her right hand, as with her left she reached down to the open zipper, put his penis back into the suit, and zipped it up. Then, with a long red fingernail, she intercepted a thick tear on his cheek, which like so many others before it was about to roll down his contorted face.

"Don't worry about a thing. It will all be fine. I'll take care of you. This is something we both deserve, you and me. With our combined forces, my dear, we will make our dreams a reality!"

And before anyone could blink, Felix was gliding off behind Dr. Tomič and her assistants to her car.

Tomič's ambitions went far beyond her scientific career. Not long after finishing her doctorate, she had resolved to devote her life, not to reproducing the human race, but to producing energy. After a few years she realized that her office was too cramped and she would do better to pursue her goals through politics. The bigwigs in the center-left party soon took note of the liberal views of her charismatic personality and included her on their ticket. "Any good political operative knows that an ambitious, intelligent, and sexually uninhibited woman of mature years is a priceless asset in the strategy of any party," a well-known psychologist-slash-pundit had once observed with respect to her media presence, adding that Dr. Evica Tomič was the very embodiment of all these qualities. She ably defended the party's political and economically sound interests, and did so as fiercely as any Spartan mother. But at the same time she was constantly searching for that extra something to establish not just her role as a member of the party, but herself personally, as a scientist and energy expert—as Evica Tomič, PhD. So it was that, at the symposium, with her sense for logistics, which included as well her inestimable intuition, she saw at once that this timid man was just what was lacking in her climb up the career ladder.

Of course he would sign anything, would do anything—whatever Dr. Tomič desired. He could even repeat the experiment, not once but countless times, Felix Gril told her. Initially, he was terrified that she was about to take him herself, personally, to the asylum or the police, but when he found himself in her office and saw that Dr. Tomič had no such intention, he became even more confused.

The scientist incorporated Felix's invention in her political program. At first this program encountered serious reservations and doubts within the scientific community, as well as harsh moral condemnations. Men said openly (even her party colleagues, though of course not in public) that they had a pretty good idea of the sort of energy device Tomič really needed to have plugged into her. And women turned bright red whenever the scientist showed up on television to explain, without a hint of shame, the way her energy system worked; the feminists attacked her mercilessly for merely inverting the sexist patriarchal model but by no means doing away with it; the church denounced her loudly and threatened eternal damnation, while the humanists claimed that her system was just another form of human exploitation.

But when her advisors skillfully calculated the percentages by which air, water, and other forms of environmental pollution would be reduced, not to mention unemployment and poverty, and the amount by which social prosperity would be increased, the counterarguments began collapsing one after the other and her opponents—in part because of some nimble maneuvering by her party, which may or may not have been entirely consti-tutional, but who cares—had no choice but to relent.

And thus the global transformation of society could begin.

In towns and villages across the country construction began on huge power stations. There was work for anyone willing to roll up their sleeves and spit in their hands, said the minister of labor, family, and social affairs and Tomič's party colleague. And it wasn't far from the truth, either, for these were no empty promises. From now on, formerly unemployed men could earn enough for mothers to stay home and devote themselves entirely to their families, and in the evening they would tell their spoiled children to eat their supper, since, to put it colorfully, it had been cooked on their father's fire. Hard-working male students could ease the burden of their studies, while female students who usu-ally waited till the last minute to write their term papers found it easier to keep awake through arduous all-nighters knowing that their computers and desk lamps were powered by the youthful energy of cute male classmates. Foreign workers' dormitories (the theological seminaries categorically refused to participate) supplied energy to hospitals, daycare centers, and kindergartens, while many young men opted to fulfill their national military obligation by grabbing not guns but their own penises.

This humane and eco-friendly universal system thus produced an energy that brought warmth to the lonely, gentle healing to the afflicted, and even greater riches to the rich.

As for Felix, he simply blossomed. All his illnesses and pains disappeared. There was no more self-recrimination, no more pangs of conscience. He often thought that, useful as he was now, he would make even his mother smile. And on the day when he received the Gold Medal of Freedom from the hands of the president, the new minister of energy, Dr. Evica Tomič, kissed him on his burning cheek right in front of everyone and said into the microphone: "Felix, I am so very proud of you!"

His life had turned around completely. In addition to this national honor, Felix also had a new job and a new home. He was in charge of technical maintenance at the National Sanitarium for the Treatment of Drug and Alcohol Addiction. And at the orders of the energy minister, the sanitarium's board of directors had given him lifelong use of a freshly painted apartment in the building's attic.

And he never again had any worries.

He did all his work with love.

A Swarm of Fireflies

SHE HEARD THE sound of a motorcycle in the driveway. She threw off her ragged track suit, slipped on a formfitting blue and white dress, and in front of the mirror swiped a pale lipstick across her lips. She didn't know he'd be coming this afternoon. Her son had called in the morning to say that practice was going to run late and he'd get a ride home in the evening with his father. She opened the door. In the driveway the boy was taking off his helmet. No, he's not back yet, she said and instantly lied that her son had told her he should wait for him. She suggested he put the motorbike in the garage. Not only because it was starting to drizzle, but because she didn't want anyone to see that he was here when she was alone. That they were by themselves.

As he was parking the bike in the garage, she recalled that hot September afternoon when she brought her son's freshly ironed shirt into his room; her son had gone out a little bit earlier to the store. Stretched on the leather recliner, wearing red linen pants and a black T-shirt, he was resting his head on his crossed arms and listening to music with headphones over his ears and his eyes closed. He couldn't hear her or see her. She had stood in the doorway looking at his smile, his oblong face, his tan body splayed over the leather, a body that over the summer had grown long and firm. She had felt something in her gut then, something she had forgotten even existed. Something that had not happened to her in a long time—not since she had been his age—an exciting pleasure hard to describe, pulsing with the desire to approach him, to touch his body and kiss him on his thin, slightly parted lips. She had hung the shirt in her son's wardrobe, gone into the kitchen, and carefully started arranging thin slices of ham and cheese on pieces of toast. When she heard her son's footsteps on the stairs, she had followed them with an uneasy feeling in her throat, knocked on the door, and entered. You're probably hungry, she had said, avoiding the boy's eyes. As her son was pouring the Cokes, the young man had looked at her, grabbed a sandwich, and smiled. His smile was different too, she had noticed. He wasn't smiling just with his lips anymore, but with his whole face, including his warm, slightly angled, brown eyes. That hot September afternoon a cocoon had woken within her, the kind that can lie dormant for years and then, at some unforeseen moment, even decades later, as happened with her, start twitching, wake from its dry, unmoving sleep, and life completely changes: colors are more intense, sounds are purer, a swarm of fireflies spreads through the body, and you start glowing.

When he put the motorbike away, she invited him into the living room and, her voice trembling, offered him, for the first time ever, not juice or a soda, but a beer. He took off his black leather jacket—the same jacket she had so often removed from the coatrack in the front hall so she could bury her face in its smell—and she went into the kitchen. When she was at work, for the past two months, whenever she expected him to stop by, she would already be thinking about what to make that afternoon: apple strudel, pizza, maybe a rich chocolate cake. She couldn't remember ever cooking for anybody with this much care. Or feeling anything like this. Maybe she had forgotten. When a person falls in love they think they have never before experienced anything so intense, so strong, so overwhelming. Especially if as in her case it happens after such a long time. At forty-seven. Which was terrible—not her age but the fact that the boy was only seventeen and her son's classmate, that he was still a minor and she was married.

Whenever he was there visiting her son, she'd find all sorts of excuses to go into her son's room. Sometimes she would maternally close the window, and then come in a second time to open it, or she'd come to get the dirty laundry or bring in the clothes she had ironed; she'd ask how their classes were going and try to catch the boy's eye. Had he just now looked at her differently? She was sure his pupils were more dilated. What was he trying to tell her with that gesture, when he quickly touched the corner of his eye? Had he maybe winked at her confidentially? Or had she imagined the whole thing? Because it was what she wanted. And nothing she had seen was true. One evening when she brought them fresh-baked ginger cookies and cocoa, and then half an hour later two Cokes, her son gave her an ugly look and yelled: "Can't you just leave us alone!"

"I'm sorry," she had said to him. "I'm sorry," to both of them. She had blushed, caught the young man's inscrutable smile, and on her way to the bathroom heard her son and his friend making fun of her, his mom. She had sat down on the edge of the tub and burst into tears. For the first time she was really afraid that she had lost control of herself—that something she would only later call love had been in control of her ever since that sultry afternoon.

She came back to the living room from the kitchen with a cold can of beer, poured him a glass, and sat in the recliner opposite him. Nervously, a little maternally, she started asking about school, and about how he could still ride the motorcycle in late October, now that the weather had turned and he could catch cold.

"Don't worry about me, Mom," he said casually.

"Please don't call me that." She was hurt.

"But that's what you are."

"Sure, but you can call me by my name."

"Fine, if that's what you want," he said indifferently.

So what did they do in the evenings, where did they go, him and her son—out with girls maybe? She could hardly form the words. He talked to her about the motorcycle, snowboarding, music . . . Absorbed in the movement of his slightly wet lips, she thought how her husband had long ago lost the strength these young men had, these boys, a strength born of passion for the things they desired, which made it seem as if they were willing to sacrifice safety and comfort for anything they believed in, but they would never sacrifice their desires, not under any circumstances. Was that what so enchanted her in this boy, what she saw in his warm, unreachable eyes, in his body on these early autumn evenings when his skin exuded an intoxicating scent? Had he brought something back to her, something she had thought was lost forever, lost a very long time ago? What she had discovered decades ago with the boys of her own generation, when they were his age—no fear of the future, outrage at anything more than twenty-five years old, the sense that you are part of the chosen race of youth who would never grow old because you would never let yourself be trapped in the nets the adults were setting for you. In a few decades, he would probably be the same as her male contemporaries, the once angry young men in their torn jeans, army boots, battered leather coats splitting at the seams, anarchist badges, who reeked uncontrollably of beer and cigarettes at night, who went to punk concerts—Pankrti, UBR, Via Ofenziva, Berlin Wall—and spit at the performers because that's what you did back then, who drew anti-government graffiti on the walls of underpasses, and who today sit on corporate boards and supervisory councils, run political parties, and edit newspapers. Had it really been about nothing but seeking pleasure and banishing boredom? From time to time, whenever she'd run into them at the market on a Saturday morning, they were usually in a rush, always about to go somewhere—skiing, an afternoon game of golf, or down to the coast to work on their sailboat. Sometimes, too, she'd run into the ones who had managed to avoid the system's sticky spiderwebs and today were panhandling on the streets along with the same, now aged, bums they used to buy cheap wine for in their youth, or they had over time given up alcohol for some more lasting anesthetic. And there were those she never ran into anymore, whose lives had ended in overdoses, road accidents, or disease. Yes, disease—in their late twenties and early thirties her generation saw the first signs that they were not immortal. And maybe fear of death is why they started fucking differently, with a life plan they would never have contemplated ten years earlier, and didn't want to contemplate, let alone imagine themselves living the same life drama their parents were living. So today these forty-something, fifty-something men, yesterday's rebels, were coming home at five o'clock to their kids and middle-class wives, the very sort of women they used to mock and despise, and turning up with them at public events and in gossip columns. And when they got together for a game of soccer, they still patted each other on the shoulder, as if to say they're the same as ever. And in fact they were right. Today she knew that that boyish rebellion in their teens and early twenties was mostly the effect of testosterone, which a decade later settled into a career and a family. That's the way it's always been and always will be. They kill their fathers so they can take their place and become just like them. Today they no longer smell of cheap cigarettes and beer, but aftershave. They no longer use bikes to get around, or beat-up old cars, or motorcycles—at the very least they drive mid-size vehicles. And they don't walk around the house in shoes anymore, but as soon as they come in the door always change into their slippers.

No, her husband had not been a rebel. He kept his hair short, sometimes shaved his head, went to concerts, listened to Joy Division, Dead Kennedys, The Clash, the Sex Pistols, The Fall, etc., and supported whatever the other guys did. He was an observer, same as her, only she was a young woman. She dyed her short hair red, or sometimes peroxide blonde, wore heavy makeup and a leather miniskirt with black stockings, and drank beer with the boys. But when she finished university, there was a feeling of emptiness. The morning of her first job interview, she stood in front of the mirror and, for the first time in her life, thought she looked like her mother. With exactly the same short hair, only younger. By the age of twenty-six, she had a full-time job and yet had nothing. She had known him for a long time, but only by appearance, from concerts and art shows, and from the very start, theirs was not the kind of stormy love she had had before, with the angry rebels who had softened over the years and who by the age of thirty—after the collapse of the old regime, in the new country—were already pushing baby carriages, climbing out of cars bought with bank loans (and then only subcompacts), and, like her, working at their first jobs. It was at the age of thirty that she first realized that their world had changed, that her generation of rebels had vanished forever. But now, with this teenager, the lost feeling had returned. Even if he knew even less than her generation what he was rebelling against. Even if she knew that what she saw in him, just like what she had seen twenty-five years ago in her male peers, was an illusion. But this feeling—that your entire body, down to its last nerve ending, was inhabited by a swarm of glowing fireflies, even if the source of their light is false—this feeling was true some twenty-five years ago, and it was true too, here and now, with this boy.

He had stopped talking. An awkward silence filled the space between them. She stood up, went into the kitchen, and came back with another beer; she placed it in front of him and sat down next to him on the sofa. He gazed at her fearlessly. She wasn't sure if it was desire she saw in his eyes, but at that moment she knew without a doubt that he knew that she wanted him, and had known this for weeks, maybe even as far back as that afternoon when, lying on the recliner, he had possibly not had his eyes all the way closed but had watched her through his eyelashes as she observed him from the door. The last time she and her husband made love, a month ago, she had been thinking of the boy's smooth, hairless chest, his slightly angled eyes, his long, dark curls reaching to his shoulders, and what might happen if she ever found herself, like today, in the house, with him, just the two of them . . .

"So what are you thinking about, Mom?" He startled her; he was looking straight into her eyes.

"Don't call me that," she snapped and was starting to feel sick to her stomach. She wanted to ask him if he had a girlfriend, if he had ever slept with anyone, but her vocal cords seized up and she couldn't speak. Her body had started to slip out of her control and behave as if something outside of her was operating it. Her hand, trembling, moved away from her body and stroked him on the cheek. He did not even flinch. It slipped down his shoulder, down his skintight T-shirt, and then she leaned over and, cautiously, kissed him.

"Are you out of your mind, Mom!" He pushed her away.

"Stop with the 'Mom' already!" she stammered out with a sob. "You know what's going on."

"I don't know what you're talking about," he said gruffly, then jumped off the sofa and walked over to the window.

"I love you," she said timidly, probably for the first time in a decade.

"Leave me alone," he replied coldly.

"Why? Because I'm your friend's mother?"

"You're not my type."

"You mean I'm too old for you?"

"Yeah, probably that too. With that motherly-sweet servility, you come off as too old, but you're also annoying, coming on to guys who could be your son."

"Please," she cried, "I beg you. If you don't touch me, I think I'll go crazy." She unbuttoned her dress, tossed it aside, and stood before him in her underwear.

He took a long look at her, sized up her body, and made a sour face.

"Don't look at me like that!" She ran to him, threw herself at his feet and embraced his knees.

"You even smell weird," he said harshly.

"What kind of smell?" She looked at him.

"Like an old woman."

"What are you saying?" she cried and started to unzip his pants, but he roughly pushed her away, and she fell with a thud next to the television.

"If you could see yourself now, just how miserable and pathetic you are, you wouldn't even think about touching me!" he hissed at her with contempt. A moment later his phone rang. He answered it calmly, as if nothing had happened. She could tell from the conversation that he was talking to her son.

He told him they needed to meet right away, but not here, somewhere outside, that he'd wait for him, that he hadn't known he had practice.

She grabbed her dress, ran out of the living room, down the steps to the basement, and from there to the garage, where she collapsed beside his motorcycle. She had no idea he could be so cold, so cruel. He had known all along; he had intentionally been luring her, toying with her. For the pure evil of it. But all she had done was follow her feelings, feelings she had never felt so strongly. Which had possessed her completely and about which she had had no choice. There had been no evil in it, except, perhaps, the fact that she was married and, probably, also that the boy was still a minor . . . But some boys at the age of seventeen aren't children anymore, and he certainly wasn't, not since last summer, when she had noticed more than once a reddish-blue spot on his neck, so with her it definitely, probably, would not have been his first time . . .

She wrapped her arms around the motorcycle, placed her tear-stained face on the leather seat, and kissed it. He was so mean. After that first beer he could have stood up and left; he could have stopped coming there weeks ago, stopped smiling at her, stopped looking at her in that very particular way. But he couldn't wait for her to humiliate herself in front of him, couldn't wait for her façade to crumble. So is that how the little rebel intended to get his revenge on women, and maybe on his own mother, a woman her own age who, people said, had had affairs with men much younger than herself, which is why everyone was laughing at her husband, although maybe it was the oldest son who was suffering the most? Was he trying to get revenge through her on the world of old people, who have a weird smell and who should never intrude on the world of people who aren't yet adults but are no longer children?

Never again would she be able to look him in the eye; never again would he smile at her. Without love, her world would be nothing but pain, but even that was better than the anesthetized world she had been living in before the boy awakened her desire, and she didn't want to go back to that world ever again.

She heard the sound of her husband's car in the driveway. She grabbed her dress, ran from the basement to the front hall (the boy was still in the living room talking on the phone), climbed the stairs to the bathroom, locked the door, leaned over the sink, and threw up.

From outside, through the closed window, came the sound of the front door opening and then loud talking. He would blab everything, first to her son, and then her son, who had probably seen what was going on, would tell his father. Life with them would become impossible. And worst of all, the thing she couldn't bear, was that people would be laughing at them because of her, because like a teenage girl she'd fallen head over heels for her son's schoolmate, a boy who was almost a child.

She heard the garage door open and the motorcycle revving up. Her face flushed, she held on to the radiator by the window and struggled to lift herself up; there was a jolt of burning pain in her stomach and she vomited on the window glass. As the motorcycle drove out of the driveway—the boy behind the handlebars and her son behind him clinging to his waist—the colors around her began to melt into gray, and sounds were blending into a single meaningless hum. She leaned on the sink and in the mirror saw that everything that had been burning in her eyes these past few months was now ash. Her body was getting heavy and the heat in it was going out. She turned on the hot water in the bathtub, took a box of sleeping pills from the medicine cabinet, and swallowed them all by the handful, each time washing them down with water. By now she couldn't hear the footsteps on the stairs or, later, the furious knocking on the door. In a daze, she took off her underclothes, picked up her husband's razor, stepped into the tub, sank down into the water, put the blade to her wrist, and shut her eyes . . .

Repetition

SHE IS LYING on the bed, and the late-afternoon August sun
shines on her face through slightly open Venetian blinds. These
past few days she has noticed the shadows of the houses getting
longer, and since the storm last night there is, for the first time
this year, a smell of autumn in the air. She lifts herself up with
her arm, grabs his shoulder and bites into his neck. Her lips glue
themselves to his throat and slowly, very slowly, suck on it. With
her tongue she lashes smoothly at the taut Adam's apple, which
she squeezes between her teeth, so the soft cartilage has no choice
but to give. He winces with every squeeze. Blood floods his muscles and the warm flesh beneath his clothes stiffens against her
body. Convulsively, he thrusts at her hard, flat abdomen.

"No," she says, firmly pushing away his hand when it slides
down to the metal zipper on his pants.

"Why not?"

She bites him harder.

With a love whose form never matches its content. She thinks
of a distant place. *By a road. A few houses. Next to the cemetery
. . . a gravestone . . . probably marble . . . a name, years of birth and
death . . . or something like that . . . probably . . . She will never go
there. It's impossible to understand everything. The man who sleeps
a while inside you and then is completely gone.*

"Aren't you going to take off your gloves?"

"No, sir. You said you don't like my hands and that you enjoy
feeling the soft leather against your skin."

"I like it when you call me sir."

"I like it when you like me."

She unbuckles his belt, pulls out his thin white shirt, and takes it off. Gently, she lowers her entire body onto his burning chest.

"You're wonderfully hairy, sir."

At once he grabs her and presses her tightly to himself. She wrenches away from him and pulls the black leather belt out of his pants. She binds his hands with it and then ties them to the vertical black metal bed frame.

"What do you have in mind?"

"Nothing you wouldn't want, sir."

His breathing is clipped and strong. The sunlight through the Venetian blinds falls across the sweaty surface of his skin.

"You're not afraid, are you, sir?" she whispers coldly and strokes his inner thighs with her hand. She plunges her tongue into his mouth and flaps it around in his saliva like a seal.

"I love you."

"No, sir. You don't. Nevertheless, I will do to you what you want me to do."

He has the cold, fresh smell of mountain conifers. She runs her wet tongue down his chin, along his neck, licks the taut lymph nodes of the neck, slips over the left shoulder to his breast-bone, licks the spot beneath which his heart is rapidly beating, moves even lower, circles the navel, and stops at the bushy base of his slightly hairy belly. She opens the zipper and, like a cat with a kitten, drags his penis out of the slit in his underwear with her teeth.

"It's welling with tears, sir. I will make it sob."

She takes it deep into her mouth and sucks. She slides her tongue along the smooth underside and with her front teeth gently bites the shaft. Then she releases it, swollen and throbbing with reddish-blue veins, and dries its tender, sticky surface with her cold breath.

"It smells like chestnuts, like the fall," she says and kisses it.

She unbuttons his pants and removes them, then the gray underpants and socks, so he is completely naked. He looks at her with wide eyes, the way they have all looked at her in similar moments, waiting for their surprise. It is always about the surprise. Which is very pleasant. The first time. And a few times after that. Until the last time. They watch her with bulging eyes, like young calves unaware that when the owner unties them he will take them to a yard in which the butcher will cut their throats.

Do they have any premonition? Do they realize, if just for a moment, that last time, what's in store for them? Later, once the thing is done, she has sometimes wondered if they suspected, right before it, what was going to happen. In her memory, she looks into their eyes but can never quite decide what she sees in them. A vague fear, undoubtedly, that for sure, but there's nothing unusual about fear of uncertainty. Nothing special. There is desire too, and a hint of uneasiness, and even, for a moment—but not with all of them, just a few—regret. For having ever become involved with her? Maybe. But never regret for leaving her, for wanting to be free of her completely. No, she has never seen *that* in the eyes of any of them.

She unbuttons her close-fitting dark blue dress—it has a round neckline and a hem that falls two inches above her knees (she never wears miniskirts, which are tacky and attract too much vulgar attention)—and slips it off. His moist eyes inspect her simple, turquoise-blue silk underwear.

She lies down beside him, her damp, curly hair falling luxuriantly over his abdomen. She bites his waist, wets her middle finger with her tongue, and slips it beneath the rim of her panties down to her crotch.

"What about me? Aren't you going to . . ."

"When it's your turn," she sighs, "at just the right moment . . . I'll do my very best."

With her moistened middle finger she tickles her crotch. She shut her eyes tight, as she always does, whenever the outlines of the world begin to throb and everything around gets blurry, in colors that awaken her anxiety.

As she lies there beside him, the shadowy parts of her body begin to slowly open.

Slowly, very slowly, the man approaches. He is of medium build, more slight than not, with strong lips and eyes that always look green in the dark. Only in the dark, when he kisses her on the sprucewood bed and does what a man does with a woman he loves. But he doesn't. He doesn't love her any more than he loves the other women he brings to his apartment from time to time. With her, it's not from time to time, but regular. Once a week. For almost three months. He liked her because she wasn't afraid (at least she didn't look it), because neither of them were afraid of anything. Except love. And because she didn't ask many questions. At first. Because it was just a game. At first. Because it was a love whose form didn't match the content. At first. Then not any longer. When is this "next time"? How soon? It seems like something has changed. Like I feel something. Like I care about you. Maybe even love you. After that, nothing stops her. Not even the cold, biting pain when her head flew into the sharp metal ribs of the radiator. Nothing is important anymore, she told him. I don't care, not even about that, so long as I'm with you . . .

Whenever he doesn't call for a few days, she lies for hours on the bed at night, her hand on the phone, in her thoughts trying to summon him from a different part of town.

This is because he doesn't spend enough time thinking about her. Less than he did at the beginning and, especially, much less than she spends thinking about him. Which isn't good. She never forgets him, not for a moment, and even when she's asleep she dreams about him, but he only thinks about her when he feels like it, and that's bad. Very bad.

After a couple of hours she always dials his number. Are you alone? I'd like to see you. Can I come over?

He is usually sitting at the computer or watching TV. With hardly a word, they undress. Words come later. They're part of the game. But part of the game less and less. Later, in the middle of the night, he goes over to the bureau, where there's a stack of journals with his articles, and grabs his car keys. Time to go, he says.

Only once did he allow her to stay the night. She slept in the bed with him. She had cautiously, very cautiously, snuggled up to him, but he pushed her away. It's not good for a person to get used to such things, to get attached to them, he had told her, and added that he'd probably sleep with some other woman the following night.

Lying next to him, she does not touch his body. He is only a touch away from her but infinitely distant. She looks through the window above the bed and listens to his dog whimpering in the front hall. And she wishes he were dead.

In the late August afternoon, smelling of fall and dwindling into evening, the man beside her, whose hands are tied to the metal bed frame, is kissing her nipple.

"Are you close?" he asks.

She opens her eyes and thinks that rarely has she been as close to everything as she is now.

She licks her middle finger and slips into *a humid August evening, right after the man with the dog has undressed her, when she is dizzy with anticipation that they will finally touch the boundary they have been inching closer and closer to. Which is the only thing they have in common. He binds her hands and ties them to the wooden bed frame. He starts by tenderly kissing her neck and stroking her hair. Then he pulls at his swollen penis, holds it above her torso, and urinates on her breasts. She covers her face with her arm so the bitter droplets won't irritate the mucous membrane of her eyes. Then he thrusts himself deep inside her. As he makes his rough, repetitive motions, a dark haze wraps itself around her body, her heart is wildly pumping blood to her body, a spiral of heat squeezes her like a boa constrictor, strangling her body in a tight embrace, until coil after coil it relaxes its grip. She exhales, and softly, darkly, the bedroom subsides.*

He lights a cigarette and goes to the window. She looks at his frail body. Why doesn't he love her the way she loves him? He prefers the woman he'll be sleeping with tomorrow night. She can tell this from how he mentioned her. Maybe it really was just a game at first, but the rules changed. And now there simply aren't any rules.

The motion of her finger is more and more accurate; she is breathing faster and faster, each breath louder and more convulsive than the last. After she comes, she slides up to his neck and tenderly kisses his thin lips.

He gives her a friendly look.

"You know . . . the thing I said today on the phone," he whispers in her ear, "I didn't really mean it that way . . . not really . . ."

"You meant exactly what you are trying now to tell me you didn't mean."

"That's not true."

"Oh, please," she replies, as her hand searches the nightstand for a lighter and cigarette, which she lights. The gray band at the tip of the cigarette is expanding like mercury. She sits up, takes another deep drag, carefully brings the cigarette above his body, and flicks the ash onto his penis.

"You're insane!" he cries.

"You're afraid. That's good . . ."

Since that summer when she went on warm nights to a neighborhood of tall towers on the edge of the city, a few more summers have passed. The first began without him, on a warm June day when he was taken in a metal urn (the body was extremely disfigured, she had read in the newspaper: eleven stab wounds in the lower region) back to the place from which he had come to the city ten years earlier, with too great a desire for danger and too little a desire for life, as he had once told her.

She puts the cigarette out in a crystal ashtray on the nightstand, stands up and goes into the bathroom. She squeezes green toothpaste onto a red toothbrush and brushes her teeth. She looks in the mirror. Her pupils are so dark and dilated the green-gray iris is almost invisible. Her features have changed, so much that the person she sees is almost someone else, not completely her, even though she knows that she is looking at herself in the mirror.

She leans on the light-brown sink and closes her eyes.

She is twenty-six and he is twenty-nine. They are in his apartment, with the big dog; there's a two-and-a-half-liter bottle of cold Coca-Cola on the table. She is sitting on the sprucewood bed; there are melted Swiss chocolates on the cream-colored sheet. He suddenly tells her she should go. Already? she asks. It hasn't been that long since she got there. Had he opened the door for her because he thought it was somebody else?

He takes a step away from her, holds her face in his hands, and tells her again that she must go right away. No, she replies, it's not so simple. She grabs his hand and he pushes her away. She goes into

*the kitchen, picks up a glass and takes an unopened bottle of mag-
nesium pills from the shelf. She tries to pull off the plastic ring that
seals the lid to the container, but she can't. She opens a drawer, takes
out a knife, slices beneath the plastic lid, and shuts her eyes: . . . She
is nineteen years old. Gripping the railing, she goes down the stairs
from an old, shabby apartment. She feels nauseous. She stops and
looks into the abyss where the staircase curves in a spiral like the shell
of a sea snail. Her stomach trembles and, as she clings to the railing,
she throws up. On her dress too, a dark blue summer dress of rayon.
And on her skin, which is scratched up and, in some places, bleeding from open wounds. She struggles to remove her white summer
pumps and, holding them in her hand against the metal railing,
slowly steals down to the first floor and across to the main entrance.
Bearing down with all her weight on the handle of the door, she lets
out a deep sigh and tears start welling behind her closed eyes: . . . She
is fifteen years old. It's Tuesday afternoon. She is at home, standing
in front of the medicine cabinet. Opening bottle after bottle. She
pours bright-colored capsules into her hand and gobbles them by
the fistful, sometimes washing them down with booze. Next to her,
a dog (now long dead) is whimpering; the dog is licking her feet,
but more and more she doesn't care about anything. She is drifting
away with her eyes closed: . . . She is eight years old. She is lying
next to some sheep in a mountain pasture (now long overgrown),
and her mother (dead now) sits next to her with slightly curly, very
blond hair and fair, very fair, somewhat pinkish skin. They're on
vacation. High in the mountains. They are talking. At first it seems
that she doesn't understand her mother. She can't understand why
her mother doesn't understand her and doesn't even want to. The
high mountain sunshine dazzles her, bringing tears to her eyes. She
closes them: . . . It is summer and she is three years old. There's a
baby on the floor in the room: her little brother, who is crying. He
slipped out of her hands, or maybe she let go of him because, when
she lifted him from the crib, she thought he was too heavy. She can't
stand hearing her brother cry. She covers his mouth with her hands.
She hears footsteps hurrying up the stairs. She presses her hands more
tightly over his mouth and now, for the first time, hears the voices.
They could be human voices, but she knows very well that they are*

not coming from outside. They are from inside her head. At the age of three she has already learned that people can tell the difference between things that exist and things that, even if you hear them or see them, simply do not exist . . .

She rinses her mouth with tepid water and spits out the frothy liquid. In the white foam around the drain she sees red threads of blood and runs her tongue across her damaged gums. She glances at herself in the mirror, puts her hair in order, and goes back to the room.

She stands in the doorway and stares at him.

"What's wrong? You're not upset, are you? . . . Because of what I said when you got here . . . You know, sometimes a person just says things. Stuff happens . . ."

"Sure. Sometimes a person just says: I want to forget you, I want to forget all about you. I never want to see you again. In fact, I never loved you. It was all just a game . . . And stuff happens."

She goes up to him and with her cold breath kisses him on the lips. Then she bends over him and again swallows his penis, which grows hard beneath the tingling menthol.

"I love you."

"That's not true, sir, and you know it."

She gets up from the bed and goes to the large black wall cabinet. She pushes open the sliding door, which has a mirror attached to it, and takes a thick cord from the bottom shelf. Her eyes are as murky as the lake she swam across a few hours before. She approaches him, her lingerie unbuttoned, ties the cord in a knot around his penis and tightens it a little. Tears are running down his face.

"Goddammit! You gonna break it like that!"

Outside, the night animals are making their noises. The little rodents are squeaking in muffled tones. The night birds have arrived from the city park. She covers her ears and the sounds she hears are like voices at an airport terminal or railroad station. She glances at the window and sees a nearly full moon gliding across the sky.

"They're not asleep. Do you hear them, sir? It's warm out. Do you feel how different the world is at night? Things happen that would never happen during the day."

She sits on top of him, puts his penis inside her, and begins to jerk up and down on his belly. The rough cord cuts into her groin. She shuts her eyes and every so often, using both hands, tugs the ends of the cord.

"This is hell!" he grimaces.

"No, sir. There is no hell, none at all. Nothing. Total nothing. Nothing of the sort. Not even after death. One endless nothing. You will forget all about it, sir. Instantly. You will forget about me, and not just me; you will forget about everything."

She tugs the cord harder. His penis is hot and swollen and the veins are throbbing a purply blue.

"Will you be soon, sir?" she asks.

"Yes . . ."

"Tell me when."

With her left hand she takes the other end of the cord as well; then her right hand slides over to her white handbag and feels for the deerhorn handle. Her eyes are motionless and glassy, like the eyes on those plastic dolls in long pleated skirts, which twenty or thirty years ago, as was the fashion, people would place on the marriage bed. Most likely, he barely notices her right hand slipping into the white handbag.

The pleasure is so great he does not notice the sharp metal crescent in her hand as it slips past his head towards his abdomen.

"Are you getting close, sir?"

She is moving harder and faster on top of his body.

"Oh yeah," he cries. "Now . . . now!".

She lifts her hips and his penis slips out of her. Then, right at the knot that is strangling the swollen penis, she holds both strands of the cord in her left hand and with her right takes a swift, strong swing. Once. Then, quickly, a few more times.

Just one scream. And nothing else. Not another sound.

His body is twitching convulsively. The open vessels between his thighs foam with dark-cherry blood. A few more minutes and everything will be forgotten. She counts them in her mind. The seconds. In life, these can be extremely important sometimes . . .

It is getting light outside. Now there are different animals. Making brighter, clearer sounds.

She uses the damp sheet to wipe off the body, which is bloody and sticky. She picks up the blade with the deerhorn handle and goes into the kitchen. At the sink, she turns on the faucet, squeezes a few drops of dish soap onto her gloved hands, and washes them. On her palms she feels the coolness coming in from the outside of the gloves. Then she washes the blade with the deerhorn handle, wipes it with a towel, and dries her gloved hands. She returns to the bedroom. She gets dressed, picks up the white handbag, goes into the bathroom, empties the ashtray down the toilet, and goes back to the kitchen. She fills a glass with cold water and drops in a magnesium pill. She waits for the liquid to turn fizzy orange and drinks it in long gulps. The magnesium clears her head and makes her feel as though she is being cleansed of everything. She opens the handbag, takes out a light-brown case, and inserts the deerhorn handle. She wraps the case in a plastic bag and puts it away in the handbag.

She runs her hand through her long, curly, light blond hair. It is almost dry. It is a little sticky, though, from sweat and blood. Maybe she should cut it or dye it. Or maybe not. Maybe that's not it at all.

She never forgets anything. Never loses anything. She values precision. And can't abide carelessness, not towards people, animals, objects, or obligations.

She washes the glass, places it on the drying rack, picks up the handbag and, without another look around, without going back to check the bedroom, leaves the kitchen, goes to the front hall, and stops in front of a photo of a dark-haired woman, which is hanging on the wall at a slight tilt. She takes a few steps back, looks at the picture, goes up to it, and straightens it. She doesn't like leaving things half done. She goes out through the front door, locks it behind her, calmly as usual (her hands are not shaking any more than then normally do), gets into her car, turns the key, and drives home.

At home she falls asleep. She sleeps for a very long time. A few days. A few months, maybe. And doesn't dream of anything.

Not until she meets him. He has reddish-blond hair. He is a year older than her. Of medium build, his face a little freckled, his eyes light blue, and the past ten days they have been avoiding her when he talks to her. She smiles and looks away. Nothing new. The same as all the others.

She knows what she has to do. Only what she always does. Even before he tells her, she'll have everything prepared. She smiles. Not out of spite. Not out of vindictiveness, but because things are so clearly and so precisely repeating themselves. Because she does not have a choice. Because she always does only what she has to do. What needs to be done.

She opens her eyes and gets out of bed. She opens the window all the way. The shadows are falling more and more at an angle. She will probably drive to the lake and swim across it. Swimming is soothing. Very soothing. The senseless repetition of movements calms a person down. She looks for a towel and her black one-piece bathing suit. It looks good on her; it goes with her complexion, which in June is still very fair, and with her hair, which is the color of cold beaches. She puts a pair of gray and white gloves in her handbag, as well as a clear plastic bag, a dark-green leather case, and a full bottle of fizzy magnesium pills.

She picks up the telephone and punches in nine numbers. She knows that for the past few weeks he has not been waiting. It's the same every time. No one ever says anything to her. They act as if everything is fine, but then suddenly they have less and less time for her, or no time at all. And then one day they want to have done with her for good.

When she notices objects starting to bleed into each other right before her eyes, and when the voices she hears are getting louder, even when she has music playing at full volume, she knows it is time. They make that very clear to her.

No metaphors. Only calm, precise instructions. She just needs to take the time to prepare everything carefully. Every gesture. From start to finish. Every step, even the smallest movement.

Lying on the bed, she calms herself and waits. People say life repeats itself, and for her the repetition is very predictable. She always meets somebody with whom it does not last forever. As if they become bored by the repetitiveness of life with her. But she does try. She tries very hard. That's why she always has to finish it herself. She feels no pleasure in this, no delight of any sort. On the contrary, the thing she desires is a man who will love her, who will live with her as couples do, in an apartment or a house, in the city or the suburbs, preferably in a big house by the lake, with children, a dog, and, well, all the rest. But they don't want to. She does nothing to them except fulfill their desire—and sooner or later they all desire the same thing: I want to forget you, they say; I don't ever want to see you again; it was all just a game. But it is not possible to simply erase someone from memory. It is not right. It is not good to cross out every-thing in a single day, especially to cross out someone whose body has been breathing closely with yours. She herself never forgets anybody. And she will not forget him. His reddish-blond hair, his long, thin limbs, his soft fragrance of meadows in June, his smooth, pink chest.

She is always precise and careful. She never plays with a per-son's life or emotions. They, however, when they talk about love never mean it seriously. And they can even laugh at it. Which is not good. Such hateful, cold emotions turn people ugly. Not just on the outside, but also on the inside they weave cocoons that eat at the body. Which can look disgusting. And this is something she always prevents from happening to them.

She listens to the telephone signal, and then hears a man's voice.

"Hello, sir. Can we see each other today? . . .

"Yes, when I get back from swimming . . .

"You don't want me to call you 'sir' today? . . .

"Things are different? How are they different? . . .

"Enough? . . . Enough of what? . . .

"I should have sensed it? . . .

"Sure . . . we can get together . . .

"One last time? . . .

"Didn't I realize? . . . Realize what exactly? . . .

"I understand . . . of course I do . . .

"Be calm? . . . The stupid repetition of movements kills the body . . .

"I said *calms* . . . I meant, *calms* the body . . .

"Everything is fine . . .

"When I'm done swimming I'll come straight to your place . . .

"No, I didn't cut my hair . . . I didn't dye it either . . .

"Because that's not it. I'll probably do something different . . . It'll be a warm night, and there will be a lot of animal sounds . . ."

Her Hand

I AM TWENTY-NINE years old and I weigh two hundred and thirty-six pounds. I have a feeling I won't be gaining any more weight from now on. At least I don't think so. After what happened I feel lighter, regardless of my weight. But it's too soon to say anything, since I still don't know exactly what did happen or where I stand in this story and its future. Yesterday I was taken before the examining magistrate, who asked me about the details. I didn't tell him anything new, nothing I didn't tell the detective the day before yesterday. I was calm and not too talkative, but that's how I was even before it happened. That's just the way I am.

When I got out of the elevator Monday afternoon, people were already gathered around her in the courtyard; they included an elderly woman from our building and a young father, who had forgotten that he was holding his daughter's hand and should probably have prevented her from seeing anything like that. I never imagined that a body could make such a loud noise when it strikes concrete. Her body was weirdly twisted and the only thing left of her head, I think, was the face. As I walked around her body, I had the feeling that her eyes were watching me, following me. That's how I felt my whole life, that her eyes were following me, even when she was nowhere near me physically. Her mouth was stretched into something that could even have been a smile—a nasty smile, the kind of smile she had whenever she was putting me down, especially these past twenty years. Her face didn't seem all that different from the one I had looked at every day, the one I was afraid of—yes, I was terribly afraid of her; I never knew when she was going to raise her hand against me, or yell at me, or do something else to hurt me.

I don't know what happened, I told my elderly neighbor; I don't know, I repeated later in the apartment to the police officers and the detective. When I got into the elevator with them—since they wanted to inspect the apartment and have a chat with me—I overheard the young policeman whisper to his colleague that it was hard to believe such a small elevator could carry such a heavy load. He didn't hurt my feelings. Remarks like that haven't hurt me in a long time. There was a time when I would have been hurt, just a few years ago even, especially if I liked the boy, if he seemed friendly, and then it turned out that he was interested in me and acting friendly only because he had not yet found the right name to insult me with or because he wanted to remember what I looked like so he could tell his friends about me later. Mostly, the insults were delivered in a soft voice, but always loud enough so I could hear them. Lots of times I simply had the feeling that people were talking about me, about how much I disgusted them. And that I smelled too, and that would happen on hot days, which is why as much as possible I avoided the bus and the subway and went to wherever I was going on foot—to work, to the grocery store, to the bank, the post office. Or to the cemetery. I never met anyone at the cemetery who was rude to me, or rather, there it was easy to keep my distance from people. I don't know if I believe in life after death, but if my father is anywhere, I think he is most present there. From what I recall, *he* loved me; at least when I think of him, I don't remember anything so terribly bad. But if there really is an afterlife, as some people say, then he should have been present somehow at home, too, in our apartment. But at home, when it was just the two of us, after he died, he definitely wasn't there anymore—which doesn't mean he wasn't constantly present in a different way, as somebody who wasn't there. And I'm to blame for that, for the fact that my father isn't around anymore. I used to sit on his grave and talk to him. For nineteen years I talked to him, about how unbearable it was, how afraid I was, afraid not only that she didn't like me but that one day she might actually kill me. And I would tell him I missed him, I missed him so much, although I don't know what he would have been like later. If he had lived. And especially, I told him I didn't know what to do, that I was doing my best to please her but it didn't make any difference because I could never do anything right, and there were lots of times she would attack me for no reason at all. I also told him how really sorry I was that I had stayed in the park that day after school with those other girls from my class. It was a warm spring afternoon and none of us were anxious to get home. Even though we knew our families would be worried about us, especially after what had happened two days before. That girl had not been one of our classmates; she was in a different class. And she wasn't our friend either, but everybody knew her. People said she was one of the most popular girls in school, and it had happened in that very park, next to the school, at seven in the evening when she was going home from gymnastics. None of us would have had the courage to be in the park by ourselves, especially not just before dark, but we were fascinated by the crime scene, which was still surrounded by yellow tape and guarded by policemen. We stood about a hundred yards from where the incident occurred and talked about what had really taken place: what had happened before he killed her? We were nine years old and knew that whatever it was, it was connected to why our parents had forbidden us to talk to strangers and warned us not to get into cars with people we didn't know and not to accept anything from them.

I think that's when we first understood the reason for all those prohibitions, what might actually happen to us—although none of us had a very clear idea about it and we kept repeating and trying to connect the snippets of conversation we overheard in the corridors, when our mothers were whispering together in front of us. We looked at the placed marked by yellow tape and tried to picture the scene. We weren't all that frightened, since there was a police officer guarding the area, but whenever we tried to describe out loud the event that we had not seen, our imaginations never went any further than him undressing her and starting to touch her. And we remembered how she had chatted with the bus driver on one of our school trips, and another time in front of the grocery store with a man who was as old as our fathers. We didn't notice that it had started to get dark—it was probably eight o'clock because the policemen were changing shifts. I knew I'd get an earful when I got home and probably a beating too.

The apartment door wasn't locked. When I went into the kitchen, there were two policemen sitting with Mother, who was hunched over the table crying. The older policeman (I know today that he was a detective) came and patted me on the head. I knew something had happened. I suspected it had happened to my father. I had seen similar scenes on TV and in the movies, when mothers would be crying like this because someone in the family had died.

"What happened?" I asked.

"It's Daddy . . . Daddy is gone." She could barely get out the words before she started crying even harder.

The older policeman told me to sit down; then he slowly and carefully explained that my father had been hit by a motorcycle.

"Where?" I asked, unable to imagine such a thing.

"On his way to the park . . . to get you!" Mother screamed. And I realized that in some way I was responsible for his death.

"He had gone to look for you!" she yelled. "Because we were scared something had happened to you, because you weren't anywhere to be found, because you were out wandering again—and now he's dead!"

The police officer tried to calm her down, and not too long after that, the doctor arrived, talked to her a bit, and gave her an injection. After the police and the doctor had left, two neighbors came by and then my father's brother, my uncle. I was sitting in a corner, in a daze, and nobody paid much attention to me. Eventually my uncle came over and tried to hug me. I pulled away. Everything was getting mixed up—I was still thinking about the conversation I had had with my classmates about older men who touch girls, and then about my father dying, and I was just beginning to realize that he would never hug me again, would never hold my hand again and take me out for a walk, or to the movies, or to the store. At some point, my mother and I looked at each other, and I could see in her eyes that she hated me. A few times before then, all I had seen was that she didn't especially like me, that I got on her nerves, but now, for the first time, and definitely not the last, I realized that she really and truly hated me. I was the one to blame, it was because of me that he had left for the park and then, where the road bends in front of the grocery store, been killed by a motorcycle.

A little while later my aunt came. I think she saw what was happening with Mama. She was a nurse. She took me to my room, gave me half a sleeping pill, and stayed with me until I fell asleep. I don't remember the next few days very well. Not much has stayed with me except a few images from the funeral, in particular, Mama standing at the grave with an ashen face and clenched lips. On the day of the funeral, my aunt had come over and helped me get dressed—in the dark blue dress I always wore for school events. She tied back my long brown hair with a black bow and brought me my cousin's blue overcoat, which more or less matched the dress. Even though my cousin and I were the same age, her coat was a little too big for me. No, I wasn't fat back then; my height and shape were completely normal for a nine-year-old girl. I think my aunt was worried about me, and about my mother's attitude towards me. I think she knew my mother well and had picked up on some things even before my father died, but before his death maybe she didn't wanted to interfere in our affairs, our family business. We stood next to the grave, my mother on my right and my aunt—today I think she must have placed herself there intentionally—on my left. When the undertaker put the urn in the niche, my mother started sobbing loudly. I reached out my right arm and tried to hold her hand, but she pulled it away as soon as I touched her. My aunt saw this and took my left hand and squeezed it tightly. Tears poured out of my eyes; I don't know which was more painful: the fact that what was left of my father was being laid in the grave, or the knowledge that my mother was determined to be my enemy. Because I had killed her husband, my father, because I had killed her man.

For weeks after the funeral she didn't say a word to me.

Whenever I asked her something, she acted as if she didn't hear me, and when I tugged at her sleeve or stood right in front of her, she would look me up and down with her cold eyes, to let me know that from now on we were at war and I would pay for what I had done.

A week or so after the funeral, my aunt stopped by with my two cousins. She pressed a brand new xylophone in my arms, with a music book, and asked me if I still felt sad. I told her I was even sadder.

"Because of your dad, right?" She looked at me, and I said it wasn't just that. She glanced at Mama and whispered, "Are you sad because she's sad too?"

"Yes," I replied, "because she's sad and doesn't want to talk to me."

Then my aunt whispered something to my mother and they went into the kitchen; my cousins and I stayed in the living room and watched TV. I sensed that the two women in the kitchen were talking about me, and I hoped my aunt would soften her. A few days later, Mama changed; she started speaking to me again but was still cold. And she was right. If I hadn't lingered in the park that afternoon, my father wouldn't have gone out to look for me and what happened to him would not have happened.

I offered to clean the bathroom on Saturdays, I went to the store, washed the dishes, but she never said anything about it unless she thought I hadn't done a good job—good by her standards, which were becoming harder and harder to make sense of. No matter how I tried, she would still fly into a rage sometimes and start tearing me down, telling me what a slob I was, that I was dirty and lazy. She never gave me pocket money, but then nothing like that ever happened when my father was alive either. Once, when I told my parents that my classmates were receiving monthly allowances, she yelled at me, saying that only people who worked got paid, and since I didn't do any work I wouldn't be paid, but that I should finish school as soon as possible and then I would have whatever money I could earn on my own. That's why my aunt always gave me money whenever my mother and I visited her, or when she came to see us, and during her visits, no matter what season it was, I always felt like our chilly apartment became a little brighter and warmer.

The week before my mother's birthday all I could think about was what to give her. What should I buy her, what could make her happy? Of course I couldn't give her the things she always wished for when she was complaining about her life—to go and live somewhere on the coast, to take a trip, go somewhere warm, to Spain or, if she had more money, to Bali; how she wished she could buy the kind of clothes she really liked but this was out of the question because she had to take care of me all by herself; how she wanted to live in a house with a yard because she thought working in a garden would relax her, and so on. In a nearby store I found a turquoise headscarf, the color of the sea, just the kind of sea she wanted to experience, and a box of the chocolates she loved, and some primroses in a flowerpot—they were yellow and orange, the colors of the blazing sun she wanted to bask in. I wrapped everything up in orange tissue paper and added a postcard with a picture of an exotic island; on it I told her how much I loved her. That I wanted her to love me too—I didn't write this, but it's what I was thinking. I drew a big heart and signed it: *From your darling daughter*. I got the gift all ready the evening before her birthday and was intending to give it to her in the morning, before I went to school. I woke up an hour earlier than usual. I slipped into the bathroom, got dressed, and put the water on for her coffee. Half an hour before I had to leave for school, because she still hadn't appeared from her bedroom, I cautiously knocked on the door, and when she didn't answer, I went in. She was still asleep. Cautiously, I moved closer, went right up to her, gently touched her and kissed her on the cheek: "Happy birthday, Mama," I said, but she did not move. I wondered if she was even breathing and was scared she had died. I was so frightened, I shook her—maybe too hard. She turned around in shock. I don't know, but maybe she'd been dreaming about something, about my father maybe; it was her first birthday without him.

"Have you lost your mind?"

I felt my stomach tighten. "I was frightened. I thought something was wrong—"

"Everything is wrong! It's been wrong for over a year!" she shrieked.

"It's your birthday today." I struggled to keep from crying, but when Mama yelled at me to get out of her room, I burst into tears. I don't recall how I got to school that day; I only know that when I was called to the blackboard in math class I couldn't remember anything. The teacher was saying something to me, asking questions, and in the end, she gave me a failing grade and told me that if I wasn't smart enough I should try even harder and at least be conscientious and consistent.

When I got home from school that day, I tidied the kitchen and washed the dishes she had left before she went to work. Then I made her bed and waited on the bench in the kitchen; her present was on the table. Never before, not even at school, had I felt such fear. Just before she came home, I took the pot with the stuffed peppers out of the fridge and put it on the stove. While I was setting the table I heard the jingle of her key in the door. She came in, pale, with no word of greeting.

"Did you burn the food again?" she hissed at me, then hung up her coat and put her purse on the shelf. She went over to the stove, stirred the pot with the cooking spoon and added some cold water. "I tell you over and over: if you're going to cook, you have to concentrate, you have to pay attention, but just like always, you are careless and whatever you cook gets burnt." I felt like she was slicing up my heart into little pieces.

"Happy Birthday," I said in a low voice.

"Thank you," she replied dryly and barely looked at me.

"There's a present for you."

"What present?" she barked. "Where did you get the money? I hope you didn't steal it."

"No . . . my savings," was all I could get out.

"You mean the money you get from your aunt, and now you've gone and wasted it."

I ran out of the kitchen, through the hallway and down to the courtyard, where I collapsed on the concrete pavement behind our building and burst into tears. Back then, I still didn't realize that even with the best intentions, you can't soften the heart of someone who hates you. No matter what you do, the result will always be the same. It would take me a few more years, an entire decade almost, to learn that, and until then I kept endlessly trying and trying, but without success. When I came back to the apartment that evening, she didn't say a word to me. I saw that the pot of primroses was on the kitchen shelf, but what she did with the chocolates and headscarf, I have no idea. She never wore the scarf.

But there were also some nice times. Every once in while, on a Friday afternoon, she'd come home from work with a smile and tell me to get changed because we were going shopping in town. We would stroll past the window displays, try on clothes, and sometimes actually buy something. When she was trying something on, she would look at herself in the mirror and laugh. She liked the way she looked. And it's true; my mother was very beautiful. At least I thought so—tall and slender, with short, dark, almost black hair. But even on those afternoons, when we were walking around town and I tried to hold her hand, she would pull it away each time. And that always hurt, but all the same, I was happy because she was happy. But most of the time, I was sad. Or afraid. Afraid of a lot of things. That all of a sudden she would start yelling at me, hit me, punish me, but I was also scared that something might happen to her. Yes, I was terrified that she would hurt herself or be in an accident. Or just suddenly die.

A few years later, when I was fourteen, a man appeared in our life. Up until then, I don't think she had gone out with anyone, or at least I didn't know about it. My mother was glowing. I had not seen her this happy since my father died, or later either. He was her own age, a little over forty, and for a few weeks he was a frequent visitor to our apartment. In the evenings too. But he never stayed the night. He wore a ring on his right hand, and I had to wonder what my mother really expected from him. The man was nice to me, but I could feel that he did not intend to become my father. Once, and only once, he even took my mother and me on a day trip. We climbed into his car and he put down the roof. Mama wrapped a dove-gray scarf around her head and put on sunglasses. She had a tremendous time as we drove to the seaside and was constantly making jokes. And later, when we were swimming and lying in the sun on a deserted part of the seashore, she was very nice to me and very affectionate with him. It didn't bother me at all when she touched him with her hand; on the contrary, I hoped she would caress me sometimes too—and I was happy because she was happy. On the way back home, however, the trip was ruined. I don't know why, maybe the man wanted to show off in front of Mama, but at some point he started driving faster. Mama tried to get him to slow down, but he just laughed and teased her and pressed harder on the gas. I was in the back seat like I was frozen, but my mother became louder and louder until she was screaming at him. I covered my ears and watched them quarrel. He dropped us off in front of our building and never came to see us again. And there was never anyone else. Her glow disappeared. Forever. And her anger became worse and worse, and our life more difficult.

School, too, was becoming more difficult for me. Subjects I once easily understood, I just couldn't get into my head. I would spend the entire afternoon sitting with a book and the next day at school all I remembered were the pages or shape of the text, but nothing of the content. When I completed middle school, I enrolled in a high school for management and administration. That was her advice, so I could find work as soon as possible, and also because, given my academic success, it was a school I could get into. Because I wasn't exactly bright. But if I applied myself, and worked very hard, I might even be able to graduate. She was nearly wrong about that. I did apply myself, and right after school would go home and study, but when it came to final grades, I was always on the border between passing and failing.

My obesity started with high school. Whenever I was most depressed, I went to the wardrobe in my bedroom, took out a box of chocolate cookies, and stuffed them in my mouth; initially, I felt better, but then I usually started feeling sick and would have to lie down because I was so tired. In high school, she started giving me part of my father's pension, which I spent on school necessities and food. I couldn't wait for the school day to end so I could run off to the store and buy, not just cookies and pastries, but jars of pickles and mushrooms, cold cuts, cheese, and bread, and then when I got home I would eat everything right away, in secret. These orgies lasted only the first ten days of the month and then usually my money ran out; since I didn't have a lot of money to begin with I'd buy the cheapest food in the largest possible quantities. I think she saw what I was doing, but she didn't say anything. Not until one Saturday morning when we got into another fight and she scolded me for being lazy and not looking after myself and said that all I ever did was make my big ass bigger. That I looked awful, and that being as fat as I was, it was a sure bet that nobody—no man—would ever like me. These attacks of hers were happening again and again, and after every such outburst, I'd run to the nearest store, buy things to eat, find a quiet spot, and gulp it all down. At first I wasn't throwing up, but after a few weeks, every big eating binge was followed by vomiting, and then another binge. A few times when she wasn't at home, I emptied the entire fridge, and she yelled at me, saying that she had to work and go to a job just so I could gorge myself and if I intended to go on like this, then I had better move out.

Once when we were watching TV together, she gave me a sharp look and said that, clearly, I had stopped washing too, because I smelled like a cadaver. She was partly right: I was seventeen years old and, at five foot eight inches, was approaching two hundred pounds. My body disgusted me; I didn't want to look at it or even touch it. And so sometimes I would go for days without washing or showering. On that occasion, she sent me into the bathroom and ordered me to take a shower because my stench was making her sick. To me, my body was like some disgusting, derelict apartment in which circumstances forced me to live. It's been years since I really looked at myself in the mirror. I don't know my own body, especially not my private parts, which I never touch except with a sponge.

But my stench, or smell, whatever you want to call it, wasn't the only thing that made her feel like throwing up. In a little drawer in her nightstand, I was finding more and more boxes of tranquilizers and antidepressants. I also noticed that bottles of booze, especially brandy, were starting to collect in her bedroom wardrobe. At first, she never drank in front of me, but later the bottles were arranged on the kitchen counter. And after lunch—she was cooking less often, and when she did, it would be something you could heat up for a few days—she'd sit down in front of the television with a bottle and a glass and watch soap operas. When she got home from work, she didn't go out again; she just stared at the TV without saying a word. I could see she was following the story very closely. I never sat and watched with her; that way, I could have some peace from her, plus I knew she wanted to be alone. She was disappearing deeper and deeper into a world of simplified good and evil and transferring the personalities of the TV characters onto herself, me, and my departed father: she saw herself in the victims, me in the evil bitches, and her husband in the good-hearted men.

After graduation, I got a job working in the office of a small construction firm; it was about a half-hour walk from home. I could have found a room somewhere and moved out, but I never really considered that. More and more, I was afraid that something might happen to her, especially after her retirement. At the age of fifty-six, her malice started losing its vigor, probably due in part to the pills and the alcohol, with longer and more frequent periods of lethargy followed by sudden outbursts of rage. Nobody came to see us anymore: my aunt took ill and died a few years after my father, my mother lost all of her female friends over the years, and I hadn't had any since the end of middle school. No friends, either female or male, and certainly no man. Apart from my dead father and her murdered husband, there were no men in our life anymore. My mother and I were turning into parasites feeding on each other, and it was only a matter of time and strength as to who would devour whom. A few times I thought about ending it all, about going into her bedroom, stuffing myself with pills, falling asleep on her bed, and never waking up. Once I even tried, but I got such violent nausea that I barely made it into the bathroom before vomiting everything up.

After she retired, she would sit in a stupor in front of the TV for whole days, nights too, often falling asleep in her clothes with the television still on, and the next morning when she woke up she just kept on watching. And then, after a few days like this, when she had not said a single word to me, she would suddenly for no real reason fly into a rage and start ranting that I wanted to put her in her grave, that I was spiteful and with my disgusting, fat body I was stupid too. Mother was right; everything she had been constantly telling me since my childhood, since the death of my father, had proved true: I wasn't particularly bright, with my two hundred and thirty-six pounds I was repulsive, and over the past few years I had very probably become spiteful too. Just as she hated me, I had begun to hate her. Well, not entirely. The truth is that, even if I did hate her whenever she insulted me or slapped me, I felt sorry for her. And wished there was some way I could help her. And I knew that despite everything, despite hating her, despite her malice and anger, I still felt so much love for her. And would never abandon her, because I couldn't leave her by herself, because I didn't think she could survive on her own and would certainly die without me. I felt this even if sometimes over the past few years I wanted exactly that—for her to die, to go away and finally leave me alone, to free both herself and me.

That Monday afternoon I was lying in bed eating custard cake and reading the horoscope in a women's magazine. All of a sudden the door swung open full force and Mama came bounding into my room, screaming that I had intentionally washed her white silk blouse with the other whites in the washing machine. That I had ruined it, either on purpose or because I knew nothing about clothes and couldn't even tell silk from cotton. I did not look up. As she yelled at me, with me not reacting, she started to thrash me with the wet shirt. I stood up and went out on the balcony. It was a pleasant June afternoon, about seventy degrees, and the warm afternoon sun was shining.

"Leave me alone," I said calmly, but she kept on yelling and every so often would lash me with the blouse. At two hundred and thirty-plus pounds, I was twice her weight. I had never tried my strength against her before, was never able to hit her back; instead, I would always shield my face and, if necessary, run into the bathroom, lock the door, and stay there until it blew over. This time too, I went into the bathroom, picked up the basket of just-washed laundry, took it out to the balcony, and started hanging the things on the line. She was following me, badgering me, screaming that I had destroyed her blouse, her youth, her life, everything.

"The only thing I regret," she hissed, "because then my life would be entirely different, is that when I was pregnant with you, I didn't have an abortion."

I looked at her. "What did you just say?"

"Being pregnant with you was a total nightmare, and then because of complications with the delivery I couldn't have any more children. And I wanted them! I wanted a son, at least one son, but you spoiled everything! First you destroyed my uterus and reproductive organs, then you killed your father!"

It was first time she had ever said straight out what I always knew she thought. How different it is when somebody finally says what you know she's been thinking! I knew she had never liked me. But even more than her wanting to abort me and regretting that she didn't, the real blow was what she said about my father. It was as though I had been waiting all my life for her to finally say what had made her treat me so horribly. After she said it, she struck me again with the wet, ruined blouse, and it really stung. Not so much the blow itself—she smelled of alcohol and, besides, was getting physically weaker and weaker—what stung more were the words she had said. Something shifted inside me; something that for decades had been asleep rebelled. When she tried to strike me again with the blouse, I grabbed it and pulled it towards me, and Mama with it. She wouldn't let go, she was trying to hit me again, and in that tug-of-war, I calmly pushed her towards the balcony railing. She managed to hold on to the metal bar with both her hands but was in such a stupor she lost her footing. Her body swayed there like a poppy in a windy field. Her body was swaying between life and death. Between her life and my future. I looked into her eyes, which were tired and cloudy. She had never had such a look in her eyes; there was neither rage nor terror there. What was there, was death. My mother was tired. Very tired. I saw in her eyes that she didn't want to live anymore and maybe didn't even know that for a very long time she had not been living. I stood in front of her and instinctively reached out my hand. Mama glanced at my open palm, lifted her eyes, and looked straight into mine. Not shifting her gaze, she opened and slightly raised her right hand. For a moment I thought she was offering it to me, but a second later, the corners of her lips spread into a defiant smile, she lifted her right hand over her head, unclenched her left, and tumbled into emptiness. When the thud came, I caught my breath. I didn't look down. For a few moments, until I heard the screaming, I stood frozen on the balcony; then I left the apartment and went down to the courtyard.

Some of our neighbors had undoubtedly heard us quarreling—again, one more noisy quarrel. At least the woman next door must have heard; the sound of the radio was coming from her apartment. Half an hour later, like almost twenty years before, I was sitting with the police officers and the detective in the kitchen, calmly describing what had happened. How Mama had been drunk and in a stupor, and not just that afternoon but constantly for the past few years. The detective did not entirely believe my story. Nor did the examining magistrate later; he watched me closely, trying to detect in my gestures at least a trace of agitation, a feeling of guilt or confusion.

"Are you sure you didn't push her off the balcony?" the detective had asked me that Monday afternoon in the kitchen; later the autopsy confirmed that there had been large amounts of tranquilizers and alcohol in her blood.

"Yes," I answered. "She was high as a kite and lost her balance. But then she lost her balance ages ago," I added, thinking: even before my father died, maybe even before she met my father. Her life before our family, even before it was just the two of us, was pretty much a mystery to me. I never knew my grandparents, and she had never talked about it—her previous life. As the detective studied me, I noticed her photo on the bureau through the open door of the kitchen. It had been there all these years, but only now did I really look at it. Or maybe I just saw it differently now. It had been taken when Mama was around my age. I had never asked her who took it or where exactly it was taken. In a close-fitting suit with her hair cut short, Mama is standing on the steps of a stone medieval wall; she's not looking at the camera but gazing into the distance. She is smiling, and it seems like she sees something on the horizon that she likes, something she is looking forward to. Maybe by then she already knew my father; maybe she had just fallen in love with him; maybe she was thinking about how they were going to start a new life together; maybe she was pregnant and, when the photo was taken, didn't know it yet. Or maybe she did and that's why she was smiling . . . I felt the detective's hand on my shoulder; he was offering me a tissue.

"I'll ask you one more time. According to the statements by your neighbors, the two of you often quarreled. They heard fights too. So tell me the truth: did you push her over the railing, maybe just by accident?"

I was looking at the photo and started crying even harder. "No, it wasn't me who pushed her to her death. She was my Mama. And I loved her so much."

Pinewood

"WE DON'T HAVE any choice. It's the only way I can be at the hospital in less than an hour if there's an emergency."

Firmly and with no possibility of objection, his wife laid out the facts for him every year—now for the eighth year in a row. She was one of the very few female surgeons at the regional medical center, where men ruled the roost and competition was fierce. It drove him crazy even to think about spending yet another summer at that *pension*—a four-story lakeside villa with a spacious yard and beach surrounded by a wire fence to keep out uninvited guests. And there was something else that really bothered him: not far from the villa, just a fifteen-minute walk from the edge of the tidy, quiet little village, there was an unsupervised beach, a hideout not only for nudists but (as he had heard) also for the sort of men who made his stomach turn. He didn't even know it existed until five years ago, when he was complaining to some friends about the penal colony that again awaited him that summer, in that boring rancid swamp-hole, and one of his friends, with a meaningful grimace, said that he had heard there was a notorious place not far from there where the faggots liked to gather. And not just the faggots you could recognize from a distance by that disgusting way they flapped their arms and wiggled their unfurled butt cheeks, but people said that even respectable men went there, when their wives were snoozing on beach recliners or occupied with the kids.

"I had no idea. Really, I didn't," he said sheepishly. He had been very embarrassed and was furious at his wife, who was dragging him by force to that goddamn Pension Blauer Enzian, which was owned by a heavyset hypochondriac called Frau Brigitte. Apart from burying her husband and inheriting the huge villa by the lake with a view of the Karawanken Mountains, this woman had done nothing in her life except obsess over her illnesses and make bundles of money off tourists. Her health always improved a little in the summer months, especially during the three Valium-paced weeks he spent behind that wire fence, when Frau Brigitte would analyze her diagnoses in endless detail, shower his wife with compliments—along with special complimentary treats ("Oh my dear doctor, it's on the house of course!")—and gossip with her and two other silly cows about incompetent surgeons, slipshod interns, and lazy medical staff. One of the cows, whose husband spent two weeks there every season catatonically imbibing beer, worked in the office of the president, while the other, who was divorced, owned a health food store that sold not only ecologically produced food, but every sort of nonsense a warped mind might crave, from amulets for guarding one's aura, to energy jewelry, to paraphernalia for exorcising demons and neutralizing evil forces. He had never understood his wife. Publicly, she swore allegiance to science and Western medicine, but when her friend, the witch with the pendulums, confirmed her suspicions that one of her work colleagues—her rival to head the gastroenterology clinic—was using black magic to undermine her, the two of them got to work on a voodoo doll (for eleven euros), which they covered in candle wax, dribbled milk and honey on, and then with malicious glee, while directing ruinous thoughts at his wife's rival, set aflame. As for him, who worked in pharmaceuticals, even those lotions made from mare's milk and goat's milk represented total idiocy and commercial quackery, so he had little patience for the deluded voodoo operations his wife employed whenever she was riled by something at the hospital. The quartet of snooty witches was thus complete, and, as a first-rate medical specialist, his wife reigned over the other three. He himself was just an analyst at a pharmaceutical company and of no interest to the women—except when it came to small errands. Every day they sent him from the beach into the village to fetch the tabloids, and then they would spend the next few hours in irrepressible joy gossiping about the people mentioned in them, especially when they knew them, however slightly, or knew somebody who knew them, and so were able to supplement the photo-illustrated article with some yet unpublished juicy morsel.

So it was now the fifth summer that he had felt trapped between the middle-aged women who lay with their thickened soles on the best part of the private beach and, as he had heard, that invisible multitude of men who, though they might look entirely normal, were secretly disappearing into the little pine grove on the lake's western shore, where all sorts of things supposedly went on. A few times over the past few years he had even swum in that direction, so curious was he to see those goddamn faggots who had found a place for themselves amid the lakeside pines. His curiosity was only further piqued by something that had happened three years ago: a drowned naked man had been pulled out of the lake—a young Turk, it turned out, who had been strangled and whose killer had never been found. The women had talked about it the entire second half of their vacation and later on the phone, too. He had gone there merely to observe those men at a distance. From the lake, and to all appearances completely by coincidence, in the guise of an avid long-distance swimmer, he had taken a few quick glances at the shore, where men of various ages were sunbathing, some younger guys too. Yes, much younger guys— he realized for the first time that summer—boys the same age as his son, who had recently turned sixteen. Just a few months ago he had begun to notice that, apart from a classmate—a skinny, nerdy girl in glasses—no females ever called his son at home, nor had he ever mentioned anyone, let alone brought someone by for him to meet. It's not that he was criticizing the boy or any- thing, but it seemed quite natural that, by the end of his sopho- more year, his son would have a girlfriend, just as he had had at the polytechnic: a normal, teenage love with occasional clumsy sex, based mainly on walking around town together, going to the movies, biking and skiing, which after a year or so, with no particular melodrama, had ended. But his son? Nothing. Just

school, sports, computers, and music—always with other boys
from his class and his buddies. But no girls.

This summer, as he lay on the beach by the lake, he started
observing his son more closely. It didn't surprise him that the boy
was hanging out with the son of the health-food witch, and not
with her pudgy daughter, who when she was on the beach would
bashfully wrap herself in robes, towels, and long-sleeve T-shirts.
Nor, on closer inspection, did the two boys' relationship seem
suspicious. But the way his son walked, suspiciously weaving
his legs, did not seem at all natural or normal. The boy rotated
his pelvis much too dynamically, and he could at least chop off
that little raven-black ponytail. His misgivings were only further
confirmed by the arrival of some new guests.

In advance of their arrival, Frau Brigitte had rigorously prepared her little club, acquainting them with what, in her firm
opinion, were all the essentials regarding the famous moderator
of family-themed TV discussion programs and her husband, a
surgeon at the neurology clinic in Vienna. His wife didn't find
the neurosurgeon especially interesting, probably because she
didn't want anybody competing with her in the medical field,
but also because she knew that any information she needed about
Viennese neurology could be extracted inexhaustibly from the
TV moderator's lips. The women added another beach recliner
to the four beneath their umbrellas, and for several hours after
the couple's arrival they inducted the moderator into the club;
he noticed that a few times she even overshadowed his wife. At
foreseeable intervals, the neurosurgeon would bring them cold
drinks, comment on a news item or two, and generally behave
like a well-polished gentleman. But more and more, the man
was glancing over at the recliners next to him where his son
was playing cards with the witch's kid and another boy. Doctor
Heino was a tall, gray-haired man in his fifties, who came to
breakfast wearing long white pants, a cream-colored shirt, and
ocher moccasins. The ocher moccasins (and that was their precise color) and the gold-set ruby on his right hand were the
first alarming signs that Doctor Heino was one of those men
who would disappear in the afternoon from the fenced-in lots,

allegedly to have a little stroll or get a newspaper, but in reality to gallop off to Pinewood, as that disreputable place was called. The surgeon was very polite to him; every morning at breakfast he would greet him amiably, and during the day, too, they would exchange a few well-chosen phrases on the beach. But every night before falling asleep, he would reflect on the fact that the moderator did not have the faintest idea that her husband, who was just then climbing into bed with her, all nice and showered in his striped silk pajamas, had during the day been sticking his dick up men's butts just a few hundred yards from Pension Blauer Enzian. He was revolted by the very thought of the sex act between men, and more and more he had the firm conviction that Doctor Heino was suggestively glancing over to where he was reading newspapers and his son was playing cards and listening to music with his friends.

That Friday at breakfast, as he poured himself a cup of coffee at the buffet table, he saw Heino go over to his family's table and make some seemingly casual remark to his son, who gave him a big smile and laughed and then said something in reply. He couldn't hear what they were talking about. It irked him that he wasn't there, but the degenerate bastard had probably seized his chance at his brief absence and, with the help of some carnal gesturing, let loose an arsenal of jokes especially designed for innocent minors. He didn't let the man out of his sight all day. He watched his every movement—his sycophantic servility around the women's club and the two times he poured drinks for the boys, and a drink for him too. He naturally declined the beverage, offered with Heino's piercing gaze, and then dashed into the villa and ordered himself two spritzers. Completely out of breath, he drank the first in a single gulp and raced back to the beach with the second—lest that pedophile queer try something. Doctor Heino, sunk in his recliner, was blithely turning the pages of some novel and, when he saw him come back, gave him a baffled look. After that, everything started unfolding with unstoppable speed. The boys put down their portable CD players, the witch's son picked up the windsurfer and ran into the lake, and his son and the third boy went off in the direction of

the woods. Less than half a minute later, Doctor Heino set off
in the same direction. He quickly downed the second spritzer,
shouted to his wife that he needed to stretch his legs, and went
after them. You fucking faggot bastard, I'm going to catch you
in the act, he kept repeating to himself as he approached the
little pine grove, now on foot for the first time. After about ten
minutes he saw the first couple a little ways off the path—a man
and a woman sunbathing naked on the grass—and then a few
more naked people of both sexes. But the further he went, with
every few yards, there were fewer and fewer women. When he
realized he had lost all trace of his son, his son's friend, and the
neurosurgeon, he heard a sound coming from the direction he
had just come—the unmistakable sound of heavy breathing.
He doubled his pace and, since he could not turn back, went
forward, reckless with fear, straight into the heart of Sodom on
the Austrian Riviera, until finally, in the undergrowth—by now
he had gone off the path—he nearly tripped over a pair of warm
male bodies. He leaned against a pine tree and saw a sight that
made him go completely numb. For the first time in his life he
saw, in the flesh, two male bodies writhing and winding themselves around each other like furious vipers in a tense, hissing
rhythm. He couldn't think; he could only watch, as his throat
tightened and burned and a cold sweat beaded his forehead. He
gripped the trunk of the tree with both hands and wished that
he had never plunged into the dark branches of Pinewood—and
that what he was seeing in front of him would go on forever. He
felt a warmth spreading from his abdominal cavity; his palms,
touching the bark, began to sweat, and his body became rigid.
From somewhere behind his back he heard twigs breaking. He
did not turn around. In a gesture of surrender, he laid his face
against the tree trunk, and when from behind a strong hand
caressed his neck and then slid down his bare chest and he saw,
in the late afternoon sun, the red gleam of a ruby on the ring
finger, for a moment he shut his eyes.

"I thought you would be the one to take the initiative," came
the soft tones of a man's voice, "from the way you kept looking
at me—at breakfast, on the beach—but then when I offered you

a drink . . ." He was caressing him with his voice, caressing his chest, and pressing his pelvis against his buttocks. A violent heat flooded his body. He wanted to grab that hand, wriggle free of its grip and flee, but he couldn't move a muscle.

"Where is my son?" was all he managed to say as he stood there wedged between the pine tree and the taut male body.

"Having fun somewhere I'm sure."

"But I thought you had your eye on—"

"On your son?" the man chuckled, stroked his butt, and turned him around so they were facing each other. "For heaven sakes, he's still half a kid, and besides, I don't think he's one of us," he whispered, and then ran his tongue up his neck, kissed him passionately, and dived into his body.

My Dearest

THE MOMENT HE walked into the auto showroom Monday morning at five past eight, the salesman he had signed the deal with three days earlier waved at him amiably from behind the counter and hurried over.

"Come with me," the man said, pressing the fob with the blue and white logo into his hands. From it hung the key he had dreamed about for twenty years. In the canopied parking area, shining in the early morning sun, stood a brand new, never-driven BMW 5 Series sedan. They went over to the car and the buyer stroked it gently, running his hand over its body, and it was only at the salesman's encouraging gestures, as if to say, Go ahead, unlock it, it's yours! that he inserted the key in the lock, unlocked it, moved a step away, relocked it automatically, and then some six feet away, again unlocked the car. The gleaming interior smelled of fresh leather. He got in, started it up, and blood raced through his body and he began to sweat.

"Splendid, isn't it?" said the blond salesman, as he strolled around the car.

"It's the best!" he replied, with a smile stretching from ear to ear.

The low hum, which he modulated by pressing on the gas pedal, only enhanced the feeling. As they examined the dashboard, with the salesman's manicured hands skating back and forth across it as he demonstrated the lights, he distractedly asked a few questions—as if he hadn't scrutinized every detail three days ago and then over the weekend studied all the finer points

on the BMW website. The salesman had plenty of experience
with inaugurations on the purchase of mid-size luxury vehicles,
especially such a rare gem as this. So he adroitly conducted the
inevitable protocol in such circumstances, and not just because
the automobile's electronics had to be explained—the right customers would already have thoroughly researched everything,
down to the smallest detail—but also because of the stress triggered by the ineffable happiness associated with purchasing a car.

"You've made a superb choice, sir. A silver arrow, I tell you!"—
words that so caressed the buyer's soul that for a second he was
in love with the salesman.

He drove out of the dealership's enclosed parking lot and at
once felt that from this moment on he would be gazing down
at the world from on high. The look in his eyes as he now sur-
veyed all that lay beneath him was exactly the same look that
years ago, when he was still getting around in humble, nondescript tin cans, he had imagined was in the eyes of the people
who drove BMWs. As a student, the car had been a beat-up
jalopy more than fifteen years old, the make of which he could
barely remember today. Then at twenty-five, when he got his first
full-time job, he was driving a Citroën DS that was seven years
younger than he was. But six months after his son was born, he
took a loan out to buy a Renault 5 subcompact—a brand new,
light blue R5. As he drove it around, he would repeat to himself
the R5 advertising slogan and was extremely happy—this was
his first truly new car—but at intersections he was still glancing over at the cars next to him and checking out the ones in
his rearview mirror. Most of them were large, noble beasts, the
finest of their kind, while he was scuttling down the road like
an insect. Yes, "less is more and smaller is better," he said over
and over to himself, his wife, his friends and acquaintances, but
he knew it was a lie. No, for real drivers, who link functionality
and safety to aesthetic design, when it comes to automobiles, less
is not more but always and absolutely not enough. Slogans like
that, in ads for tiny cars, are merely mantras for soothing the
frustration of penniless buyers at the sight of bigger and more
powerful models.

FRAGMA 107

He felt no different about the cars he bought later. Some of them were not even new, but two or as much as four years old; back then, sadly, there had been no other choice. The image would constantly appear before his eyes of young fools, men just under thirty, who packed themselves and their young families into an R5, and as they drove along, everyone would be merrily singing, the kids waving their arms, but for the driver himself, even passing a truck was a remarkable achievement. First he would check the rearview to see if behind him there was anyone more powerful (which in those miserable R5 days meant almost everyone) who similarly intended to pass. Then he would hold down the pedal as the needle on the speedometer climbed slowly to eighty, shift into the left lane, and with all his strength press down on the gas as he passed, while firmly gripping the steering wheel so the car wouldn't be pulled into the truck by vacuum forces, all the while praying that some goliath wouldn't suddenly come up menacingly on his tail. Meanwhile, the kids would still be singing and sticking their arms out the windows. It was terrifying and humiliating, he thought each time it happened, and he knew there was only one way out of the situation: career advancement. So two years ago, with a twelve-thousand-euro loan, he went for his MBA and, after completing the degree, was promoted to purchasing manager at a large retail outlet. It was an excellent job with better pay. But still he could see no path that led to ownership of the car he had desired with his whole being ever since second grade, when he and the other boys would collect the automobile trading cards hidden beneath chocolate wrappers. The best he could do with his MBA was a new Renault Mégane. But there was one more trump up the narrow sleeve of his fate. He just had to wait a bit. This involved the now-capitalist country's denationalization of property as it related to his paternal grandmother, a penny-pincher who fifteen years before her death was buying noodles and canned goods that many a dog would turn up his nose at and who spent her days calculating the costs of the basic necessities. The news of her death, and even more the invitation to appear in probate court, delighted all her grandchildren, grandnephews and grandnieces (she was

the last in a family of four siblings), who viewed the court proceedings as a way to finally right old wrongs. His grandmother,
it turned out, had been sitting on real estate—residential buildings and land—confiscated after World War II by the voracious
communist government. Invitations to the hearings went out
to all corners of the country, and even abroad, and the large
number, and large appetites, of the potential heirs meant that
the process dragged on three whole years at great expense. For
him, the outcome was favorable. Very favorable. He was entirely
satisfied with what he received: a parcel of land in a well-known,
first-class tourist area, where a throng of potential buyers were
prepared to pay sixteen euros twenty a square foot. And there
were lots of square feet—nearly ten thousand of them. At the
end of the arduous and lengthy probate process, which left the
cousins quarreling for the rest of their lives, as soon as he left
the courtroom he was converting the square feet to euros in his
head. He had truly had one of the very best lawyers, who had
done a superb job, even bringing up his client's care for the
deceased in the last years of her life, an argument that won the
day only because the lawyer had somehow managed to hypnotize
the female judge. The truth was that his grandmother, afraid that
one of her relations might do away with her before her time, had
never let any of them near her. When her health started visibly
deteriorating and her malignant phantoms and delusions led to
a diagnosis of paranoid psychosis and hospitalization over the
five years before her death, he too started seeing visions, on the
movie screen of his consciousness, in the rounded amount of
one hundred and sixty thousand euros.

"Fantastic! We did it!" His wife greeted him at home that late
afternoon when the court process was over. She was all smiles
and expectations, with a thoroughly worked-out plan for spending and investing the money.

"We'll divide the parcel into two parts, sell one part and
build a vacation home on the other. And we'll invest some of
the money for the children's education."

"We're not doing any of that," he snapped back. "We're going to sell the entire parcel, put one part of the money into mutual funds and use the dividends to pay off our loans, but we're going to use most of it to buy a car. A brand new car!"

"Not in your dreams!" his wife objected. "We bought our new Renault less than two years ago."

"In my dreams? No, thank god, not anymore! Because I'm going to buy the car I've dreamed about my entire life—a BMW 5!"

"You're crazy! You're just as crazy as that grandmother of yours!" his wife retorted, watching him closely and checking his eyes to see if maybe he had not gone out to celebrate the successful settlement, which had ended in the morning, with his lawyer, who was not just an infamously successful wheeler-dealer but also a notorious alcoholic. No, her husband was completely sober. She swallowed her anger and ran up the stairs in their small, one-family, duplex. But, from the top of the stairs, she yelled back that he was nothing but a big macho jerk and slammed the bedroom door.

She'll survive, and it won't take her long to get used to the comfort, he thought, browsing through the BMW website for his chosen model. Even before the end of the court proceedings, when things began looking very positive for him, he had thought it all through. At first he had considered buying the sporty BMW M3 coupe, but he soon changed his mind: it would be hard to squeeze a family of four into that car, let alone luggage. But after some exhaustive research, he decided to go with a tried-and-true family car: the BMW 530i. Spacious enough for comfortable traveling, it was still a nimble steed, equally capable on both highways and country roads, as well as in the variable traffic of city streets.

The silver four-door sedan BMW 530i with 230 horsepower at 5900 revolutions per minute could do up to 160 miles per hour. For the first time in his life, he did not worry about fuel consumption when he was planning to buy a car. His German love, indeed, was a real gas-guzzler that got no more than seventeen miles a gallon. But in the midst of such happiness and triumph, who thinks about gallons when there are hundreds of miles of anxiously awaited pleasure to be had?

The next day his wife still wasn't talking to him.

"Why would you want such real estate anyway?" he told her that afternoon. "It's like a spoiled baby: it gives you a few hours of happiness on those rare weekends you can get away or when you're on vacation, but every other day of the year it's an unending headache, and besides, the property taxes ruin whatever pleasure you get out of it."

"But what about the kids, you selfish jerk?"

"I thought about the kids. Right now, let them grow and mature, and when they're teenagers, we'll use the dividends from the mutual funds to send them to language classes, and then later, if they study hard and get good grades, maybe we'll send them abroad to university."

"Asshole!" she barked at him, on the verge of tears.

"Don't forget, it was me who inherited the money. I can do what I want with it. But don't worry, honey, there'll be something left over for you, too. What were you telling me about, some operation for your eyelids? Or was it liposuction for your hips? Listen, I'll pay for it. Just tell me what you want."

"Even so, the kids and I would rather have a cottage. You know, where they can enjoy the seaside. Especially the little one—it would help his sinuses and allergies. And besides, being outdoors is good for my nerves. And like I've been telling you for five years now, if I had a vegetable garden, it would be a well-deserved rest from my stressful work week, relaxing among eggplants, tomatoes, and lettuce."

"Come on now, I'd hardly say your job is all that stressful. Look at all of my responsibilities, especially on peak business days when I have to work late in the evening. Compared to that, your work at the Chamber of Commerce is a walk in the park. Anyway, there's no point growing vegetables—the produce we offer in our supermarket is the cheapest in the entire city."

"Sure it is—frozen, half thawed, flavorless, probably even genetically modified—"

"My dear, as a business rep, you can surely see from a simple calculation that with the amount of hours it involves, having a garden just doesn't pay. Plus, there'd be enormous work with the cottage, and besides, we'd have to spend our vacation in the same place every year. How boring is that? But with the new car we can go wherever you want, somewhere different every time. And it'll be so much safer and faster than the Renault Mégane— which I'll give to you; you'll have it for doing errands around town. And tomorrow we'll get rid of your Punto, so it doesn't eat up the space in the garage. Because that's where I'm parking the BMW, and you can keep your Renault in the carport from now on."

"Idiot!" she hissed, then quickly changed her clothes and left the house. To her mother's, probably, or one of her girlfriends', to pour her heart out and complain about him, but that didn't bother him in the least, and it certainly didn't throw him off track. His time had finally come. After so many years he would again be getting something he really wanted, with no worrying about having to be good or how much it cost or anything like that. The last time it had happened he was nine, when St. Nicholas brought him an electric train. The same one he had seen in a catalog and for which he had been pestering his father for two whole months before December came. After that, getting what he wished for always meant compromise, whether financial or behavioral, which, when he was a child, was called "being a good boy." But now there were no such stipulations. And he knew what a snob his wife was, and that when she saw the car parked in front of their house and later, in the days that followed, saw the admiring and envious looks of her relatives, friends, acquaintances, work colleagues, and neighbors, she would be more than satisfied with his purchase.

The land sale went off without a hitch, and the very same day that he signed the purchase contract, on a Friday afternoon, he drove to the BMW dealership. The salesmen, bigoted pigs that they were, must have seen him climbing out of the Renault because he was forced to wait while one of them first handled a customer who had arrived a minute after him in a BMW M3 convertible. Only later did a salesman waltz over and ask if he needed any help or advice.

"Nope," he said decisively. "Everything's clear: I want the BMW 530i, metallic silver."

"Ohhh," the blond salesman fawned. "A customer who knows his mind—that's the kind we like best. An excellent choice for a family man on the threshold of his mature years. With that automobile you'll have everything: a sports car's thrust, power and elegance, and total safety for your family. But"—he looked at him from head to toe—"are you sure it's the 530i you want, and not perhaps the much more economic 530d?"

"What! A diesel? A real BMW runs on gas!"

"Right answer! I can tell you're a true connoisseur, a real expert. Many people believe it takes money to buy a car. Not so. A car must be bought with feeling, and you only know it's right when your whole body starts to vibrate when you choose it and you can feel how your own energy is in perfect tune with your chosen, new, never-before-driven car, and you are vibrating together in harmony." Gesticulating expressively to illustrate what he was saying, the man slithered across the showroom and invited him to follow.

"Kindly come this way. Although I can see that you are thoroughly familiar with the car," he said between deep inhalations and exhalations, "nevertheless allow me to show it to you." He slithered his way past the vehicles on display until he reached a 530i model.

"This way, please," the man in the Hugo Boss suit was hissing like an excited viper as he pulled him to the car. "Have you ever . . . actually . . . sat in one?" The blond man held his breath.

"Never. Not once." The customer bent over and was already opening the door, about to climb in.

"Careful. The filigree gray leather seats are delicate and extremely sensitive. Any unclean fingerprint will leave its mark. Just feel this leather, dear sir," the man salivated as he opened the sedan door. "Just touch it." He tenderly stroked the leather seat. "Like the skin of a sixteen-year-old girl." The words almost dripped from his molars. "Come on, then. Put your hand on that gearshift. Just feel it. Feel how perfectly it fits the masculine hand. All right, here you are." He handed him the key. "Now stick it in and just listen to that sound, like a herd of wild Mongolian horses. And look at these silent controls," he hissed on, as he started deejaying the dashboard. "Of course, I don't expect you'll be declining the extras?"

"I'll take everything that comes with it."

"Everything?" He looked at him in amazement and determined that he was dealing with a special caliber of customer. "That's very wise of you. With six airbags you'll be as safe as in an armored tank, and in the hot summer when you open the retractable electric roof, no matter where you are, you'll feel like you're gracefully taking the curves on the French Riviera as if they were nothing. Automatic transmission, too?"

"Sure, but I want to keep the gearshift."

"Quite right. That's the bridle—but also the spurs—on this bold, irrepressible stallion." The salesman drew a breath. "But you are the one who sets the rhythm, you are the one who rides him . . . with cruise control, I assume?"

"Naturally. Cruise control and the alarm system too. I hope I can rely on it."

"Fifteen thousand percent. Be assured: the satisfaction you will get from this vehicle is like few things you have ever known."

"I don't doubt it."

"Glad to hear that. You really do understand everything perfectly," he continued to fawn. "So how should we arrange the payment? The price is, after all . . ." and again, a little uncertainly, the salesman gave him the once-over.

"I know the price. Sixty-six thousand euros. You can put my company's name on the invoice. I'll be here tomorrow to pick it up."

A few years before, he and three colleagues had set up a shoe store for just such potential transactions—buying a car with the costs covered by the company or concealing certain revenue on their tax forms. And besides, the cheap, half-plastic shoes they bought at discount stores in Italy did surprisingly well, as did the clothes, the wine stoppers, and the plastic bags, all of which his colleagues sold at a substantial markup in the retail outlet where he worked as the purchasing manager.

"I'm sorry to tell you, sir, but this particular beauty has already been sold. You'll have to wait for another one to arrive."

"What's the fastest I can get it?"

For the wily salesman, this deal, which to all appearances was nearly done, was nothing but a test run, merely foreplay. It was a rare opportunity, he knew, to do business with customers of this man's ilk. Whether it was a matter of lottery winnings, or underworld dealings, or an inheritance, that was of no interest to him.

"Three or, I'd rather say, five months," he replied, deliberately stretching out the delivery time.

"That long? I'm supposed to wait half a year for it? That is not an option!"

"Just hold on, now!" The viper coiled around the customer's arm and began pulling him, as if in confidence, to another part of the showroom. "Come with me. There's something I want to show you," he said, tugging at his sleeve, "something I'm sure you haven't seen yet." He stopped in front of a vehicle that was, at least to look at, not unlike the first.

"Now this is our newborn baby: the BMW 545i. He's still warm—got here only yesterday, direct from Munich." He opened the door automatically. "A real purebred. Just look at those colors: Titan Silver Metallic on the outside and, inside, the leather is Dakota Granite. The beast you see before you comes fresh from the stable with the power of three hundred and thirty-three racehorses, with an electronically limited top speed of a hundred and fifty-five miles per hour. But you know,"—he took a quick glance around the room, as though he was selling him some exclusive illegal goods under the counter—"I know a guy who can train these horses for you so they do as much as a hundred and seventy-five."

While the viper hissed on, the customer stood in front of the new BMW model with a wide and fully compliant smile on his face, like a child in front of a Christmas tree, and the viper, knowing he had struck the right spot, went on discharging his venom into the customer's sensitive consciousness.

"With this vehicle, dear sir, you will avoid all compromise and get not only a beast with the strength of a bear but also an Aryan tank that offers a man luxurious comfort even as it keeps him safe as a baby in his mother's womb. Of course, this very special BMW does cost a few grand more," the salesman hurried on, "but instead of six airbags, it comes with eight, and the options also include a television and DVD system, so on long drives you can distract the kids and forget completely about your family."

The skillful salesman had obviously read his mind. With such a machine, it was like getting the sporty M3 and the safe, family-friendly 530i in a single package.

"If I were you, I wouldn't refuse the automatic transmission, although, of course, the gearshift should stay. That way, as you're driving along, you can safely devote yourself to entirely different things, while your new and most valued friend takes over and does all the work for you."

"How much do you want for it?" He gazed at the miracle of the BMW company like a saint waiting for beatification.

"Seventy-nine thousand," hissed the viper, who clenched his teeth and, with his eyes shut, hoped that the venom was oozing into every part of the customer's body and, most of all, into his brain.

"I'll take it!" At these three decisive words, the funds for the children's education at prestigious foreign universities vanished instantly and irrevocably before his eyes. Let them make their own way, he thought, just as he had had to do, just as everyone has to do in life.

"Done!" the black viper hissed. "The key will be yours on Monday!" And knowing that this deal would reward him with a large commission, he was already imagining himself on the prowl, fangs full of venom, slinking around the bushes of Ibiza.

He gave him his business card.

"Here you go. I'll draw up the invoice for you, and if you have any questions at all about the car, feel free to call me over the weekend. Regardless of the time. Day or night," he said with a slight smile, and walked him to the door with quick, short steps.

When he turned into the driveway late Monday afternoon, the two children darted across the yard, ran up to him with squeals of delight and were already trying to squeeze into the car.

"Stop right there, dirtbags!" he yelled. "First, take off your shoes, change your clothes, and wash your hands. Then we'll go for a little spin." Saying this, he glanced at the kitchen window, where the curtain moved, and soon his wife came strolling out of the house.

"Well . . ." she began a bit tentatively. "It looks all right, I suppose. I just hope it's a good car, given the astronomical price you paid for it."

"It's excellent, honey," he whispered. "Go upstairs, put on something nice, and get the kids dressed too, and we'll go for an afternoon drive somewhere."

She cocked her head seductively, looked at the car, then at him, and went into the house. While he was waiting for his family to put on clothes appropriate to his new acquisition, he saw his next-door neighbor, with a knife and bowl in her hands, looking at the car from her vegetable garden, and soon her husband appeared behind her holding the water hose.

"Oh, wow! What's this I see?" The man couldn't conceal his amazement. "I don't suppose that's yours?"

"All mine!"

"So you're the lucky fellow who won the Sunday lottery?"

"Nope. I worked hard with my own hands to get this."

"Who could believe it?" The neighbor had put down the hose and was already sidling around the car and, like an expert, examining it from every angle. "This couldn't have been cheap . . . Such a beauty, brand new . . . Don't tell me you just drove it here from the showroom floor!"

"Sure did!"

"You're one lucky guy." He looked at him suspiciously. "It's a fine machine." He kicked a tire twice, but the new owner stopped him at once.

"It's brand new, with only seven miles on the odometer."

The neighbor, whose Passat station wagon was parked in his driveway, looked at him beseechingly. "You don't mind if I join you, do you?" And he ran into his house, changed quickly from the track suit he was wearing into shorts and a polo shirt, and a few minutes later was shoving himself into the front seat next to the driver. But when the owner's wife appeared and looked daggers at him—and at her husband, too, for welcoming this intruder—he squeezed into the back with the kids.

As his neighbor commented enthusiastically from the back seat on the car's abilities and breathlessly shared his expert advice, the man who was driving felt like he had moved to some new, unknown city. It was a fantastic feeling. Never in his life had he been so much the center of attention, and never had he so directly controlled, with his own hands, something so powerful, so beautiful, and so valuable. At the end of the demo ride, he drove into the city and parked in front of a café. They sat on the patio so they could look at the car. Nothing could distract him or make him redirect his gaze, which pored over the new BMW 545i—neither the analytical technical comments of his neighbor, who was already pawing his third beer, nor his wife's attempts to restrain the children, who, possibly from a lack of attention, had started smearing ice cream on their faces. Like a Carthusian monk, he sat motionless in his chair, absorbed in the car's silver body, which in the summer light, he noticed, dazzled even the eyes of random passers-by.

Lying in bed that night, he felt a strange excitement, such as he had not felt in a long time. He grabbed his wife and, for the first time in months, so thoroughly performed his husbandly duty that his wife, perhaps more from surprise than anything else, fell asleep right away. But for him sleep would not come. Whether his eyes were shut or open, he saw nothing but soft leather in a shade of light granite gray and the illuminated dashboard. He got out of bed and, still in his pajamas, went to the

garage. The moment he saw it, his body was flooded by a tsu-
nami of warmth. Gently, he opened the door and carefully sat
down. He stroked the gearshift with his right hand, then he took
firm hold of the steering wheel and inserted a Modern Talking
CD into the stereo. He closed his eyes and, caressing the steering
wheel with his left hand and stroking the leather on the passenger's seat with his right, began to sing along:

You're my heart, you're my soul,
I keep it shining everywhere I go,
You're my heart, you're my soul,
I'll be holding you forever, stay with you together . . .

It was as if he had woken from a coma of many years. And it
was just what he expected. The world had become courteous and
respectful towards him. No longer did Fiats and those conceited
Opels brazenly butt in front of him on the road, the way they
had with the Renault Mégane; now they very nicely and deferentially let him go ahead. On the highway, when he shot into the
passing lane at an acceleration of 0 to 60 mph in 5.6 seconds,
the others smoothly retreated before his presence and arranged
themselves neatly in the driving lane. Every single one of them,
or nearly so, except for the occasional fancy sports car trying to
strut its stuff like a young bucking bull, but every time, to teach
them a lesson, he pressed down on the gas and nearly struck them
in the rear, and instantly they repented and got out of his way.
And of course there were his more powerful kinsmen (if only
a few), whose superior strength he was obliged to acknowledge
and to whom he always politely yielded. In fact, there was only
one serious and troublesome clan of rivals: Mercedes. When his
purchase was still very much up in the air, he had wavered a
few times between Mercedes and BMW, balancing horsepower,
price, and the capabilities of the individual models, but in the
end he had made his decision with no reservation. After all, as
everybody knows, Mercedes are for granddads. Yes, they say, we're
done with all that adolescent drag racing; that's why we sold our

BMWs and in our mature years now lead settled lives with our safe and reliable Mercedes. Fuck you, you impotent old fart! he would shout every time a Mercedes passed him, and then, accelerating, shift into the passing lane, cruise for a while next to his opponent, and when he saw the old fart trying to pull ahead, floor it with all his might, drive for a bit in front of the guy's nose, just to show him who's boss, and then disappear into the distance. The Mercedes ideology was for him nothing but the usual sanctimonious catechism. Of course, they had settled down—their reflexes had become so slow they spent half an hour just looking for the gearshift and finding the right gear, which is why so many of them had to drive automatics. While they were still trying to coordinate the operations of checking the rearview and side mirrors, there was very often such a time lapse that, if their Mercedes hadn't had that powerful motor, any simple Ford Fiesta with a 1.1-liter engine could easily have overtaken them. He knew damn well why they had exchanged their BMWs for Mercedes. When these granddads noticed (along with their disappointed wives and mistresses) that their dicks were losing the battle with gravity, when they realized they were coming in late to work because they had spent half an hour poking around the house trying to remember where they'd put their car keys and eyeglasses the night before, then, if they wished to honorably maintain the image of a respectable gentleman who cherishes his personal safety, they had no other choice but to sell their BMW and get a Mercedes. For him, however, those years were still far, far away. At the age of thirty-seven, he looked good and felt great. Better than he ever had.

Other cars presented no serious threat. The men who drove Audis, of course, were all frustrated admirers of BMWs and Mercedes, neither of which they had the balls for, so they turned instead to the safe-but-boring four-wheel drive. English Jags were driven by old Oxford fags—and anyway, he would never consider buying a British car if only because the steering wheel was on the wrong side and you can't shift with your left! The people who preferred Renaults (he had driven one only by force of circumstance) were guys with little dicks who wanted big ones, which is why they found comfort in the slogan "Size doesn't matter"; the crappy cars Fiat put out he had always viewed with contempt; the Japanese built genetic mutants and had recently even transplanted Renault engines, while the Koreans only made cheap knockoffs of Japan's transgenic monsters; up north, in the frozen climes of Europe, you had your Saabs and Volvos, which might be perfectly good if you needed your car to start at sixty-below temperatures but otherwise they were as ugly as Scandinavian moose. As for those American oil tankers, they were, for one reason or another, beyond any sober consideration, just as America itself was completely incompatible with the rest of the world.

It was just such thoughts that now ran through his mind when he was driving, unlike the past, when, in the Mégane, he was always worrying about a strategy for paying his monthly bills; the teacher's notes about his son's fighting; his daughter screaming that they had to buy her a piano because she couldn't, and wouldn't, and absolutely refused to practice on the piano at the music school; his wife whining that no matter what diet she went on she just couldn't lose that pound of cellulite on her thighs; his mother pushing him to talk to the stonemason about a decent gravestone for his father, especially now that his grandmother was buried there too, which according to the estimate cost over four thousand euros; as well as pressures from his job, pressures from all around. But everything works out eventually. Take him, for example: in a single day, everything worked out just as he had desired all his life. Yes, you simply had to desire something—that's what he had been reading over the past fifteen years on his vacations, in those inspirational newspaper supplements. You just have to firmly focus your desire on a goal, and sooner or later it was sure to come true. Nothing simpler. Easy as pie.

But it wasn't all so very easy. Things soon started getting complicated. After the initial excitement, when his body was exploding with libido like never before, his desire for his wife—which he hadn't even known was still there somewhere, languishing in the protected reserve of his body, on the edge of extinction—that desire slowly began to fade. It just wasn't happening. At first, he didn't know why since there had been times in his life when he had desired her with true manly passion, and had done a good job of it too. When he was performing his marital duties, he would try to help himself by imagining the different places he and his wife had done it before their marriage, like their very first time, in the busted seat of that old jalopy, which was particularly unforgettable because for the whole next week he couldn't tie his shoes like a normal person. But for some reason that trick wasn't working. Some nights the picture that appeared on the screen of his thoughts was his wife in a tight red dress with black lace underwear protruding from beneath it, along with a bit of extra body mass, lying in the front seat of his BMW. Mysteriously, the miracle formula worked. Whenever his wife gave him the sign that she wanted him—which often enough involved a certain amount of bargaining, including demands like driving the kids to their afterschool activities the next day, paying the bills at the bank or, even worse, Sunday dinner with his in-laws—he shut his eyes and, like the director of a television commercial, began composing a script and filming a scenario that guaranteed a pleasurable and satisfying outcome. And without fail, the story was set in his BMW 545i.

One day, after they had agreed the night before that she would pay the bills, go to the store, take their daughter to music, and come home and cook, after which he would drive her to the post office and, with her waiting in the car, since it was always hard to find a parking space in front of the post office, run inside with the delivery slip to pick up the book of sheet music they had ordered—his well-tested scenario became fatally complicated. He had noticed over the past few weeks that, during their relations, his wife was inching more and more towards the car door. She had somehow started getting twisted up and no matter how hard he tried to correct her position in his mind and place her directly in the middle of the passenger's seat, she was pressed more and more up against the door, until one night it had finally opened and her head fell off the seat and out of the car.

That Wednesday, the post office was incredibly crowded.

Obviously, the last and poorest income bracket of the population had received their tax notices. Milling in line in front of him were a bunch of scruffy guys and the kind of women he would never want to touch, not even if he was a castaway on a desert island. To relieve his eyes from the sight of this rabble, he turned his head towards the large window in the post office and admired the tree leaves, which were slowly turning yellow and dropping from the branches. But his gaze soon spontaneously shifted from the processes of nature to his silver German. And he froze. Sitting in the passenger's seat of his BMW 545i was a woman of early middle age with dyed streaks of red in her brown hair. Her pointy nose was poking towards the windshield, while her other features, as much as were visible, displayed a disappointing, tedious air of something that had always bothered him, which he had tried at all costs to avoid: mediocrity. Never before had he seen her the way he did now, as she sat alone in the BMW. At once he concluded: no sir, that woman does not belong in a BMW Series 5. This was something he had clearly been sensing for a long time, if not actually seeing it.

With the book of sheet music in his hand, he returned to the car, sat down without a word, and turned the key.

"Is something wrong?" she asked.

"Oh, there were just so many people in there, it almost frazzled my nerves," he answered blithely, conscious of the full weight of his decision. But he had not bought the car just so he could polish it in the garage with a deerskin cloth, drive back and forth to work, go on family visits and trips, pick up the kids from music and sports, oh yes, and drive to his badminton game twice a week. And that was all. Just boring, dependable stuff. But that was not who he was—he adored challenges and never stopped at anything.

The following Thursday, after the badminton tournament, he asked his buddies if they wanted to go somewhere for a drink. Sorry, don't have the time, just can't, family, the wife, half of them said, but two of the fellows were fully in support of the idea. The bar, which had been open for less than a year, he had read about in some gossip column, though he had never been there. As soon as they entered, the clientele were checking them out and the usual sort of glances were exchanged. He suggested they sit at a table where the light was brightest. While they sat there, he thought he would test a move, a trick, which he'd seen in some comedy, and to his surprise it worked. Where the light shone the brightest on the table's surface, next to his wallet, he placed his car keys, with the blue and white BMW checkerboard gleaming, and at once he could feel soft glances caressing his hand. It couldn't be that easy, he thought. He looked around a little and saw that he was far from one of the oldest men there and that, at some tables nearby and at the bar, there were even a few granddads with dyed, thinning hair. Then he saw which direction the glances were coming from: three young women, between the ages of twenty and twenty-five, were at the table just behind them. He ruled out the redhead right away—he had always found redheads too aggressive; the brunette he might have tried his luck with once, in the Mégane days, but the blonde, who was casually but unmistakably flashing her light-blue eyes at him, he recognized immediately. She was one of those girls, models of a sort, who the past few years had been circling like satellites around beauty pageants and fashion competitions. After the badminton game, he was feeling both sporty and elegant, especially in the company of his two buddies, who had parked their cars out front: the first, already quite bald, drove a four-year-old Volkswagen Golf 4, and the second, who had a beer belly, a Peugeot 307. He waved the waiter over and told him to give the ladies at the next table whatever they wanted. When the three models were sipping their clear beverages, he raised his glass of cognac to them in gentlemanly fashion, and since they toasted him back, if somewhat shyly, with what were probably gin-and-tonics and not mineral waters, he stepped over to their table and gallantly invited them to join him and his friends. Sitting down at the men's table, they at first pouted uncertainly as they inspected the terrain, checking to see if their hosts were not perhaps loser douchebags, who in a few minutes would pay for the drinks and trot off home to put the kiddies to bed, or maybe they were just petty fuckhunters whose wives had extended their curfews and who hoped to use the opportunity for a quick screw in the back of their Hyundai. The women were careful, experienced observers, whose eyes had instantly zeroed in on the logo on his car keys, although not without some hesitation at first—there were, after all, sickos walking around out there who put BMW fobs on their Škoda keys—but eventually their attention focused on him. And his on the blonde. After half an hour or so of conversation, about nothing really, he offered to drive the young ladies to their respective homes. There was general assent to the idea, and their eyes glowed with expectation and curiosity about the order in which they would be delivered. They told him their destinations and he worked out the route: first he would dispose of the redhead, then he'd drop off the brunette, and finally he'd invite the fair-haired one to join him for another drink. The plan succeeded, smoothly and completely. Forty-five minutes later, the two of them were sipping cognacs at another popular bistro, even more expensive than the first. He talked about his stressful job and his responsibilities, explained the basic rules of business to her, and every so often would puff up her self-image, starting with her looks, and the girl began to melt like a beeswax candle. He said that he'd never met a woman who was so very attractive, and intelligent too; that someone with such irresistible magnetism and remarkable beauty needed to be treated well, and that he remembered her from TV and the newspapers, and did she live by herself?

The girl, a little flustered, winced and said, no, she lived with her parents.

"That's a bit awkward," he replied, "but it's understandable since you're so young."

"But maybe not as young as I look," she rejoined, and he realized that in fact she was much younger than he had first thought. I hope she's at least eighteen, he prayed, but he had no serious intention of raising the question. Since the girl really was more used to mineral water, and he was already plying her with her third cognac, and since he himself had not been sober for a few hours, he suggested a nearby hotel. The sex was nothing special, but towards morning, as day was breaking and she was getting

into his car, she seemed to him like an exclusive BMW acces-
sory. She had already given him her phone number and, while
they were still at the first bar, he had texted his wife to say that
one of his buddies was having a birthday and they were going
to celebrate a little and she shouldn't worry if he got home late.
So just one more thing needed to be taken care of: swearing his
buddy the Golf driver to total secrecy, he made an arrangement
with him for the occasional use of his apartment (the man's wife
had left him for a coworker).

Everything went according to plan. The model was available
whenever she didn't have a photo shoot or pageant preparations,
and his wife, too, had no suspicions and believed unconditionally that he was working longer hours due to the company's
expansion into southern markets. And then one Saturday he
had the chance to spend an entire weekend with the model away
from the surveillance of his family. Two weeks earlier, he had
learned the date of his father-in-law's wine harvest and delib-
erated started coming home late from work—although a few
times he was just killing time at a bar near the office or browsing
the internet—and at home he would talk about the enormous
amount of work he had because of the new shopping mall they
were opening in Serbia. Which wasn't far from the truth. So not
long before the harvest, he announced to his wife and her family that, since he was so backed up with work, he unfortunately
wouldn't be able to help out that year. His father-in-law was
offended and grumbled something, his mother-in-law looked
doubtfully at her daughter, but because his wife showed no signs
of suspicion, they all accepted the situation.

"So that means I can take the BMW to the wine harvest," his
wife said, "and pick up my cousin and her friend on the way."

"I'm afraid that won't be possible," he replied. "The car is
registered to my company and you're not authorized to drive it."

All obstacles were thus cleared away and less than an hour after
his wife drove off with the kids early in the morning, he got
into the BMW and picked up the model at the place they had
agreed on; then, taking the bypass around the city, he turned

onto the highway that led to the coast. As soon as the young
woman, whom he had only known a few weeks, sat in the car,
he thought she seemed different, a little plumper, especially her
breasts, which was unusual since just a couple days earlier they
had looked entirely normal. She was also less talkative than usual,
and on the way there asked him, not once but twice, to stop. As
he waited for her, he leafed through BMW's annual catalog. The
second time, when she returned from the bushes, he could see
from her face that she clearly wasn't feeling very well. Today of all
days, he thought, when he had gone to such trouble to organize
a free weekend, she had to make a face like that. He didn't ask
what was wrong; he only hoped the girl wasn't going to become
hysterical, which can happen to people of her sex with no warning. They were already descending the steep road to the sea when
the girl made an awful face and ordered him to pull into the
first gas station they came to. It looked pretty serious. When he
stopped the car at the gas station, she ran for the restroom as fast
as she could. As he was calmly turning a page of his catalog, his
eyes fell on the passenger's seat. He couldn't believe what he saw.
The light gray leather seat was soaked in blood. He closed his
eyes, opened them again, but the bloodstain was still there. He
jumped out of the car, opened the door on the passenger's side
and continued staring at this unbelievable phenomenon. When
she came back from the restroom, she had just started to explain
that it had caught her a little off guard when he turned to face
her, grabbed her by the head and, as if she were a bad puppy,
nearly shoved her face in the menstrual blood.

"What is this?" he howled at her. "You ruined it!" And she
burst into tears.

He held his head in his hands and started shrieking as if
somebody had butchered his child in the seat, and three men
from the gas station hurried over to see what was wrong.

"Are you insane? You destroyed my car! It will never be the
same again," he was yelling. The gas attendants tried to get him
to calm down.

"What's the matter? It's only blood."

"Only blood? Yes, it's blood! Blood on the seat!" he shouted. "You're never going to get that out! You filthy bitch!" he screamed, and the girl's tears soon turned to rage and even spite.

"You're such an asshole! I knew you were a total idiot, who fucks women only because he can't fuck his stupid old car."

"What? What did you just call it? Say that one more time, I dare you! You fucking whore!" he bellowed and, right in front of the gas attendants, started shaking her like a wet rag, so she was barely able to wriggle out of his grip. But the model knew some defensive methods, including a few retaliatory measures.

"That word you just called me? I swear you will never say it again!" she hissed at him in fury. Then she reached into her bag—from which tampons came tumbling out—found her house key, ran over to the door on the driver's side, and started dragging the key along the silver body. As the steel edge dug into the metal, the piercing sound was like somebody plunging a knife into his liver. He lunged at her and as hard as he could punched her in the face, so that she collapsed on top of the hood. Two of the gas attendants jumped on top of him, while the third helped the girl detach herself from the car.

"I'm calling the police," he said, as he helped her to her feet.

"Oh no, please don't the police," she cried. "Call the mental hospital for him, but I beg you, not the police!" Her helpless-victim eyes entranced the gas attendant, who ended the phone connection and walked her to the restroom.

"But your nose is bleeding," he persisted.

"No, it'll be fine," she said, and repeated: "Just don't call the police. Please, no media, no cameras . . ."

The other two attendants eventually relaxed their hold on him and, when they saw the disgraced leather seat, agreed that a girl should know when such things are about to happen to her and maybe it really wouldn't be so easy to remove the stain completely. Then they told him how to get to the nearest car wash.

With a sob he sat down in the car and sped off to the car wash, got out, and told the fellow there to clean up that filthy mess and charge as much as he liked. Then he went to a nearby eatery and ordered a double Jack Daniel's and then a bowl of stew, since he already had a bad headache and didn't want to be sick to his stomach too.

Not long after he ordered, a girl came in—she seemed a bit disheveled, in a long, dark green skirt and a white blouse, with a colorful backpack in her hand. He gave her a cursory glance and didn't pay much attention to her. But since there were only three tables in the place, and the other two were occupied by locals drinking beers and spritzers, she came over and asked if she could join him.

"I guess," he said indifferently. She sat down and ordered a juice and a hot sandwich. As she was pulling at the melted cheese with her fingers, she asked him gingerly if by any chance he might be traveling in the direction of the capital.

He didn't answer at first, but when she asked again if he could give her a ride, since she had missed her bus and needed to be in Ljubljana that night because she had an exam early Monday morning at the university, he nodded yes but showed no interest. Judging from her appearance he thought she was telling the truth, and anyway it might not be such a bad idea. It would certainly be better to have a road companion than be thinking all the way back to Ljubljana about the disastrous weekend that had blown up in his face before it even got started.

The guys at the car wash had done their very best: where before there had been blood, now there was just a wet spot on the seat, which still needed to dry, they explained as he took some twenties out of his wallet and placed them on their eager palms. He told the girl glumly that if she wanted to go with him, she would have to ride in the back, and then vigorously put his foot on the gas.

"Just like in a taxi." She began with some trite observations, and the first fifteen miles he didn't look at her once in the rearview.

"So why did you have to take it to the car wash?"

"I spilled some red wine. The bottle wasn't properly corked."

"Oh, well, that's nothing to worry about. And here I thought someone had bled out on the front seat!"

"Actually . . . almost," and for the first time he looked at her in the mirror. If she trimmed her hair a little and, especially, put a comb through it, and if she wiped off that circus makeup—the girl had dragged the lipstick across her mouth like a bricklayer with a trowel—she wouldn't look half bad, he thought. She was obviously some sort of budding intellectual. "So what are you studying?"

"Ethnology and anthropology."

He almost veered off the road. He couldn't believe there were still fools in the world who went off to university to study something you should do in your spare time, since any idiot knows you can't make a living from it.

"You must have wealthy parents if you chose a subject like that. Who's going to support you when you graduate?"

"My parents were opposed to it. As for how and what I'll be living on, I'll figure that out when I finish my studies and find a job."

"Come on, now, really," he said, becoming a guidance counselor. "There's no real bread in that sort of profession, just crumbs that fall off the tables of the people who actually create the money. Or maybe you're planning to live off the state, with social assistance and some sort of special cultural status or whatever it's called, riding on the coattails of the people who work for a living?"

"So what is it you do?"

"I'm the head of the purchasing department at a well-known retail outlet, where I bet even you do your shopping."

"Not me. I despise those huge outlets, like I despise all of turbo-capitalism, the way it throws its weight around, like you're doing now."

Oh my, he thought, a woman who thinks, and thinks for herself too. Of course, these headstrong girls always philosophize like that until they graduate, if they even manage to finish. But when they can't find a job—or if they do, it's usually in some library—many of them soon realize that they don't want to live a life that's measured by the painful month-to-month struggle to pay the bills. So they find themselves a lawyer or economist, get pregnant as fast as they can, and thus secure and protect their standard of living once and for all.

"But why did you decide to study those things?"

"Because I was interested in them."

"When I was a kid, I was interested in being a jet pilot and a race car driver. But today I'm neither. But what I am is very successful and satisfied, living a life of dignity. I've got a family, a wife and two children, an excellent job, and the car I've always wanted."

"And you're so proud of it, too! Yeah, I saw the way you stroked it at the car wash, when they drove it up. But I think you're going to have to take it to a body shop too. There seems to be some sort of signature on the door."

"Now don't you start giving me trouble!" he snapped at her. "Just two hours ago, the person who did that was given her walking papers and tossed out, and so will you be too, if you give me any lip."

"This car is a weak point for you, isn't it?"

"No, this car is my strongest point. A point you will never have—unless you marry well after you graduate."

"What, you think I'll get married for a car?"

"You'll see. Somewhere in your thirties, with the kind of degree you're going to have, you'll be ready to get married for a beat-up Citroën. You clearly have no idea how hard a person needs to fight in this life. But why am I telling you this—you probably don't even have your driver's license."

"Sure I do. But a car is just an object, a commodity; it's not some holy statue you bow down to every day."

"That's what you think now, when you only need it for going to parties, but you'll change your mind eventually. And don't tell me you don't have any aesthetic feeling, that you don't see the beauty and power of certain models. When I see a car I know exactly the sort of person the owner is, his work habits, standards of hygiene, lifestyle. Show me your car and I'll tell you who you are."

"Oh, is that the tinplate psychology they teach you at business school?"

"You haven't got a clue. Right now you still think that driving around in some farting old wreck is an adventure, but it won't be long before you think differently."

"Don't get me wrong: I have nothing against automobiles in principle. But what I find sad are guys whose identity is inescapably wrapped up in their car. So when some guy buys a new Ford Focus, he feels like his life is in focus now; all at once, he's sure that his presence in the world is sharper and more visible . . . and don't tell me this is all because of a Ford Focus. But that doesn't mean I'm some stupid girl who objects to the very existence of cars. According to the Jewish Kabbalah, the whole of being is made up of four intersecting worlds. Not even the smallest strand of being—let's call it a mile, so we'll understand each other better," she paused to adjust her long brown curls and went on, "can for a moment exist without the will of God. Not even evil, which also has a cosmic role to fulfill. The Kabbalah says that creation is governed by the laws of God, which are based on ten *sefirot*, or divine attributes. The configuration of these divine attributes contains all the laws that govern existence, for it reveals the cosmic process of the harmonic mutual interaction between higher and lower, active and passive principles. And just as the human body is the pure expression of the sefiric laws in the physical world, so too other organisms and organizations are expressions of the laws of God. Therefore, according to the Kabbalah, even the automobile is an expression of God's laws. Whoever can perceive the workings of the *sefirot* in human products and machines, such as the automobile, will comprehend the workings of God's law in the very lowest world, where we humans manifest our will by creating things, just like our Creator does, just like God."

"What sort of bullshit is this? And who is this Jewish chick Kabbalah, anyway?"

"Let me tell you something, Beemer Boy: knowing about the Kabbalah, at least recognizing the name, is part of what it means to have a general education. But I don't suppose you have a clue about the Kabbalah because you don't stock it on the shelves at your megamarket. To put it another way, if you understood at least a little of what I was just telling you, you'd realize that even the crap you sell in your store is part of the Kabbalistic concept."

"I don't understand what you said, but wasn't there something about how this Kabbalah believes that man and machine, man and automobile, are somehow spiritually connected, are similar in some way? This maybe I could accept."

"The structure is the same, but instead of veins, cars have pipes and tubes, and instead flesh, they have sheet metal. And at the same time, just as humans are made by God, cars are made by humans. But what's really remarkable in this respect is that in the Kabbalah the ritual of meditation and self-contemplation is called 'contemplating the chariot'—in other words, the car. Through this ritual it's possible to move from the physical world into the spiritual realms. But the driver has to be well prepared for this inner journey. If the driver isn't ready, if he's unbalanced or doing it for the wrong reason, then the journey becomes extremely risky, and the driver can totally freak out and even die."

"Jesus, girl! You've got some imagination! Look, if you can't find a job, here's my business card—just call me. We need offbeat types like you, people who think outside the box and can come up with new ways to sell our stuff. Don't lose my card."

"Do you want me to read your palm?"

"What, you're a psychic too?" And keeping his left hand on the wheel, he reached back his right hand for her to read. "Well, what do you see? Anything?"

"Hmm, hmm, very interesting . . . I don't really know what to say . . ."

"That's what all fortune tellers say."

"I see that you're about to come to a turning point in your life, which involves a spiritual experience that will completely transform you. No, I don't see death; that's not it. But still, be careful on the road. Here, take this. It's called a *hamsa*, and it comes straight from Jerusalem." And on his still open palm she placed a metal pendant in the form of a hand. "I suggest you put it on the key ring with your car keys, as extra security."

"What, hang this piece of tin next to the BMW logo?"

"I would absolutely do that if I was you. The moment I got into this Beemer, I saw a picture in my mind and it's why I'm urging you to drive very carefully. And just now, when I was examining your palm . . ."

"Well, little soothsayer," he said as he pulled up in front of her building in Ljubljana, "at least the time passed quickly, even if you have been chattering for the last forty-five minutes about things that I don't think even you understand. But you're definitely not stupid. Good luck on your exam, and hold on to my card—I'm sure it'll come in handy one day."

She got out of the car, leaned over, and said through the open window, "You just be sure to attach that *hamsa* to your car keys. I wouldn't even drive out of the garage without it. Good luck to you too, Beemer Boy."

As she was leaning against the car to say goodbye, he glanced at her cleavage and went numb, his head riven with pain, as if Moses had smashed the tablets with the Ten Commandments against it. Among all the other cheap jewelry hanging around her neck, a pendant had started swinging back and forth and it gave him chills. It was the mark of the hated enemy: Mercedes. But a moment later he calmly concluded that the chick must have been wearing that hippie peace symbol, which had merely gotten tangled and twisted in some weird way.

The pain in his head did not completely go away but only transformed itself into a terrible pressure. He shut his eyes, breathed deeply for a couple of minutes, and then drove home.

The encounter with the girl, which at first glance seemed so trivial and innocent, had got him thinking. The trip to the seaside had been a fiasco and ended in a way he could not have foreseen. Even before the girl's ridiculous blather, he had asked himself more than once, in deathly horror, what if something happened to the car? What if somebody, maybe from envy, did it harm? Or even worse, what if he and the car were in an accident? Just as parents worry about their children, now, because of that crazy chick, he was worried about his car. At home, before going to sleep, he turned the *hamsa* around in his hand a few times and then, after careful thought, added it to his key ring next to the BMW logo. It didn't look great, he thought, but it couldn't hurt, and after his wife's call to check up on him—what had he been doing and how was he?—he slept restlessly and woke up a few times during the night.

The headache was still with him the next day. It was not strong, but the pressure was like somebody chiseling on his skull from the inside. He took two general pain pills and then, since they didn't help, two of his wife's prescription painkillers for migraine. During the day he watched a little TV, without really knowing what he was watching, dozed off a few times, and in between thought about the stain on the car's upholstery and how it was a bad omen. He ran down to the garage; the gray leather again seemed to have a slightly reddish tint. Those bastards didn't clean it at all, he thought; they just sprayed something on it so it looked clean, and now that the spray's evaporated the stain's come back. And not even come back since it's been there all the time; it never went away. He went down to the garage a few more times to see if the stain was still there and was horrified to discover that not only had it not disappeared, but that the red spot was getting bigger and corroding the leather.

In the afternoon his wife telephoned to say there was heavy congestion on the road and they'd be getting home later, sometime before eleven. To clear his head, he got in the car and started driving nowhere in particular. He turned on to the bypass that circled the city and about ten minutes later noticed a silver Mercedes S-Class coming up behind him. He deliberately slowed down, and the Mercedes put on its turn signal and started to pass him. He pressed on the gas, and for a while they drove side by side, but when his challenger tried to move in front of him, he accelerated, so it was only with extreme difficulty, less than a hundred yards before the exit to the south side of the city, that the Mercedes managed to move ahead of him into the right lane and turn off the bypass. All the while, he was laughing his head off and giving him the finger, which he wiggled tauntingly.

A couple of miles later, another Mercedes S-Class came up on his right. It was also silver. He didn't see that it had a different license plate number and was sure that the impotent bastard had come back for revenge. He let him get in front and then, a second later, speeded up. He drove so close to the car that he nearly bumped the fender a few times, and the gray-headed driver had to scramble to save himself.

"Can't do it, can you?" he shouted at the car, as the granddad crossed the solid line onto the shoulder and picked up speed.

"What's the problem, Mercedes, no power in your engine— or in your balls?" he yelled, and again gestured rudely with his middle finger, as the Mercedes finally reached the exit for the north side of Ljubljana.

Eventually, after a few hours of wild driving, he headed home. In the garage, he again inspected the passenger's seat, which he had somehow managed to forget about while he was driving. The stain had spread even more. He decided that first thing in the morning he would take the car to the car wash. He lay down on the sofa in the living room and slept for nearly two hours in front of the television.

"Are you ill?" his wife startled him from his restless sleep.

"Me? No. Why?" he said, waking up in shock. She leaned over and examined him thoroughly.

"You're so pale. Did you get any sleep at all?"

"Of course, all day," he almost said, but stopped himself just in time. His wife seemed different somehow; her face was narrower and her nose even pointier than usual. "I'm just tired . . . from working," he lied, then headed off to the bathroom, gulped down three sleeping pills, and went to bed.

The next morning he woke up at five in a thick daze from the pills. For nearly an hour and a half he stared at the ceiling, thoughts racing past him as if he was riding in a supersonic jet. At six-thirty he got up and, without taking a shower or drinking his morning coffee, got dressed, climbed in his car, and went to a service station not far from work, parking in front of the car wash.

"Here are the keys," he told the attendant. "Give it a thorough cleaning so it looks like new. Especially the stain on the passenger's seat in front!"

"What stain?"

"The bloodstain! What are you, blind?" he barked at the man, who humbly swallowed the abuse as just another example of the high-strung arrogance of wealthy car-owners.

He then went to work on foot, where he did nothing that

day except doodle pictures of his BMW 545i as seen from different angles.

At four-thirty he was back at the service station's car wash, where a different employee drew up his bill. He thought they had done a good job cleaning it. The seat in particular.

He drove over to the gas pump to fill up the car, but was stopped by some red and white barrier tape, and parked behind the tape he saw a real behemoth—a Mercedes!

As he waited, Modern Talking was singing, "*Baby just we two / All my dreams come true . . .*" and as his own gas tank was filling, he saw the driver of the Mercedes talking to the fellow who a few minutes earlier had handed him the keys to his just-washed car. Both of them, he noticed, kept looking over at him and his BMW. He opened the window, but he still couldn't hear what they were saying. And when the Mercedes driver started coming towards him, he shut the window as a defensive measure and anxiously waited in readiness. The brazen asshole tapped on the glass with his greasy fingers, and he lowered the window a crack.

"This beast of yours isn't the usual Series 5, is it?"

"What's it to you?" he replied.

"Forgive me, but the fellow over there was telling me about the top-of-the-line features you have built in."

"That's none of your business!" he snapped back, looking at him with distrust. It was true, though. When he bought the car, he had intentionally asked them not to put the little tag on the back that would betray his darling's noble lineage to any old busybody. He hoped that such a ruse would protect the car from potential thieves and ill-wishers, who might well devise some unpleasantness for him. But he also enjoyed using this concealed identity to pull surprises on other drivers, which he had been doing more and more recently to seemingly more powerful challengers.

"Just another idiot in a top-of-the-line model!" the Mercedes driver snarled and returned to the car wash attendant. That fellow had obviously been snooping around the BMW while he was at work and passed his information on to Mr. Mercedes. After the behemoth left, he finished filling his car and raced down the two-lane road to the bypass and headed home. On the way, he overtook the Mercedes behemoth and harassed the car so horribly and dangerously that the terrified driver pulled onto the shoulder and stopped, while he, meanwhile, tore off at full speed through the roundabout. A moment later, a Mercedes SL sports car appeared in his rearview mirror from nowhere. So they've sent one of their special agents after us, he thought, as he accelerated even more, but the SL nimbly followed him. Of course, now they want revenge. After his assault yesterday on the Mercedes S-Class, the industrial spies at the service station car wash had searched the BMW and dispatched a commando to capture and destroy both him and his car.

"You will not succeed!" he bellowed into the rearview mirror and swung off the bypass going a hundred and seventy miles an hour, not slowing down until he was on the local two-lane road. He heard a police siren somewhere, but the police were too weak to come anywhere near them. From the two-lane road he deftly steered the car onto his home street and parked it safely in the garage. As he was getting out, he glanced over at the passenger's seat and noticed that again it looked red. He should have known. They too had simply sprayed it with something so they'd be able to examine the car thoroughly and pass the information on to Mercedes. He took a bottle of bleach and poured it over the seat; then he went into the living room and sat in front of the blank television screen. The phone rang. His wife told him she would be home around seven, after she picked up their daughter from music and then, half an hour later, their son from volleyball.

Of course, he thought, for a few days now, they must have had him and his baby under their watchful eye. Even the hippie symbol around that chick's neck—it really had been the Mercedes logo, and the Jewish sorceress had been wearing it backwards to disguise it.

He heard the Mégane in the driveway and went to the window. As his wife and children were getting out of the car, a big black sedan turned on to their street and parked across the road. Two tall men in dark clothes got out and went into the duplex opposite theirs. And right after that, another sedan drove up and parked behind the first. It was also black, and a man stepped out who was dressed like the first two. All three seemed strangely, and very suspiciously, similar. More than similar, maybe identical. His wife put the kids to bed and told him a few stories from her father's wine harvest, but as soon as she went into the bathroom, he slipped out of the house with a notebook and pen and walked stealthily around the two parked vehicles. One of them had Serbian plates from Belgrade, the other, Croatian plates from Dubrovnik, and he jotted both numbers down in his notebook. But the most suspicious thing of all was that both were Mercedes. He hurried back into the house and nearly collided with his wife.

"Where were you just now?"

"Nowhere. I just popped out to check something . . . Weren't you in the bathroom?"

"I took a shower," she cooed, seductively inviting him with her eyes to come to bed. He followed her into the bedroom and lay down, but the moment she touched him, it all came to him in a flash, like a bolt of lightning, and he pulled away from her. She was being too nice to him; it was weird. Maybe she knew something he didn't know?

"Just a second," he said to her and jumped out of bed. He looked out the window and saw that the cars were still there. It was clear; it was all clear; it was all coming together in his head. It had started with the blonde they had set him up with in the bar, when he laid his keys with the BMW fob on the table. Her assignment was to ruin his car at the first stage. After her, the Mossad agent appeared; she had only sat next to him in the eatery so that, when he wasn't paying attention, she could spike his stew with a drug that would give him a splitting headache when he got back to Ljubljana; by attacking him, the pure-blooded owner of a German BMW, she was avenging her Jewish forebears who had died at Auschwitz. And then today his wife came home suspiciously late—their daughter didn't even have piano lessons on Mondays—and immediately afterwards the Serbian and Croatian Mercedes appeared. He went over to their landline telephone and called the police.

"I'd like to report the theft of a car."

"Your information, please. Your name, the make of the car, where and when it was stolen . . ."

"It hasn't been stolen yet, but they're going to steal it; that's their plan."

"Hold on a minute. How? Who? . . ."

"I don't know, but I can tell you the license numbers of two Mercedes from an international crime syndicate, which are parked just outside my door. The house across the street is dark and now they're waiting for me to fall asleep so they can attack me and my BMW 545i."

"Are you nuts?" his wife interrupted him. "Who are you telling this nonsense to?"

"The police."

"Hang up! What you're saying is insane!" She went over to him, grabbed the phone, and hung up the receiver. He stepped back and looked directly in her face.

Now everything was clear: the link between the global spy rings of the pernicious organization that was trying to destroy him and his BMW, the supreme coordinator of the Mercedes Intelligence Agency was none other than his own wife!

"You've been orchestrating the whole thing! It was suspicious how fast you came around to accepting the purchase, and then you sent me that blonde whore, and the secret agent from Mossad, who even let slip the word *organization*, and now you and those Balkan mobsters out there are just waiting for me to fall asleep so you and your Mercedes pals can break into my garage, into my bedroom, and finish your dirty work."

His wife anxiously tried to get him into bed, but he tore himself away from her and, dressed only in pajamas, grabbed his keys, ran into the garage, got into the car and drove off at great speed. From the bypass he turned immediately onto the highway and felt as though with every mile he and his BMW were escaping their pursuers and kidnappers, escaping the wicked world that was planning to destroy them both. Modern Talking was coming from the sound system; he pressed down on the gas pedal and sang along—*You are not alone, I'll be there for you*

... *Half-way to your paradise* ... and with each new acceleration he felt the tingling ants of fear coupling in a bliss that could only be compared to the height of sexual arousal. He could feel himself getting hard and pressed down even more on the gas pedal. Together they were racing down the straight highway into the night. And as Thomas Anders and Dieter Bohlen sang, "*Fly me to the moon, I'm coming soon ... We two are one ... Together strong ...*" his body was flooded with such immense delight that tears came to his eyes. He closed them, placed his right hand on his swollen dick, and was suffused with a boundless sense of oneness, the feeling that he and his BMW were becoming one, one organism powered by the same fuel, one mind and one body. But the very next hundredth of a second his moment of cosmic crystallization was interrupted by the right edge of the road, from which he instinctively veered left and then right, and a second later he and his BMW were tumbling through grass into a cornfield.

The first thing he saw were the policemen, who suddenly appeared next to the unharvested corn. They were standing beside his BMW, which was mangled beyond all recognition and from which his body was being pulled by firefighters and quickly surrounded by paramedics. He moved closer to them and, in their midst, saw the face that greeted him every morning in the mirror, only it was horribly battered and bloody. As they were putting his body on the stretcher, he tried to tell them not to bother with him, that they should instead check on his BMW, call the towing service and some German mechanics, make sure that it didn't explode ... But nobody could hear him.

At that moment, however, he was bathed from behind in a brilliant light. He turned around and froze. At the edge of the cornfield he saw the most beautiful thing he had ever seen in his life. Two blinding headlights, like gigantic eyes, were shining out of an absolutely perfect organism. Clearly, he was the only one there who noticed it. The BMW that stood before him he had never seen in any catalog. Gleaming white with a tint of sky-blue. He walked around it—and at the same time realized that he was not actually walking but somehow floating as he moved.

On the back end of the car, next to the BMW logo, he saw the numeral eight lying strangely on its side. So what he was looking at must be the BMW Series Infinity. He went up to the door and gingerly stroked the car's body, which trembled and, as if made of metallic magma, gave way beneath his fingertips. He opened the door and first patted the snow-white dashboard, which started to vibrate just as the outer shell had done, but when he sank into the seat, he could feel the soft organism's warm skin yield, adapting itself perfectly to his body. The round dial of the speedometer had only a single symbol on it: the sideways eight. He stepped on the clutch and the gas, turned the key in the ignition, and heard a sound like a fleet of jets before takeoff. He pressed harder on the gas, released the clutch, and the engine soon became quiet. A road appeared in front of him that he did not recognize. The speedometer needle started rising to the top of the dial and then descended, and then, faster and faster, was rotating with such speed that the only thing visible on the dial was a flickering light-blue circle. Next to the road he saw a sign indicating unlimited speed, and the night, which was covered in stars, became one with the road. Cornfield, paramedics, police, all were left behind. No longer did he hear people talking, the shining towns faded into the distance, and in front of him there was only the wide two-lane road; the dark-blue fields on either side were sprinkled with stars and planets, comets were shooting past, and the road was twinkling with starlight.

Apart from the celestial bodies, there was only a dark-blue abyss, and he sensed that he was operating the car with his thoughts. The needle on the speedometer kept spinning and spinning, and somewhere far, far ahead, he saw a powerful beam of light, towards which he and the embodiment of the pure idea of the BMW were moving. The nearer they came to the source of the light, the more powerfully he was bathed in its tender, boundless love, and he desired only one thing: that he and the BMW might plunge into its core forever.

They were almost there and were about to drive into the source of the light, when suddenly right in front of them there appeared a sign indicating a mandatory U-turn. He tried to keep the steering wheel from turning, but he and the sublime embodiment of automobilism split apart, and against his will the car turned on its own and began driving in the direction from which they had come. As they were speeding back to their starting point, he saw, flying past in the opposite lane, his mangled BMW 545i. A moment later the radio switched on and a woman's voice was calling to him by his first and last names, and then he was shrouded in thick darkness.

He wasn't in the car anymore. The road had vanished and through his squinting eyes he saw a new source of light in front of him, but it was cold and ugly. Yes, ugly. In front of him was a face, its lips and nose hidden by a green cover, and it kept on repeating his first and last names.

"You've come back to us!" The eyes on the face lit up with joy, and two other faces, similar to the first, appeared next to it.

"You gave us a real fright; we thought we'd lost you for good. Can you hear us?" They were talking to him. He muttered something and moved his eyes back and forth, and the first idea that came to him was that he had died and gone to some Muslim hell.

"You have no idea how incredibly lucky you are," the same female voice was telling him. But he only managed, with great difficulty, to murmur the words, "What about him?"

"Who?"

"My dearest . . ."

"But you were the only one in the car!"

"My BMW . . ."

"Oh, don't worry about your car. What's important is that it looks like you're going to be OK. You were pretty beaten up, but the operation was a success. We stopped the hemorrhaging in your brain and, fortunately, there is no serious damage to your spine," the anesthetist explained. "Everything will be OK; it all turned out remarkably well."

But it hadn't. Now in intensive care, just a few days after he gradually started to regain consciousness, he told the attending physician, who was accompanied on his morning rounds by a group of medical students, that Nurse Dyane had to be removed immediately from his parking space because he couldn't stand having that old Frog jalopy anywhere near him. A week later, Nurse Lada came to the head of the division in tears and said she just couldn't take it anymore, that she was going to have a nervous breakdown because the patient was constantly insulting her, saying she was a broken-down Russian rustbucket good only for hauling potatoes. "And this, when I change his pajamas and wipe his rear end for him!" she sobbed. So he was moved to a special room where he wouldn't upset the other patients or the staff. The division chief assigned Nurse Desa to look after him. She had a great deal of experience and was used to even the most difficult cases, not only people with post-operative dementia but also those who were crabby and mean by nature.

"We're coming along nicely," she encouraged him a few weeks later as she helped him grip the crutches and together they took his first steps, initially just around the room, then in the corridor, and in a few months they were going to the end of the corridor and back.

"Your wife is sending you a CD player with your favorite music, and your children have drawn you a picture. Oh yes, and your mother and mother-in-law—they're asking when they can come visit you."

"Desa, what was our agreement? No, I said. They are all members of an international intelligence network and are only pretending to be my family, and the leader of the spy ring is none other than my wife."

"Not even your children?"

"The children are victims of the intelligence agents and have been outfitted with high-tech equipment and trained to recite all the details of my condition. But I am still too weak, while they, Desa, are strong, because they are mercenaries for one of the world's most powerful conglomerates. Shhhh . . . I mustn't say its name out loud, Desa, or even think it, because the fluids you're putting into my body contain genetically mutated compounds that use vibrations to transmit all my thoughts and words to a certain world-famous German manufacturer."

"Well, maybe another time then, when you're feeling a little better," Desa always told him cheerfully when she left for the day. Physically, he was making good progress, and eventually, after a few weeks, he could go to the bathroom and even wash himself without assistance. The chief of the division was certain he had done well to choose a nurse whose name could arouse no doubt or suspicion in the patient. And indeed, Nurse Desa, who had the morning shift, was the only person the patient ever talked to. With the nurses on the other two shifts he remained uncommunicative.

But despite all his deliberations the division chief had not been careful enough. The patient was becoming more and more ambulatory. Gliding around on his crutches, he started sniffing about the division trying to discover how the secret organization was infiltrating the hospital personnel. The personnel, for their part, did not restrict his movements; such a desire for mobility was beneficial to his physical rehabilitation, even if it was clear to everyone that before he could be discharged from the hospital, he would have to undergo a psychiatric evaluation. During doctors' rounds, he would secretly slip into the staff kitchen, examine the packages the nurses had been given by the patients' relatives, and poke through the nurses' changing room. He found the first suspicious sign on the nurses' posted work schedule. It was there that he first learned Nurse Desa's surname: *Fuhrmann*—German for driver. So at once he began to suspect that perhaps Nurse Desa herself, who had always been so unusually open and friendly with him, was the main *driver* of the chariot, the one that that Mossad agent had been talking about on the way back to Ljubljana. He began to observe his nurse more closely and secretly watch her, until finally, on the last Thursday in December, his hypotheses were tragically confirmed.

The division was in a holiday mood. The nurses were all smiles and laughter and the air was fragrant with oranges, fresh-baked nut roll, and cookies. He was lying in bed, paging through the new BMW catalog. The sound of women's voices were coming through the open door. He listened more closely, for he had right away recognized the voice of the leader of the secret agents.

He grabbed his crutches, glanced out the door and saw the agent delivering a package to one of the nurses.

"Who did you say this was for?" the nurse asked.

"For Nurse—" the agent paused a moment. "You know, I can't remember her name. It's a bit unusual . . . like the name of a car . . ."

He was all ears.

"Well, if she's taking care of your husband, as you say, then it can't be Nurse Lada or Nurse Dyane. Oh yes, of course," the nurse now remembered. "You must mean our nurse from the coast—she's always in such a good mood. Nurse Marija. Marija Mercedes Fuhrmann, actually, but we all just call her Desa."

"That's her. I don't know why, but her name completely escaped me. These past few months have been so difficult."

"She just went to Neurology. If you leave the package with me, I'll make sure she gets it."

Pressed against the wall, almost glued to it, he broke out in a cold sweat. Everything was crystal clear now. The main collaborator from that international secret organization was the counterintelligence agent Marija Mercedes Fuhrmann, who worked undercover as Desa. He was being held in a German laboratory, where the only reason they were repairing him was so they could perform some sort of technological experiments on him. In all likelihood, Japanese experiments. He knew he had to get out of that hospital as soon as possible, but first he had to destroy the program that had been collecting data on him and sending it via their global network to the individual cells, who were then passing it on to General Headquarters in Stuttgart.

After the agent left the division and the nurse placed the mysterious package in the staff kitchen and went into one of the rooms, he slipped into the kitchen, grabbed the key to the changing room, and forced open Nurse Mercedes' locker. He took her car keys from her purse and was surprised to see that Mercedes did not drive a car that bore her name but instead, as part of her disguise, drove a Volkswagen—a red Lupo 3L, as it later turned out. With the remote-locking key in his hand and his crutches under his arms, he glided down the corridor into the elevator and went down to the basement, to the employees' parking area. For fifteen minutes, as he repeatedly pressed the button on the key, he hunted for the vehicle of the counterintelligence agent, and when he finally found it, he threw the crutches aside and squeezed himself into the car. He put the key in the ignition and turned. The German wolf howled like a wounded animal and opened its two glassy eyes.

He drove up and down between the parked cars, searching the underground lot for the ringleader, in which he expected to find the surveillance program installed. He was almost at the exit, when, in a dark corner, he saw the silver trio. A twenty-foot-long Mercedes S-Class was in the middle, flanked on either side by two bodyguards: a Mercedes A-Class and a Mercedes C-Class. He positioned the Lupo so it faced the Mercedes S and started menacingly honking the horn and revving the engine. The Mercedes S switched on and activated its headlights. A moment later so did the entire parking lot. Of course. It was the Boss. "The Boss must be destroyed!" he cried as the Mercedes' henchmen started wailing and barking submissively like wolves before the leader of the pack. If he destroyed the Boss, he would destroy the entire laboratory; he would destroy them all and then destroy the organization itself, he screamed as he backed the car up a few feet. The Renaults were croaking defensively, the Japanese and Koreans flashed their slanted eyes in fury, the Golfs howled like injured beasts, the Fiats were screeching like cats in heat. He pressed down the gas pedal, released the clutch, and rammed directly into the Boss, while the Mercedes A on the one side yapped like a miniature Doberman and the Mercedes C on the other growled like a schnauzer. With the Boss destroyed, he next took down his guard dogs; then he crushed the Renaults, demolished the Japanese, mowed down Passats, Peugeots, and Opels, then another small Mercedes, and so wrecked half the cars in the lot before the security guards and a group of strong, agile medical technicians managed to jump on the car and surround it with meal delivery carts.

The days pass quietly now, and even more quietly the long winter nights. After five days of snow, which the residents of the institution, heavily tranquilized and immersed in their respective depressions, by and large slept through, the orderlies Bojan and Erik enter the room at seven in the morning and conduct the morning ritual. First they greet Professor Marn, who is already up and sitting by the window, notebook in hand, monitoring the condition of the tiny new foliage on the plane tree in front of the hospital. The new patient is still asleep.

"Good morning! It's a beautiful day outside, dry and sunny, perfect for taking a little drive," Erik cheerfully greets the new patient, and as he shows no signs of life, the orderly gives him a vigorous shake.

"We need to get the engine running and clear out some of those cobwebs. It seems to be pretty badly clogged."

With Bojan's help, the patient slowly lifts himself up. Erik, meanwhile, gives Professor Marn his morning doses.

"Well, then, the usual procedure: first we change the oil and then have a wash," Erik says as Bojan leads the patient by the arm to the toilet and then under the shower, where he helps him wash himself.

"Oh, look, they're already back," Erik comments.

"Yes, there wasn't any line today at the car wash. So now we get the new oil, right?" the patient asks.

"Here you go," Erik says, offering him the first plastic cup. And when the patient gulps it down, he gives him another. "We also need our engine coolant, so nothing goes wrong on the road."

"Erik, are you going to check underneath?"

"Sure, just park in your regular space," Erik replies, pulling on a pair of latex gloves, and as the patient lies on his back, the orderly inserts a suppository into his rectum. "I also changed your spark plugs," he informs him.

"Professor Marn, would you like to go with us for a drive?" Erik asks.

"I am most grateful for the invitation, but unfortunately, I am inordinately occupied and cannot be pulled away. Once again, the numbers, the numerality, the numero-foliarity do not tally statistically," Professor Marn explains as Bojan helps the new patient dress.

"Why, Bojan," Erik winks to his colleague. "I think he looks as good as new."

"Like from the showroom floor?" asks the patient with a hazy stare, but already a little more cheerful.

"Like on display in a German dealership," Erik confirms.

"Erik, do you think it's going to snow? Or should I open the retractable electric sunroof?"

"Absolutely. It's a beautiful, sunny winter day, and if it starts to get colder, we'll just shut it," Erik replies with a wink at Bojan, who grabs the patient's knit cap off the coatrack.

"Are the tires all right?" the patient asks as they help him with his boots.

"The tires are fine. They're winter tires," Erik says as Bojan supports the patient. A patient from the next room is already in front of the door directing traffic like a traffic cop.

"Officer Ivan indicates that it's OK to pass through the intersection," Erik says, as Ivan rotates his right arm, holding it close to his body.

"Do you think the roads will be icy?" the patient asks.

"It's snowy outside, but the roads have been salted and they're in good condition."

"Is it safe?"

"Perfectly safe. You'll really enjoy the drive."

Yardstick of Happiness

WHEN WE FIRST started becoming closer, you had nothing. Your parents were dying, your relationship with your partner was falling apart, and you were about to lose your job. My life was the exact opposite. I had more or less everything: everyone around me was healthy, I had just gotten married and had an excellent new job at the university. I'm not exactly sure why we became closer just then; maybe I felt like I needed to pay a kind of happiness tax, and if I didn't, it might all go bad. You were terribly lonely. When so many unhappy things accumulate around a person, people tend to keep their distance; they're afraid of being infected by misfortune, as if it was a malignant virus or dangerous bacteria. But I was certain that in a well-modulated friendship with you, nothing at all would happen to me, and I received great satisfaction from helping you. Yes, and a kind of power, too. From time to time I took you out to an inexpensive lunch, let you smoke my cigarettes, and if my work obligations took me to another city, I invited you along and so gave you a rare chance to get out of town.

But in fact, whenever you were feeling most down, to the point where you could hardly speak and just sat there motionless and withdrawn with a strained look on your face, and the few words you did say were spoken in a voice trembling with fear and dread, I always despised you, your helpless pose of a wide-eyed calf waiting to be slaughtered, and I felt no sympathy for you. There had to be some reason for what was happening to you, I thought. And I would remember how it was before we became "friends." How men's eyes would be glued to you, which you never particularly noticed. Because you were afraid. And instead, you did your best to give them the impression that you were smart too. But in those days, you didn't have to do anything. They would have noticed you no matter what, whereas my charm was always connected with displays of my intelligence. And after many failed attempts, I was finally successful. In your case, however, your looks and your brains only left men confused; they didn't know which to trust, especially since you were so unsure of yourself, and in the end, when it came to the men you really wanted, you were left high and dry.

When your time of tribulation arrived, it seemed in a way fair to me. We all have our time of happiness, and you had failed to take advantage of yours. Despite every opportunity. Despite having more opportunities than the rest of us. I attended your parents' funerals, and occasionally I invited you to our home. But whenever you phoned me at night after nine o'clock, trying to keep from going crazy with fear in your loneliness, my voice would become drier, my words slower, and I very clearly let you know that you were calling me too late in the evening. Because I was not alone; I had a husband, and the evening was our time for each other. Because I had a family.

Whenever I felt afraid for my life, without exactly knowing why, whenever I was seized by some inexplicable anxiety, I would tell myself: compared to her, you have nothing to complain about; on the contrary, things are going well for you; in fact, you're doing extremely well. You were my yardstick of happiness, and whenever I doubted my good fortune, I only had to look at you and I didn't feel sad anymore. Probably not everything was really fine, and a few times I went too far. Once, thanks to my position at the university, I had the chance to significantly change your life. It was not long after your parents died, and I was on a committee for an international grant. I knew how badly you wanted it, so you could finally get away from an environment that was making you so miserable. I told you later how hard I had worked on your behalf, but in fact I had kept my mouth shut and done nothing. Because just as much as you needed me,

I needed you. And I was not prepared for us to go our separate ways. After all, we were seeing each other regularly. We were friends.

And then one Monday your face had a different sort of glow. Your expression had changed. You didn't have that wide-eyed look anymore; your eyes were angled—maybe you had done them up differently, or maybe you felt like you should start doing yourself up differently—and there was no more fear in them. Your breathing was not as shallow as it had been the past two years, and for the first time in a long time I saw a relaxed smile on your face. You had changed. I don't know if somebody had maybe said something to you about that committee, or if you had heard some rumor, but you started acting differently towards me. No longer did your voice tremble when you needed something, and indeed, you needed me less and less and were becoming more and more distant. I took this as a sign of ingratitude. After all, when you were in need, it was me who took care of you and helped you.

A week or so later, after I told you I was three months pregnant, you came to see me at work. It had not been as easy for me to conceive as I had expected, and I found this strange and suspicious. I was very frightened and very much wanted to have this child. We were sitting in my office and I don't even remember what I was saying to you, but at a certain moment, as you were listening to me, I caught you staring at my belly. There was a fixed, dark look in your eyes. You had never looked at me like that before. And even when you realized that I had noticed this, you did not look away but kept staring at my lap. Instinctively, I put my arms around my belly to protect it. Although I don't really believe in such things, I couldn't shake the feeling that there was something evil in your eyes. Something dangerous. That you wanted to hurt me. Maybe even take revenge on me.

On New Year's Eve, you stopped by with a mobile with stars and planets—it's for the baby, you said—and you gave me some sort of pink crystal. Of course, as soon as you left I took both these things out to the garbage in front of the house, and then I carefully inspected the living room and bathroom to make sure you hadn't maybe left something else behind, that you hadn't planted anything. Your gifts—and I was feeling this more and more intensely—always brought negative energy into the room. Even the card you sent me for my birthday (I celebrated it with just my family and closest friends) had some strange symbols on it, whose meaning, unfortunately, I was never able to decipher, although I checked several books. And you were looking better by the day, and visibly happier, which made me think that something wasn't quite right. When I mentioned this to my mother, she told me that she too always felt tired after your visits. As if you were absorbing her energy. And you were, too—whenever we met, I was always more exhausted afterwards, and I started feeling a strange pressure in my uterus. I mentioned my suspicions to my husband, who had never liked you and thought you were a complete loser, but he just waved his arm and said something like, there's nothing she can actually do to us, but let her know anyway that she shouldn't come around anymore. But of course I couldn't just let it go; there was too much evidence that you had done something. "We're afraid that not everything is as it should be," they told me when I had an ultrasound after New Year's. "The fetus is growing too slowly." So I decided to pay you a visit. Your apartment was meticulously tidy for the first time in years. There were some strange paintings on the wall, candles on the table, and in the middle of them, in a glass vase, there was an unusual object, something between a skeleton and a dried plant.

"What have you got here?" I asked, but you said only that somebody had given it to you as a gift.

In the bathroom, there was an open box of condoms on the washing machine. "I see you've been letting your hair down a little. I told you, didn't I? The sun always comes out after the rain." And as I watched you from the side, I thought: so that's what has put the light in your eyes, why you don't call me anymore in the evening, why you're impossible to get hold of or always have something you need to do, while I wait at home lying in bed, because not everything with me is as it should be . . . More and more I had the feeling that you were gaining power over me and my unborn child. That you had wrapped me in cloudy spiderweb, which grew thicker with every week of my pregnancy, keeping my child from growing, and that maybe the fetus was drying up. I knew how unusually gifted you were, I knew what intuition you had, and I had noticed that, when you were in close contact with death, your intuition had developed even further. That look in your eyes was intensifying. So I would probably have to do something about it—to protect myself, my unborn child, my family.

When you came by that Friday, at my invitation, you were not feeling all that well even when you arrived. It was like you were inside a balloon, you said, and you had menstrual cramps. After the first two whiskeys, I asked if you wanted some of the pain medication I had left over from my difficult fertility tests. I went into the kitchen and—I don't know, I didn't plan it, I didn't think about it, it just happened spontaneously—instead of a few drops of medicine I poured nearly the entire vial into the glass of water. You downed it in a single gulp and made a face, after which I yawned and said I was tired. You left. You drove away. You were going to see somebody who lived just outside the city, you said. It was dark and raining hard. I went to bed and fell asleep. The next day when a friend called, I almost didn't believe what had happened. Of course I didn't wish for you to die, and I rushed right over to the hospital. I felt terrible when I heard that you had probably fallen asleep at the wheel and driven off the road, and were lucky to even be alive, and that because of your severe spinal injuries you would be bedridden for the rest of your life.

Now I visit you once a week in the old age home—that's where they put you since you have nobody to look after you. Sometimes I even bring my little boy. And I know that, apart from me, you don't have very many visitors. I bring you sweets, peel fruit for you and feed you, from time to time read to you, change the TV channels for you; I tell you what's new and talk about my family, my husband, and my son. It's hard for you to talk so we don't chat very much, which is why I often take a photo album out of my bag and tell you where, when, and with whom the different pictures were taken, on family vacations, anniversaries, trips. I'm not afraid of you anymore. I'm not even

afraid of your eyes—which became cloudy after the accident and
lost all their light. Also not long after your accident, my pregnancy stabilized, and everything turned out well.

When I'm at home alone and some strange anxiety seizes me
and I feel like I'm slipping into the abyss, there's just one thought
that courses through my body: you are not doing so badly, I
tell myself; on the contrary, things are going quite well for you.
Then I rummage through the drawer and choose a few photos,
take some fruit from the fridge, and maybe a pudding or yogurt,
pick some flowers in the garden, put on some nice clothes and
makeup, and go to see you.

A Kind of Syndrome

THIS TIME SHE grew restless while they were fixing supper. She broke a nail chopping the garlic and swore loudly. They sat down at the table and when she looked at the fish's eye she felt queasy. After the first few bites she started criticizing him: the fish was too salty and he'd used ordinary vegetable oil for the salad dressing instead of the cold-pressed olive oil. Which wasn't healthy. And it didn't go with scorpionfish.

She poked at her food more or less disgustedly and barely ate any of it.

He knew the signs well. He accepted every criticism without protest, each time apologizing—he had mixed up the bottles by mistake, he said—and cautiously watched her every movement. He offered to clear the table and do the dishes himself. While he was stacking the dirty plates, she got up and went into the living room, flopped down on the sofa, picked up the television remote, and started clicking through the channels.

She stopped at a British sitcom and the next moment jumped to a channel where commercials were playing: *I had no idea what they could do for me, I'm free and easy all through the day, every day of the month, frozen pizza, Norwegian hake smothered in thin tomato wedges and sliced potato, all wrapped in aluminum foil, just stick it in the oven and bake for fifty minutes, with not a drop of oil . . . after thirty, your skin starts to age so you need to take especially good care of your body with liposome creams . . . the most natural color rinses for your hair, so you'll be just the way he likes you . . .*

He wiped his hands on the red and white checkered dish

towel, went cautiously into the living room, and sat down in the
armchair next to her. She switched to a Hong Kong film that
was dubbed in German. She seemed to be attentively following
the excited gestures of some Asian prostitutes who had been
chased off a squalid double-decker Chinese junk by the police.
He glanced a few times at the gray and black ceramic clock
above the TV and, when the hands were approaching eight-
thirty, asked in a nervous, cautious voice: "Aren't we going to
watch *The Graduate*?"

She didn't answer.

"It's twenty past eight. I think the movie has started."

"But we've seen it twice already. Anyway, can't you see I'm already
watching a movie?" she told him coldly, without looking at him.

"What, this movie? You don't even know what it's about. And
you don't understand German!"

"Oh, I don't know what it's about, do I?" She looked at him
with hatred. "And I can't understand it because I don't know
German? Unlike you: the polyglot, the intellectual, or should I
say, the genius?"

He got up from the armchair, went into the kitchen, and
opened the refrigerator. She just stared at the Chinese junks
and the policemen, who were now draping the body of a young,
dark-haired hooker in a sheet of black plastic.

She brought the ring finger of her left hand to her lips and,
like a mouse, nibbled at her broken polished nail with her teeth.

How is it that some women are able to maintain such manicured nails without them ever chipping or breaking? She looked
at the half-closed door between the living room and the kitchen.
She knew he was standing in front of the illuminated packages
of cheese and cold cuts, jars of tomato sauce, cartons of juice
and milk.

"Just get your damn OJ already and shut the fridge!" she
screamed in the direction of the kitchen.

A detective was writing something in a notebook; then he
pulled a phone out of his brown leather jacket and fired off a few
words into it in German-dubbed Chinese. She muted the television and listened to the sounds of the refrigerator door being

closed and liquid being poured into a glass, which he then drank slowly in long gulps. He went into the bathroom and turned on the water in the tub. She clicked even faster through the channels and thought how she'd like to follow him in there, plug in the blow dryer, and toss it into the bathtub.

On Channel 5 they were showing a miniseries she had seen a few months earlier on Channel 9. About a man and a woman and all their problems . . .

"Honey, are you coming in after me?" he called from the bathroom.

She didn't answer. She switched to MTV, where the young dark-haired host was cracking jokes. Nothing ever changed, not even on television. It was all the same a week ago, a month ago, a year ago.

She got up from the sofa, went to the liquor cabinet and poured herself two fingers of whiskey. For three days she has felt as if she is walking around in a big balloon filled with tepid liquid, which washes over her brain and drenches every thought before she is able to utter it.

"Honey," he called, "I'm waiting for you."

She drank the whiskey in small sips and stared at the ceiling. She recognized this feeling of calm before catastrophe. It was probably like whitewater rafting. At first you're tossed this way and that, only barely missing the dangerous sharp rocks that threaten to pierce the sensitive inflated rubber; then the river slowly grows calmer, there's no more foam on the surface, and you drift wavelessly forward. And when the water is most calm, you hear thundering in the distance, but by then it's too late. The current gets stronger, you're moving faster and faster over the surface, the sound of thundering water gets louder and louder, and you know there is a waterfall in front of you and no way to escape it.

"C'mon, dear, I'm waiting for you. I'm all ready," she heard from the bedroom.

So am I, she thought, and made her way towards the saccharine voice.

He was lying on the bed wearing nothing but white boxer

shorts. He seemed rather satisfied. She looked at his skinny, scrawny body and the hand that was stroking his distended abdomen. He was one of those men who never gained weight in the face or limbs, but only in the belly, which as the years went by was growing like leavened bread on his ever more flaccid body.

"What do you want?" she asks him.

"You know what I want. I want you."

For months now, his body has revolted her. When he touches her, she shudders, like before a thunderstorm when she's getting out of the car and her hand grazes the metal door.

He runs his hand down his sallow belly to the undershorts and pulls out his erect penis.

"C'mon, honey. Take it."

She can't remember when it started. First, it was the way he walked that bothered her. Too cautiously, with no self-confidence. Whenever he approached her, slightly bent forward, he reminded her of men with clasped hands going up to the altar to receive the Host. He would sit with his legs twisted together and his feet usually turned inwards. And when she sat on the bed dressed only in undergarments, he would kneel in front of her, open her legs, and gaze at her genitalia like a child in front of a Christmas tree. Completely helpless with anticipation of some delightful surprise. What could be hiding in there, in that present tied up with a crimson bow? But perhaps the gift is not for you, since you haven't been good this year; on the contrary, you've been disgusting, so no gifts! As punishment!

"C'mon now, sit on it. You know what to do . . ."

He lifted himself off the bed and wanted to touch her as she stood by the door.

"No," she told him, coldly and decisively.

When they first met, none of these things had bothered her. Maybe she didn't notice them. Or maybe he was different and she was different. She had thought he was very intelligent, with a successful academic career ahead of him, but mainly, he was incredibly gentle. Even after they started living together, he never demanded any special effort from her when it came to the housework. He even helped with the chores. When he had time. When he wasn't preparing a paper for a symposium. When he wasn't writing a book.

A woman comes by once a week to clean their rented single-story house in a quiet part of town. The furnishings are both aesthetic and functional. The spacious living room adjoining the kitchen, the eco-friendly solid-wood furniture in the bedroom, his light-filled office and bookshelves, an attractive room for guests, the bathroom—everything is designed, as they say in magazines, in a simple, enlightened, contemporary style, with details that lend character to the space. The sideboard, cabinets, and windowsills are adorned with all sorts of knickknacks from different parts of the world, some houseplants, lots of pictures, dried flowers—all pleasant and homey, yet also very tasteful.

Sometimes they go out in the evening to dinner or for drinks. More and more, however, she has been going out without him. To the movies, the theater, art openings. Or just going out. He never asks too many questions or even criticizes her. But the next morning at breakfast, when she has come home late, he is silent, more or less, and looks at her with the sad eyes of an abandoned Cocker Spaniel. Damn it, say something already! she wishes on such mornings. Yes, I went to a movie with one of my girlfriends, but I already told you that; so go ahead and ask me something else. The movie ended at ten, and then, yes, we did go to a bar and we stayed there until two in the morning. Or maybe we didn't; maybe my girlfriend wasn't even my girlfriend; maybe it was a man I just happened to meet at the movies, by chance, a man who is not as genteel as you, and even better, he doesn't have any academic knowledge about the human psyche or some refined sensibility about women's equality. So ask me something, damn it. Do what real men do; shove me against the wall and shout in my face, Where the hell did you go last night, you slut! But no, you hate violence, you disdain aggressive behavior, and instead you cultivate some humane, humanistic attitude and keep your mouth shut. You're so vapid I'll go crazy!

"Come here, honey. I love you."

All this babble about love and caring and similar nonsense—it completely drives her up the wall. He's the same way with his female students: always understanding, full of advice, lenient when he gives them back their term papers.

"I'm not feeling well," she says.

"What's wrong? Do you maybe have premenstrual syndrome?"

She tips the glass to her mouth and downs the alcohol. And goes on staring at him. No, he doesn't ask if she's irritable because of her period, or just happens to feel like that, or if maybe something else could be wrong—like everything, for example! No, he's an academic, so he has to ask if there's maybe some syndrome behind it. Maybe premenstrual syndrome!

"No. I'm not coming over there. But you know what I *am* going to do? I'm going to explode, that's what!"

"You're right, honey. I'm sorry, I forgot. I should have known. Of course. You always have problems this time of the month. That's OK, I won't force you. Come here and I'll just stroke your back."

Asshole, she thinks. He'll just stroke my back! If he was a real man, which he will never be, he would jump out of bed, grab me, push me into the sheets, and give me a good fucking. Instead, he's going to try to understand me, to comfort me. God, I should never have married him.

When she was twenty-one, he was a young, thirty-year-old teaching assistant. With gentle movements and trusting eyes, he conducted the seminar in psychopathology and sociopathy. He was a peaceful man with none of the intellectual male swagger she knew in boys. Yes, he was already a man when she met him, something quite different from the kids she went to class with or met by chance, incidentally, around town. They were either incurable dreamers with their mouths full of ideas they had not yet realized and never would, or ruthless macho careerists, who today had climbed to leading positions in their fields.

But he was different. He knew what he wanted but didn't push people around because of it, and what's more, he was willing to understand women. He knew how to listen to women, or at least he gave that impression. He taught her favorite subject,

or maybe it was her favorite because he taught it. But over time
everything had changed, and she had come to detest both psychology and him. What she wanted most was to pack her things
and leave. For good.

He got up from the bed and came to her in the devout pose
of the understanding man.

"Everything will be all right," he told her in a voice that at
every fourth syllable usually crackled and sputtered like a broken speaker.

"That's what you think. Nothing will ever be right again!"
she snarled.

"Honey,"—he patted her lightly—"why don't we go somewhere this weekend? You'll see; you'll feel better in nature . . ."

"Nature? That's all I need to drive me insane!"

"You spend too much time indoors. Sunshine and fresh air
will definitely relax you. And also . . . well . . . I think it'd be
good if you gave up smoking."

"Oh, you think so, do you? What else is there for me to do in
this house? Smoking is simply choosing the bad over the worse."

Better a cigarette in her mouth than his dick, she thinks, and
even smiles at the idea. How many times has she felt like she
was going to vomit her half-digested food over that thing of his?
Maybe there was a time when she actually didn't mind the taste
of his semen in her mouth, but now even the thought of touching it with her lips makes her feverish. As if his bodily fluid was a
concentration of all his arduous groveling after success, the bitter
blows he swallowed obediently and unprotestingly as he tried
to make a career for himself (which all eventually paid off), and
especially that vapid universal humanism of his, which makes
him seem like such a noble, intelligent, understanding person.

"You hurt my feelings, you know."

What fucking sensitivity! I hurt his feelings! Well, you ain't
seen nothing yet! What she should really do is bite the thing off;
then he wouldn't have the strength for such ball-less blandness.
He's got no balls, that's exactly it—he never did have any. He
just sits there on the bed, hunched over, gazing at the floor, as if
he is trying to read his fate in the floorboards. It's only going to

get worse, she thinks—nothing as smooth and polished as the bedroom's oak floor.

"I've made a decision. From now on we're sleeping apart—me in the bedroom, you in the office. That will be best for both of us."

"Don't you love me anymore?" he asks, his voice breaking.

If only he wouldn't squeak like that. She had always been attracted to men with deep voices, but then she went and married some squeaky intellectual.

"Don't you love me?" he repeats.

She knows he is only asking this so she'll say: Oh, you know I love you, but I'm getting my period and I'm in a foul mood. You understand that; you're a psychologist. You know about such things. You're an internationally recognized authority. I am so lucky to have you by my side, and with your academic knowledge and, most of all, with your love, you can help me. No, she intentionally will not reply. She'll ignore the question. Deliberately.

She takes the glass into the living room, pours herself another three fingers of whiskey, drains it in a single gulp, and collapses in the armchair. In an instant, a wave of heat courses through her body. There is a burning in her throat and stomach and she feels like she has to vomit, so she holds her breath and covers her mouth with her hand.

He puts on his gray and white striped pajamas, follows her into the living room, and gently strokes her hair.

"Drinking's not good for you; it only makes it worse."

"Lots of things aren't good for me, but I do them anyway. Like living with you, for instance; that's what's really bad for me, more than any booze or cigarettes."

The muscles on his face wince. He turns around and goes back to the bedroom. Now, probably with his jaw clenched, he's getting sheets and pillows out of the linen cabinet. He has decided to spend the night alone, as far as possible from her impudence, her insults, her lack of appreciation. Most women would appreciate living with a successful, tolerant man. But not her. Nothing can make her happy. But her husband understands these attacks. Tomorrow he won't even mention her hysterical outbursts, her crude, vile insults about how everything about him utterly and unreservedly repulses her. In fact, he has written an entire stack of articles, and several books, on the subject of women's dark moods.

She sees him carrying the bedding past the living room and into the office. So he's making up the daybed and then he'll pick up some book. No, nothing in the world will throw the scholarly professor off course or keep him from his research. Or ruin his career. So let him make his bed; let him lie in it, and stick his nose in that fucking book. She will wait; she'll wait just long enough for him to read about three pages, until he forgets, at least to some degree, about her and the psychological difficulties at home, and then at just the right moment she'll burst into his office and give him hell.

She pours herself another whiskey, and when she drinks it down in a few swallows, the living room starts to reel off its hinges. She feels nauseous. The food she ate two hours earlier is rising in her stomach. She'd really like to slam her body against the wall once and for all, one single blow, so her guts spill out across the cool plaster surface, and that would be the end of everything. Forever.

She goes into the bathroom and leans over the toilet. She feels like she has to throw up but can't. She shoves her index and middle fingers into her esophagus and imagines it's his penis in her mouth, tasting of urine and stale semen. Her digestive tract begin to vibrate, and with a few convulsions she retches up the undigested food, which is drenched in alcohol. She turns on the cold water and bends over the sink. Her head is spinning unbearably. She is extremely nauseous. As she washes her face, she feels the abdominal cramps. She opens the medicine cabinet, takes out three pain pills, and swallows them with a few gulps of water from the faucet. She looks at herself in the mirror and notices the red capillaries around her eyes, which always burst when she pukes. I am horrible, she thinks. And I look horrible too.

She goes to his office and opens the door. He is lying on the made-up daybed, reading. He does not even look at her.

"So, what, now you're offended?" she snaps at him.

He says nothing and turns away, as if she is not in the room. His face is somber, the corners of his mouth drooping—let her see that she's hurt him. She feels like picking up the chair and smashing that offended face with it.

She leans against the door jamb and barks at him:

"I suppose you're reading about premenstrual syndromes? Or maybe that's the thesis of one of your gifted girl-students, who draws her motivation for psychology from her dripping pussy?"

"You're disgusting! Vulgar!"

"Vulgar, am I? A woman who is dangerous to be seen with in your academic circles, at those pseudo-intellectual dinners where you professors try to outdo each other, bragging about the number of journals you subscribe to, which symposia you participated in last year, how many of your articles have been translated in foreign publications, how many copies of your insipid books have been published! You're embarrassed to show up at these dinners with a person who personifies the very pathology you write about in those articles, a person who happens to be your wife. A person who for some reason can't be included in your worldly conversations about boring incidents with lost luggage at airports, about multiculturalism, which to you more or less means exotic cuisines, about the services at different hotels, about world-famous places that she knows mainly from books, about the way things are done around the world. Because, of course, she lives a different kind of life. A more domestic life. Because she hardly ever travels, or travels only when she goes to some symposium with him. As the wife of the esteemed professor. Where she is never herself but merely and solely his wife. This is Professor So-and-So, doctor of psychology, who teaches at Such-and-Such University, and the lady next to him, why, that lady is his wife. First name only, no surname, since we know that already. And what field might she be in? What might the lady do? She works at the university. Oh, is she a professor too? No, nothing like that. Nothing so very important. She just works there. In the library. Oh, how interesting—that's the usual polite comment when she tells them this, and she reads in their faces that this is about the same as being a secretary, a housekeeper, a wife. Nothing more, just his wife. 'Do you have any children?' they ask. 'No, not yet.' 'Oh, no? Not yet?' is what comes next, and she knows that since she doesn't have a university career and is already thirty, there's no real reason for them not to have children. But what if they can't have them? Maybe she can't have them. What if she doesn't even want children? Well, what have you got to say to that, since you know so goddamn much about everything?"

"What things you get into your head! Nobody has anything against you. People like you; they think you're nice."

"Sure, people like people who don't pose any threat. They think they're nice. Not the least bit dangerous. And they never remember their names—'Do forgive me, but what's your name again?' And the next time you meet them, they feel like they've seen you somewhere before but can't quite place you, let alone remember your name."

"Which people? What people are you talking about?"

"People like you!"

"You really are ill," he tells her, without lifting his eyes from the paper he's reading.

"Ill, am I? Hah! A failed, unfortunate case in your psychological career, is that it? Instead of crowing about all the writing you've done, why don't you come clean and confess? In your home life, you can't even handle just one woman—let alone satisfy her—no matter how much you go around dispensing wisdom to the world!"

"How can you be so nasty?"

"Living with you is destroying my life."

"It's you who's destroying it. You didn't want to continue with your studies. You don't want to have children. You have only yourself to blame."

"It would be a crime to have children with a man like you! If I had been with somebody else, somebody less conceited, I would probably have finished my doctorate by now, instead of working in the library, where nearsighted girls take out books and go to exams only because they don't have the guts to go to bed with the professor. If they can't fuck their professor, then they'll just have to debate him in class. But first, of course, they have to study up on the subject, because they don't want to give him the impression they're not smart enough. They excite you, don't they, with their wide-eyed, admiring gazes and docile voices? But you tell yourself: I'm a married man with a strong moral character. But when they're cramming their books in their bags and putting their papers away in their folders, you check out their perky tits, and when they're leaving the classroom, you stare at their legs and their asses. You are such a prick! I'd rather hear that you had actually screwed one of these girls, instead of boasting to your colleagues about your fine, upstanding professorial attitude. That's right! If you were a real man, you would have laid one of them a long time ago, but as it is, you're always telling me, 'Honey, I'm not saying they're not cute and attractive, but they're just so young! They're so very young!'—Unlike me, is that it?—'But you know I love you. You know I'm faithful to you. I would never cheat on you.' Sure, you're faithful, but not because you don't desire them, not because you don't want them more than you want me. You say you don't mind the fat deposits on my thighs, don't mind that my breasts have sagged over the past ten years, even though I've never given birth— which means for no good reason! You don't mind my ass, which, to put it mildly, is losing its shape. But that doesn't mean you don't notice any of these things, not by a long shot. 'Your body is changing over time,' you say. 'And that's natural,' you tell me. 'It's not important, because I love you just the same as always.' And you're faithful to me, but not because the others don't attract you—you're faithful because you married me. You behave like a typical faggot. Because that's what you are!"

He does not respond. He goes on staring at the paper in his hand and pretends to be reading. She'd like nothing better than to pour whiskey and gasoline on that paper of his and light a cigarette over it. His female students would snivel into their notebooks, while his fellow professors, some of them, would be downright happy—thank god there's one less academic Rottweiler to worry about. His sappy, bearded face would be framed in a black border, and some colleague of his would give up an hour of his time to write that goddamn obituary, about how our dear colleague was overtaken by death at the peak of his career, et cetera, et cetera.

She feels nauseous again and goes into the bathroom. As she is bending over the toilet, she gets so dizzy she has to shut her eyes while she pukes; otherwise, she would collapse on the cool blue and white tiles. She drinks a few gulps of cold water from the faucet, splashes water on her face, and, sliding her hands along the walls, staggers back to the office. He is still reading.

"So what page are you on, anyway?"

"What is it you want from me?"

"Instead of pretending to read, you might at least finish a conversation with me for once!"

"It's impossible to have a conversation with you," he replies calmly.

"Is that another one of your scientific findings? So then why am I able to talk to other people? I guess it's because they're not as fucking small-minded as you are! My finding is that the more uneducated a man is—and by this, of course, I don't mean unintelligent—the more I find him attractive. Like one of the young workmen who were painting the library the other day. A young guy, around twenty-five. I felt like asking him to help me carry a stack of books to the basement. And then, just as he was putting them on the shelf, I would go up to him from behind, slip my hand over his neck and beneath his shirt, down his strong, smooth, firm chest, his flat stomach, and then with my right hand I'd unbuckle his belt and pull out his hot, throbbing dick—I could tell right away he liked me, he liked me a lot!—then I'd push him up against the radiator, crouch down, take him in my mouth, and we'd fuck and fuck like I never have with you! I was a fool not to do it, and now I regret it. I really should indulge myself like that from time to time; maybe then it would be easier to live with you."

She lurched forward and barely caught herself on the desk by the door. She closed her eyes; the alcohol was pushing its way up from her stomach through her esophagus and into her mouth.

"Can't you see how drunk you are? That's been happening a lot recently. You need to get some help."

"Hah! How very awful! A woman, and she's drunk! Disgusting, isn't it? The doctor of psychology lives on orange juice, while she, his wife, loads up on booze and cigarettes. They make quite a pair! Any other man would long ago have found a gun and shot himself, or if not himself, then her. But not you. You won't do anything that might threaten your career. You'd rather just calmly ignore the whole situation and go on studying the human psyche and writing your fucking books. Why destroy your life over a woman like that? Not worth it, eh? At least she's not. Maybe some other woman might be. But not her—not me! So you just keep clawing your way up the system, grabbing whatever you can get. And hoping nobody notices that you've got a woman living with you who you'd like to strangle with those soft, manicured hands of yours, which barely know how to change a light bulb, let alone repair a washing machine or blow dryer, because that's already getting into cutting-edge science. There are other people for that sort of thing, people whose IQs aren't high enough, whose family backgrounds aren't solid enough or wealthy enough for them to be accepted by the system or be of any use to it at all. So it spits them out into auto repair shops and construction sites where they build institutions of higher learning. You're nothing but a plain old system-climber with no fucking balls—bad in bed and just a teensy bit better in the classroom."

"Now I've really had enough of you!" He tossed the paper aside and screamed, "Get out of my office!"

"So you're ordering me around now, are you? Telling me where I can and can't go in my own house?"

"Sometimes I just want to belt you one!"

"But you never do, do you? Because you haven't got the balls. Because you're not, shall we say, primitive and vulgar like me. Because you're so very educated and repress all those negative, violent passions in yourself, so they can't possibly threaten your utopian civilization project, is that it?"

He jumped off the daybed, pushed her out of the room, and slammed the door.

"You're a wimp! Just a plain old wimp!" she screamed.

She felt the blood trickling down her thigh. She went into the bathroom and undressed, stepped into the shower, gripped the metal bar attached to the wall, and as she showered, with great effort tried to keep her balance. Resting against the cool ceramic tiles, she stood under the running water for a few minutes and gazed into the emptiness. He wasn't coming after her. He doesn't want to see her like that, in such a state. She disgusts *him*, too. And it's true: these attacks, which sneak up on her with no warning, are hardly rare; they have been happening quite a lot this past year.

She shut off the water, wrapped herself in a big orange towel, and, leaning against the wall, tried to dry herself off. Standing naked in front of the mirror, she examines her thirty-year-old body. It's repulsive. Not even she can say when the changes started. It's like her flesh is drooping from her skeleton. When she's in clothes, she doesn't look at all like she's gained weight; in fact, people generally think she's thin, but naked as she is now, she looks really unattractive. Cellulite is collecting on her ass and thighs, and the same is true of her stomach; her shapeless breasts hang loosely like empty plastic bags; on her face, her first wrinkles are braiding themselves below her eyes, and around her mouth too. Now, whenever she combs her once thick, dark brown hair, she discovers more and more gray. A few months ago this made her so angry she went to the hairdresser that same afternoon and had him cut her hair really short and dye it an even darker brown, almost black. She is afraid. When she sees signs of aging on her body, she is terrified of death. She is very good at noticing them on other people, especially women. When she first sees a woman, even a young woman, she very carefully, minutely, scrutinizes the woman's face and then her entire body. She looks for the woman's strong points and, especially, her flaws, after which she tries to guess her age and, if she can, confirm it. It makes her furious when a woman hypocritically conceals her age, but what really infuriates her are the women who look younger than their years despite living an unhealthy lifestyle. Is it expensive cosmetics? Good genes? And she cannot understand those few women who never really bother too much about aging or the body's changes, who don't care about such things—or who at least put on a convincing show that they don't. Nobody will ever convince her that aging is something natural and can even be beautiful. On the contrary, aging is disintegration, is dying; it can even be a very long dying.

Slowly and carefully she takes a pair of fresh underwear from the cabinet, struggles to get them on, and places a panty liner in them. Waves of hot and cold wash over her. She breaks into loud sobs. There will come a time when she won't be able to stand it anymore. She'll have herself sterilized, but first she'll get a lobotomy so she doesn't change her mind. She'll have everything taken out of her—uterus, ovaries, brain—everything. Clinging to the wall, she makes her way to the bedroom. She falls on the bed and cries. I can't do it anymore, she keeps repeating; one day I just won't be able to stand it anymore.

She is crying even louder now and wincing from the abdominal pains that are contorting her body, until finally the mixture of alcohol and pills begins shrouding her in darkness and slowly she calms down. The cramps in her abdomen subside. If she shuts her eyes, the wooziness isn't as terrible and she no longer feels like she has to throw up. She lies there with her eyes closed and takes deep breaths. She hopes that sleep will wash over her like a wave and she'll never again swim to the surface.

That everything will instantly disappear—the house, her husband, her past, her future—and she won't leave any trace of herself behind.

If only he had slapped me, at least once, she thinks and feels her body sinking into somewhere without memory. Not even his presence would bother her now. Not even what he would say to her. Nothing at all would matter to her. If he was next to me, she thinks, she would take him by the hand and maybe he would kiss her hair and tell her he loved her. He would pull down the blanket and tenderly stroke her back.

But it doesn't matter, she repeats to herself. She has already gone over the dam in her inflatable rubber raft and reached the foamy surface, which is slowly becoming still. For a few weeks life will again flow along its mundane course. Orderly . . . Almost without incident . . . Ordinary . . . Almost peaceful . . .

Malfunction

YOU NEVER NOTICE me secretly observing you. From the living room, stretched out on the sofa, I watch you in the reflection of the open glass door as you stand naked in the bathroom and, leaning towards the mirror, use your fingers to inspect something, probably wrinkles, on your face; then you take a step back and examine your body from different angles. I could get up, slip quietly out of the living room, and appear suddenly in front of you. I could ask you a question, one of the questions I already know the answer to, but I don't. I know you don't know that I know everything. That is my power and my advantage over you, who have no idea that we are already on the battlefield, who are still wondering when to declare war and how to arrange your forces so you suffer as little as possible, do as little damage as possible to yourself and to everything you hope and intend to hold on to from the family, which you know means that you must be considerate of me.

When you decide the time is right, you will tell me a story. Probably about how you still love me—that you love the children with all your heart and, because of the children and everything we have been through together, you still, in a way, also love me. But love—and you know this, you'll say to me, you're an intelligent woman—has not been in our bed for years and no longer flutters in the morning when you come into the bathroom and I'm drying off my body. No, it's been a long time since there's been any love between us. Don't tell me you haven't felt this way too, you'll tell me; tell me instead that for a long time you haven't felt all that much for me either. It's true. I haven't felt anything in a long time. For a long time we have been, not strangers, certainly, but coworkers, employed at the same firm, the firm we call our family. We are business partners, bound together by the need to coordinate the purchase of raw materials and the payment of bills, to organize the transport of the children to school and to their afterschool activities, and to arrange family events for relatives and friends. We are longtime colleagues, who know each other very well, who when they have finished their work obligations wish only to get away as soon as possible. To go home? Of course not home, but somewhere it doesn't feel too familiar and too strange at the same time, somewhere everything isn't saturated with that casualness which when two people live together ultimately pulls them apart. Where everything isn't permeated with that domesticity which comes with the years, comes even after a few months, when you stop feeling ashamed in front of each other not only of how your body looks but also of your morning breath and sweat after a night on the town, traces of menstrual blood on the bed sheets, the occasional fecal stain on the underwear, and when the other person's body becomes so very close to you that exploring it loses all allure. Everything that initially seemed like awkward intimacy suffused with lust and feelings of shame, becomes calcified, through years of being discovered and accepted, into something unbearably foreign. Twenty-one years ago, the first time I entered your small, rented apartment, I flushed the water in the toilet so you wouldn't hear the tinkle of my urine, and a few weeks later I was slipping my tampons into a plastic bag prepared for the purpose, which I put away in my purse just so I wouldn't leave any organic traces at your place. No, back then, we had not yet slept together; back then there was an extremely powerful desire between our bodies and many, many words. But later, my smell, which you said never failed to drive you wild, and your touch, which electrified me even before you actually touched me, slowly, over time, became routine for us. There were still words between us, but between the words there gradually appeared meaningful emphases, suspicious pauses and, between the sentences, wounded silences.

When we began, we could not imagine that one fine morning I would wake up and not desire to touch you or that you would turn away from me at night. I know that I truly loved you, maybe not more intensely than I'd loved anyone before but certainly more maturely than I had ever loved. This was not like first love, when desire beats only through smells and touches; later, in one's more mature but still young years, love is also inhabited by content, and by plans for the future. When, one warm and drizzly morning in June, we were walking through the stone-paved streets of a small, old town and caught our reflection in a store window—this is us now, and we are going to live our lives together—we were absolutely convinced, I definitely was, that that was how it would be. To the very end? To death, of course. But that drizzly June morning death was unimaginably far away; that day, there was no death in our life. No fear of death either, nothing that could threaten the project of our shared life.

There was no gradual decay of any sort, or so it seemed. Perhaps there were periods, good and worse, but in fact it was never entirely bad. Tense, sometimes, but back then we always found a reason: moving into our first apartment, moving to our second, bigger apartment, and later into our house, and in between, buying new cars, changing jobs, having our first child, then our second—these were all transitional stages, we thought, which would pass and then we would be as we were that June morning in the old square of a small provincial town. I don't know which of us first grew tired of the other, but I was probably the first to show it. I don't know. Sometimes I just wanted you to leave me alone; sometimes I said I did and desired the opposite; sometimes I didn't say anything and desired only your touch. And often I had the feeling that you did not desire me; that it was simply about the demands of your body and it didn't matter who was lying next to you. More than a few times I would regularize my breathing to make you think I was already asleep, and meanwhile I would wait, perhaps for something to move within me or for you to approach me in some different way—wait until I truly desired you and you truly desired me.

Nothing moved. And nothing changed. Except the women.

The occasional, usually one-time affairs. Whenever I suspected something, I sighed with relief. I knew that for a while, at least, you would stop putting pressure on me. And yet I hated you, because I didn't have what they had—the something in them that attracted you—and I hated myself especially, because I couldn't see in you what they saw, the thing that excited them. It's different, I know, with her. As far as I can make out, it has been going on for at least a year. I have never met her. She has black, more or less shoulder-length hair—I found just such a black hair on the front seat of the car, and even a few times on the back seat. She is undoubtedly younger than me; I know this from her perfume, which is the sort that women my age think of as aggressively cheap. She is undoubtedly not married and very likely has no children. Otherwise, how could you pull off during the week and even on weekends, with no regular schedule, all those business dinners and unexpected long lunches with your associates? I don't hate her; on the contrary, I envy her: she sees something in you that I haven't noticed for a very long time. And I am afraid, because I don't notice it in other men either. When I see a man who is considered attractive, I want something in my benumbed body to perk up and start glowing, but I am like a monolith; between me and the world there stretches an opaque shield, through which neither lust nor arousing smell can pass, but only, if anything, occasionally stench and repulsion. It wasn't you who didn't try hard enough; for a time, at least, you tried no less than I did, and in just as wrong a way. But you are a man with a life force driven by lust, and sadly, I am no different from those women for whom the only thing keeping them alive are their cold, dried out, and all too often vengeful thoughts.

My one attempt to wrench myself out of this vise-like numbness was a farce. I felt stupid, not because I had, as the expression goes, cheated on my husband, but because I had slept with a body that was not my husband's. I did everything that was expected: lust, passion, and some of those positions I'd seen in films. But I felt nothing—not lust, not passion, not guilt, not desire to do the thing again with him even one more time. And maybe it was because of my playacting, because I gave the impression of keeping everything under control, that he liked it so much. If I had spilled my emotions out in front of him, he would surely have grown tired of me after only a few encounters, while I never grew tired of him, since from the start I felt nothing for him.

Your leaving will be a relief for me too. Touching your body makes me uncomfortable; it's like touching an enormous living tissue. But I don't want you to leave as the winner, with me left behind as the loser, in this house with two nearly adult children. I cannot easily, just like that, put aside two decades of us staying together, when I didn't leave, first of all because of the children, but also because this isn't something one does just like that, for no obvious, real reason, and because I believed that sooner or later something would change. When you finally start dropping hints and then tell me straight out what you mean to do with your life, with your new life, I will trigger that sense of guilt in you: I don't know what you're talking about. It never even occurred to me. I thought we were fine; I thought everything was OK. We've both been so extremely busy, and when it comes to husband-and-wife matters, well, we often just didn't have the time or the energy. This will surprise you because you think things will be easier. It's so patently obvious that you are bored with me and I am bored with you. But why, of the two of us, who have been together for over twenty years, should I be the only one to suffer? Suffer not because you are leaving, but because you are managing to do something that slipped out of my grasp a long time ago: you are leaving into the future, while I am trapped in the present and unable to make even the slightest move out of it. No, it won't be easy. For the next few years we will be meeting each other in courtrooms, paying lawyers and appraisers. Because there is something I want to hear from your lips, the only thing I do not actually know: What was the malfunction in our life together that made us year after year, each on our own separate, parallel paths, keep glancing over at the other covertly, waiting for one of us to finally make up his or her mind? What was it that seemed, on that distant June morning as we walked over the wet pavement of a provincial town, so very impossible and as far away as death? I want to hear an admission from you, that it was not just me who failed, but that you failed too, and, especially, that I am not cold by nature but something has made me cold, something that wove its cocoon between us, some creature which you yourself have managed to escape from but which is still sucking on me, still feeding on me. I am not in a hurry to get anywhere; I have nowhere to go. I have plenty of time, until the moment I die—and death, as on that drizzly morning in June, seems unimaginably far away. Death, after all, can only squeeze the life out of people who risk something, who before it's too late make up their minds—even if they do so in fear, regardless of what pain might come—in order to survive. But with things that are dead, with people who are alive despite having died many years ago, it can be a long time—sometimes, often, a very, very long time—before they fall apart and finally decompose.

More than a Woman

"WHO IS THAT woman?" I wondered in amazement the first time I saw you. As I was returning to my chair with my paper and spotted you in the back rows. No, you had not been there before my talk. I would definitely have noticed you.

You were exactly what I fantasized about. That woman without a face who, piece by piece, whenever I closed my eyes and held my dick in my hand, would touch me out of the darkness—with her full lips, with the look in her green, angled eyes, with her long eyebrows and high forehead, covered by a shaggy mass of light blond hair. With the separate parts of her face and body, which, until I met you, I could never join into a single whole. You were that woman, and it was better with her, in fact, than with any of the women I actually did it with. And there were plenty of those, as I told you once when you asked. No, I did not keep that a secret from you.

I don't need to worry about becoming more closely attached, or even falling in love with any of those women. That simply doesn't happen to me. And with you, too, I did not desire love. It would have been too complicated, impossible even. We live hundreds of miles apart, in different cities, different countries, and in fact we do different things.

As soon as my talk was over, our eyes met, and the language of looks slipped smoothly and quickly into words. In our first conversation, you told me you were reporting on the symposium for one of your local newspapers, which naturally I had never heard of. I invited you to join me for a late lunch, and you said that first you needed to drop off your luggage.

"I can go with you to your hotel," I suggested, and almost regretted it. The hotel wasn't even a real hotel but a rundown guesthouse—true, it wasn't far from the cultural center where the symposium was taking place, and with rooms at fifteen euros a night it was surely the cheapest, and shabbiest, hotel in the entire area. The moment I set foot in it I felt uncomfortable, and for good reason. The corpulent man at the desk, with a lewd smile bordered by a thin black mustache, was speaking through the gaps in his teeth in some Slavic language as he handed a room key to a vulgarly costumed young woman, who was then followed up the stairs by a man of late middle age. As you were counting out coins (the receptionist demanded the price of one night's stay in advance as a security deposit), you laid your passport on the counter and, next to it, your return Ryanair ticket for seven and a half pounds. Before then I had no idea such cheap flights existed.

"You take care of your luggage, and I'll wait for you down here," I said and the very next moment felt like a complete idiot. As you were struggling up three flights of narrow stairs with your heavy, dark green suitcase, and the receptionist, leaning on the counter, leafed through a magazine, I stood there like a Doric column just inside the door of this hourly-rate fleabag hotel waiting for a woman who half an hour later—as you descended those rickety stairs in the murky light, your hair just washed and still damp—looked like Leni Riefenstahl in the film *Das blaue Licht*.

"That newspaper of yours can't afford to put you up in a decent hotel?" I asked. You replied that you weren't actually a regular employee but worked freelance for the paper, and that when they finally paid you, they would cover at least part of your travel expenses. Of course I couldn't allow you to sleep a single night in that flophouse. After supper, I drove you to my apartment and the next day we went back there for your suitcase. You stayed three days with me, until the end of the symposium, and after that you visited me two more times. At your own expense. You refused to let me pay for your flights.

Never had I met a person about whom I was so convinced

that despite her obvious talent she had not made even a normal career for herself and was ruining her life. When you told me you had written a few things, I asked around a little. Nobody, absolutely nobody, had heard of you; nobody could tell me what exactly it was you did or how you made your living. OK, I guess you write, but lots of people write without anybody but themselves ever seeing what they have written. I know it must be harder for you since not many people read or understand the language you write in. But when I checked, your name doesn't carry any symbolic weight even in your own country, and I surprised myself when, in a conversation with a good friend, I actually said this.

From the outset I realized I could never be in a serious relationship with a woman from a place like the country you come from. My friends and acquaintances—despite their public condemnations of racism and xenophobia, their assertions that they are feminists (the men too), their support for LGBT rights, and their openness to difference—would never really accept you. They would be polite and friendly with you at first, but this friendliness would mostly be about curiosity, reduced merely to anecdotes from yet another former communist country in transition and its culinary delights. But here in the West, we have had our fill of sociopolitical exotica; over the past ten years, far too many people from your region have settled in our country and, frankly, we have never really gotten used to them, nor they to us. Sure, my friends would be polite to you at first, but I would constantly have the feeling that I had to be your lawyer and make excuses for you, that I had to defend you. Because their enthusiasm would eventually wane; they would stop paying attention to you and maybe even start asking you some awkward questions—to let you know that, despite everything, you do not come from the same background they do. That you are not one of us. Because there are things you simply do not know and aren't familiar with. Once, when we were in a Japanese restaurant and I told you that your face reminded me of Jean Seberg in Godard's *À bout de souffle*, you had no idea what I was talking about. Even when I translated the title into English and tried to remind you what the film was about, you asked, "What did you say—Godard?" and dipped your sushi in the soy sauce rice-side down. When I pointed out to you that that's not how it's done, that you need to dip the raw fish into the soy sauce, partly to kill the bacteria, you didn't seem to care and went on clumsily poking the chopsticks around in the rice, completely ignoring what I'd said.

And your knowledge of foreign languages, too, leaves a lot to be desired; in fact, I'm constantly having to translate for you, which is tiresome and exhausting. And for the listeners, it's not just boring, but the person you're translating for inevitably ends up sounding less than intelligent and sometimes even gives the impression of being mentally challenged. I don't understand why you have never learned to speak a decent Euro-English, even with that distinct Eastern European accent of yours. You must have had the opportunity even there, where you were born and still live.

I know you are intelligent, and you have so much energy it's like you're powered by radioactive cesium, but you have done absolutely nothing with it. I admit that this duality—your quick mind and deficient education—not only baffled me at first, it also turned me on. It made you seem even more feminine. Whenever I watched you struggle to make your words keep up with your thoughts, as your sentences became fragmented and broken, and your speech harder to understand, I could see that you were very gifted, that you had abilities, which, however, would remain undiscovered. Whenever we weren't together and I was thinking about you, I'd always imagine you in a sequence from some low-budget Polish film, against a faded, desolate background of pale yellows mixed with cool greens or grays, and you would be walking aimlessly through a dusty landscape, with nothing ahead of you at all except a bleak and anonymous end. But at the same time I envied you. The two times I visited you, as I watched you sitting at your computer paying no attention whatsoever to me, or when you were reading or absorbed in worlds inaccessible to me and didn't hear me when I said something to you or called your name—all of it you did out of some incomprehensible inner necessity, which I myself have never experienced. I love my work, I enjoy being a professor, traveling, writing books, but the passion with which you work—this I have never had. You don't care if only a few people read what you write; you don't worry about the effects of your work, and when you finish something, it only spurs you on to a new project. For me this is pure madness, a waste of time, but useless pleasure is itself a kind of madness and, in this sense, I have always thought you a little mad. Not in the way people say this about someone and it sounds like a compliment. No, you move through your worlds with such extraordinary speed, but in reality you are standing in place. And you're probably lucky that it's writing you enjoy so much and not some other, far more dangerous obsession.

At first when I read your emails, I thought it was just the way you wrote, but then, to my surprise, I realized you were serious. I know it's easier for women, for most women, to express their moods and feelings, but you—you are unrivaled in this. Every time I saw on my screen that I had an email from you, I clicked on it like a sixteen-year-old boy and was filled with a bashful, gratifying warmth. Many of your email letters I printed out and read over and over before going to sleep. At night, when I was alone, which wasn't often, in my thoughts I would fall asleep with you. And even when I wasn't alone, you were still in my thoughts. You wrote in rich, clear metaphors (even if they were swarming with mistakes in grammar and spelling), but in your native language, too, maybe you write better than you speak. It's only a game, I convinced myself at first; I thought you were writing like this only for the sheer pleasure of communication.

I was wrong. More and more I began to fear our meetings. Up until then, I never knew that the worst thing that could happen to me was for my desire—or what I thought I was my desire—to be fulfilled. Other women are always somehow evasive: Let's do something else, they say, I didn't mean it the way you took it . . . Is that what you think I said? . . . No, I never said anything of the sort . . . But with you, whatever you said you were going to do, whatever you promised to do, you always did it.

Everything in your life, without additional explanation or

commentary, is so complicated and mystifying. For example, the fact that you share your apartment with a Romanian girl, whose ancestors come from Transylvania. It's true, she doesn't actually look Romanian; with her fair complexion and light-colored eyes she might look even more European than most Europeans. I have nothing against Romanians, mind you, but appearance isn't everything: what matters is language and, especially, customs and experience. And there are things that are simply impossible to forget. Once in Florence, when I was traveling through Italy, somebody broke into my car and stole essentially everything, and they were Romanians. And as for the women—in fact, I do know a Romanian woman who is an art curator, but she's lived in Europe a long time—well, Romanian women, just like Ukrainians, young Russian girls, and girls from the Philippines, most of them, when they come to the West, live lives that are degrading to women. Also, I remember the newspaper headlines from the early 1990s: "Romanians Roast Swans by the Danube in the Middle of Vienna." I think those people may actually have been Roma, but they were still Romanian citizens. And then there's that Serbian friend of yours; it's true she hasn't lived in Belgrade for a decade, but supposedly she's related to one of those notorious Serbian generals. We were all terribly upset by the violence in the Balkans—Vukovar, Srebrenica, Sarajevo, and later Kosovo—but it was actually none of our business. All the same, and nevertheless, we helped you, and not just by sending material aid, accepting refugees, and intervening militarily, but also in terms of interpretation, since we saw your ethnic and sectarian mishmash better than you did, who were directly living it.

Of course I never told you any of this. I only think about all these things, as if I'm talking to you, on the way to the university or while driving my car. None of us would ever tell you these things. It's simply not possible to express and accept all these differences, which are enormous—in culture, in history, in the present, and of course, in knowledge and behavior too.

At our first meeting it became clear to me that there wasn't much you were afraid of and you had no respect for authority. And also, you knew how to push my weakest buttons. I don't know how you did it, but I often felt like you could see right into my brain. I suppose you have that proverbial "woman's intuition" and can interpret exactly what someone is saying; you observe the details of their behavior, the small, almost unnoticeable gestures, and then work out a story. In the stories you tell, you are strong, you are stronger than I am, stronger than most people I know. And I know that these stories require courage, a special kind of courage; you need to know the boundaries and how to transgress them.

"So what do you write about?" I once asked you.

"They're just stories," you said.

"Stories about things that happen to you?"

"No. I make them up."

"So you never write about yourself, or about people who are connected to you?"

"No, what happens to me is what I live. What I write about, I make up."

Rarely have I encountered such naïveté—someone who believes she can remove herself from the world, sit down at a computer, and simply make things up. Our two worlds—my world of scholarly analysis and yours, saturated with sensuality and emotion, with no serious theoretical basis—are infinitely distant. But nevertheless, you might not realize how precisely you struck me to the core. I did not show this to you; unlike you, I know how to control my feelings, and I was all the more careful with you. You discerned what I was convinced was hidden.

And then there was something I didn't even know existed—your sexual aggressiveness! I'm not saying I didn't desire it, that I hadn't fantasized about a woman who, not long after I met her and we exchanged a few words, would, after the first glass of wine in my apartment, walk over to me, undo my belt and zipper, pull out my penis, and drag me onto the bed . . . When that thing happened with you, it was the first time it had ever happened to me. I don't have a clue why, because I really did find you so utterly attractive. You weren't particularly upset by it; you said it had happened to you before, quite a few times, and you even tried to console me: we just need to get used to

each other, you said. I felt ridiculous. Even to myself, I felt like
a complete idiot. Like a little boy who screws up in a game
and his teacher or mother tells him, don't cry, you'll get it right
eventually, maybe next time. For me, it was like somebody had
killed me. In the morning, on my way to the university, I felt
like the whole world knew about it. That it was written all over
my face. When I stopped at a bakery and the salesgirl gave me an
apricot croissant, I could read it in her eyes: What's wrong, poor
little thing? Even this flaky croissant is firmer than you. But not
only did that not stop you, you went on—with me lying next
to you like a corpse—you took various parts of my body and, to
my astonishment and terrified chagrin, proceeded to thoroughly
enjoy yourself. The next day when we were walking around town
in the late afternoon, a friend of mine saw us from his car. And
that evening, when you were in the shower, the telephone rang:
he was calling to ask who you were, to say how good-looking
you were, and similar things. When I told him where you were
from, he didn't seem quite as interested. Oh, sure, he replied,
and with a meaningful little laugh added that women from your
country, supposedly, were very good in bed. I sort of laughed in
confirmation, and in no way let on what had actually happened
between us.

I never understood what it was about me that, despite everything, so intensely excited you. Not my professional success,
surely; you didn't care about that—or did you? I began to suspect that when you were so direct and rough with a man, you
were taking your revenge not just on men but on the entire
world—on a world of unequal chances, on the injustice of its
order. I couldn't shake the feeling that sex was your strategy
for retribution and a means of humiliation. And that falling in
love—which you say you did—was nothing more or less than
love for what you so deeply and mercilessly desire to subjugate
and destroy. Yes, you are actually a kind of sexual terrorist. Your
goal is clear, and your method ruthless and cruel: to smash to
pieces the most tender, most fragile, most vulnerable thing on
the planet: the male ego. Right from the start, I tried to keep
you at a safe distance, so you wouldn't accidentally get beneath

my skin, because you excited me so much, far more than anyone ever had; indeed, a little too much—so intensely that there were times I was scared I might even fall in love with you . . . I don't know. Could all women from Eastern Europe really be so brutal and tactless, or are you exceptional this way too?

I could never give up the world I live in, the things within reach of my arm, and I could never move to where you live, in some cramped two-room apartment. I'm not used to that anymore. When you're a student, it's a challenge; sharing a life with someone is a territory of encounters, of spur-of-the-moment acquaintances and love adventures, but now that I'm in my mid-thirties, I want peace and quiet and have no intention of adapting to anybody.

I can never explain any of this to you, although I think you already suspect a good deal of it; so maybe over the phone, or more likely in an email, I will end it with you in the fastest and nicest possible way. If we ever do happen to meet again, I expect I'll be glad to see you, at least at first—I enjoy watching you, the way you walk, the way you move your arms and hands when you speak; I like the sound of your voice—but I know that a split second later I'll feel uncomfortable and ill at ease. I won't plan to get together with you. And if you're living in my city—because maybe you will get that grant—I'll stay away from you; if you let me know in advance that you're coming, I either won't answer you or I'll send you a short text saying that unfortunately, I won't be in town at the time, or that my apartment will be occupied. In our building we all know each other well, and I don't want people pestering me again after you leave, with questions about who you are and where you are from, and I particularly wouldn't like it if, while you're here, one of my friends or someone from my family happens to come for a visit. No, my family definitely would not accept you. Not even my father and brother, and certainly not my mother and sister. I'm sorry, but it's a cruel and unjust world, and we are not going to change it.

But the world is also full of surprises and opportunities, and it's important to know how to recognize them and take advantage of them. I'm still holding out the possibility that one day I might fall in love. Probably it will be with a woman who, at least to some degree, resembles you, although she will be different. How many times have I sent you a text hoping that you wouldn't respond immediately—please not yet, I prayed, just wait a while, long enough for me to start wanting you; give me the chance to pursue you like a male pursues a female—but no, you hit back at once. With no delay. Shooting me a reply like a blast from an electric ray—not so much a letter but an emotional essay in five or six parts, sometimes completely filling up my phone. Come on, now! Do you really not have the slightest conception about the rules of desire, or do you do this intentionally? Simply to dominate a man? Once you joked that even if you don't have one, yours is bigger than what most guys you know have. Maybe you should have been a man, and me a woman, and then it might have worked out for us. Maybe you really are a man in some way, and only look female—very, very female, which I am sure only makes the men around you even more confused. In fact, you're a kind of transsexual—biologically female, but with methods that are distinctly male: you attack us with exactly the same techniques we have used throughout history to dominate women. I wouldn't be at all surprised if in a few years I hear that you are still alone, with nobody to snuggle up to at night except that pack of cats you have. With them, at least—and I saw this for myself—you know how to be gentle, which only tells me that with us the roughness is intentional.

With you, I began to understand that what a person desires most is not what he desires to have. Because having something like that is just not possible. No, a woman like you, who offers herself to me beyond all measure, is not what I want. You are not a femme fatale—they understand and have mastered the rules of the game, the techniques of attack and retreat, and especially evasion. They are like wild prey who evade only because they want somebody to catch them in the end, and sooner or later that's what happens. But you are not wild prey; it's impossible to hunt you. No, you are a beast who attacks men. First, you assault your victims with words and then, when they're half dead, you pummel them in bed. Whenever I was with you, I felt ill the next morning. You were eating and sleeping less and less; all you wanted to do was fuck and keep on fucking, even as the life was seeping out of me. It was like you were draining me—by the way you were behaving, by your riotous energy, which was your way of telling me that you were the stronger one. I completely understand the impulse centuries ago to chain up women like you in dank dungeons or simply burn them. Despite my strict scientific ideas, there were times when I seriously thought you might actually possess certain methods for controlling the souls and bodies of others, and more than once I asked myself what you were really doing to me—what you were doing with me . . .

Women like you should be kept physically out of reach—trapped on movie screens, between the covers of books, inside the frames of photographs. Women like you are meant for fantasies and dreams, but god forbid we wake up in the morning with you snuggling against us. When I close my eyes and hold my dick in my hand, I will still be thinking of something that resembles you. A likeness that will no doubt be very similar to you—but never will I let you out of my dreams. You will remain confined in the virtual worlds that exist behind my closed eyes, and when I open them, the person in front of me, the person with me, the person I am inside of, will be a different woman, a completely different kind of woman. You are simply more than a woman, and that *more* repels me; it's something I want nothing to do with.

I met a girl not long ago; she is a few years younger than you and has a beauty that is indisputable and pure. She is very attractive, just right, with no transgressive magnetism that both attracts and vulgarly repels. I'm not the only one who has noticed her. She moved here only recently and already has several candidates hanging around her. We are like a hunting party that sooner or later will attack. I have no doubt of my success. I have what women like: I can be both gentle and at the same time a total master—regardless of their world view, this elicits in women feelings of safety and protection, which they usually translate into love. And even if it's just an illusion, the illusion is effective and may even be able to turn the relationship into something like love. With you that is impossible. You let a man know loudly and clearly that you will either protect him or destroy him. And very often, no doubt, it is your protection that kills him. Your trick—and this is what's so bewildering—is that you come off as assertive, even gruff sometimes, and yet at the same moment are gentle. You don't look like a feminist, and a person might initially confuse you with something that is the very opposite of feminism. You have accepted your looks and your demeanor, and developed them into a weapon. Very often you give the impression that you are some Lorelei, and when soldiers approach, as you lure them with your long hair and sensual smile—as if to say, come closer, let me give you a blow job—it turns out that you're a Valkyrie, who calls to men only to send them straight to their graves. And then you are surprised when we make a guerrilla-like retreat and flee from you.

She too has light blond hair; her lips might not be the same as yours, and her soft body is more vulnerable, but I think it might be possible to have something with her that I haven't believed in for a long time, something that, I admit, was reawakened in me with you.

I know there will be times when I'm with her that I will be thinking not of her but of you. That, perhaps, I will be with her and enjoy it the most when I am thinking of you. When I'm inside her, it will be your image behind my eyelids. This does not mean I will care for her any less or that she will excite me any less—no matter how much time I am with her, no matter long this thing (this love?) lasts—because what drives my desire will be something that reminds me of you.

I will never forget you; it will probably be me who first slips out of your memory. But that won't matter anymore. Even if by chance I meet you somewhere, you won't be the same woman I knew; you won't be the same as you are in my dreams and fantasies, when I take you part by part . . . piece by piece . . . layer by layer . . . in small doses, so it's bearable. And pleasant. With a real and genuine pleasure . . . Yes, utterly pleasant.

The Slovenian writer and philosopher MOJCA KUMERDEJ is the author of four books of fiction, including the novel *The Harvest of Chronos*, for which she was awarded the prestigious Prešeren Foundation Prize in 2017. She also works as a critic and journalist in the fields of culture and science.

RAWLEY GRAU has translated numerous works from Slovenian and Russian. In 2016, he received the AATSEEL Prize for his translation of *A Science Not for the Earth* by Yevgeny Baratynsky. His translation of Mojca Kumerdej's *The Harvest of Chronos* appeared in 2017. Originally from Baltimore, he has lived in Ljubljana since 2001.

Selected Dalkey Archive Paperbacks

Michal Ajvaz, *Empty Streets*
   Journey to the South
   The Golden Age
   The Other City
David Albahari, *Gotz & Meyer*
   Learning Cyrillic
Pierre Albert-Birot, *The First Book of Grabinoulor*
Svetlana Alexievich, *Voices from Chernobyl*
Felipe Alfau, *Chromos*
   Locos
João Almino, *Enigmas of Spring*
   Free City
   The Book of Emotions
Ivan Ângelo, *The Celebration*
David Antin, *Talking*
Djuna Barnes, *Ladies Almanack*
   Ryder
John Barth, *The End of the Road*
   The Floating Opera
   The Tidewater Tales
Donald Barthelme, *Paradise*
   The King
Svetislav Basara, *Chinese Letter*
   Fata Morgana
   The Mongolian Travel Guide
Andrej Blatnik, *Law of Desire*
   You Do Understand
Patrick Bolshauser, *Rapids*
Louis Paul Boon, *Chapel Road*
   My Little War
   Summer in Termuren
Roger Boylan, *Killoyle*
Ignacio de Loyola Brandão, *And Still the Earth*
   Anonymous Celebrity
   The Good-Bye Angel
Sébastien Brebel, *Francis Bacon's Armchair*
Christine Brooke-Rose, *Amalgamemnon*
Brigid Brophy, *In Transit*
   Prancing Novelist: In Praise of Ronald Firbank
Gerald L. Bruns, *Modern Poetry and the Idea of Language*
Lasha Bugadze, *The Literature Express*
Dror Burstein, *Kin*
Michel Butor, *Mobile*
Julieta Campos, *The Fear of Losing Eurydice*
Anne Carson, *Eros the Bittersweet*
Camilo José Cela, *Family of Pascual Duarte*
Louis-Ferdinand Céline, *Castle to Castle*
Hugo Charteris, *The Tide Is Right*
Luis Chitarroni, *The No Variations*
Jack Cox, *Dodge Rose*
Ralph Cusack, *Cadenza*
Stanley Crawford, *Log of the S.S. the Mrs. Unguentine*
   Some Instructions to My Wife
Robert Creeley, *Collected Prose*
Nicholas Delbanco, *Sherbrookes*
Rikki Ducornet, *The Complete Butcher's Tales*
William Eastlake, *Castle Keep*
Stanley Elkin, *The Dick Gibson Show*
   The Magic Kingdom
Gustave Flaubert, *Bouvard et Pécuchet*
Jon Fosse, *Melancholy I*
   Melancholy II
   Trilogy
Max Frisch, *I'm Not Stiller*
   Man in the Holocene
Carlos Fuentes, *Christopher Unborn*
   Great Latin American Novel
   Nietzsche on His Balcony
   Terra Nostra
   Where the Air Is Clear
William Gaddis, *J R*
   The Recognitions

William H. Gass, *A Temple of Texts*
   Cartesian Sonata and Other Novellas
   Finding a Form
   Life Sentences
   Reading Rilke
   Tests of Time: Essays
   The Tunnel
   Willie Masters' Lonesome Wife
   World Within the Word
Etienne Gilson, *Forms and Substances in the Arts*
   The Arts of the Beautiful
Douglas Glover, *Bad News of the Heart*
Paulo Emílio Sales Gomes, *P's Three Women*
Juan Goytisolo, *Count Julian*
   Juan the Landless
   Marks of Identity
Alasdair Gray, *Poor Things*
Jack Green, *Fire the Bastards!*
Jiří Gruša, *The Questionnaire*
Mela Hartwig, *Am I a Redundant Human Being?*
John Hawkes, *The Passion Artist*
Dermot Healy, *Fighting with Shadows*
   The Collected Short Stories
Aidan Higgins, *A Bestiary*
   Bornholm Night-Ferry
   Langrishe, Go Down
   Scenes from a Receding Past
Aldous Huxley, *Point Counter Point*
   Those Barren Leaves
   Time Must Have a Stop
Drago Jančar, *The Galley Slave*
   I Saw Her That Night
   The Tree with No Name
Gert Jonke, *Awakening to the Great Sleep War*
   Geometric Regional Novel
   Homage to Czerny
   The Distant Sound
   The System of Vienna
Guillermo Cabrera Infante, *Infante's Inferno*
   Three Trapped Tigers
Jacques Jouet, *Mountain R*
Mieko Kanai, *The Word Book*
Yorum Kaniuk, *Life on Sandpaper*
Ignacy Karpowicz, *Gestures*
Pablo Katchadjian, *What to Do*
Hugh Kenner, *The Counterfeiters*
   Flaubert, Joyce, and Beckett: The Stoic Comedians
   Gnomon
   Joyce's Voices
Danilo Kiš, *A Tomb for Boris Davidovich*
   Garden, Ashes
Pierre Klossowski, *Roberte Ce Soir and The Revocation of the Edict of Nantes*
George Konrád, *The City Builder*
Tadeusz Konwicki, *The Polish Complex*
Elaine Kraf, *The Princess of 72nd Street*
Édouard Levé, *Suicide*
Mario Levi, *Istanbul Was a Fairytale*
Deborah Levy, *Billy & Girl*
José Lezama Lima, *Paradiso*
Osman Lins, *Avalovara*
António Lobo Antunes, *Knowledge of Hell*
   The Splendor of Portugal
Mina Loy, *Stories and Essays of Mina Loy*
Joaquim Maria Machado de Assis, *Collected Stories*
Alf Maclochlainn, *Out of Focus*
Ford Madox Ford, *The March of Literature*
D. Keith Mano, *Take Five*
Micheline Marcom, *A Brief History of Yes*
   The Mirror in the Well
Ben Marcus, *The Age of Wire and String*
Wallace Markfield, *Teitlebaum's Widow*
   To an Early Grave
David Markson, *Reader's Block*
   Wittgenstein's Mistress
Carole Maso, *AVA*

www.dalkeyarchive.com